Stories by M.T. Bass

Crossroads
In the Black
Lodging
Somethin' for Nothin'
Untethered
Article 15
Dephying the Laws of Physics

White Hawk Aviation Stories
My Brother's Keeper
Jungleland
Racing the Dream

Murder by Munchausen Series
Murder by Munchausen
The Darknet
The Invisible Mind
Motherless Children

RACING THE DREAM

WHITE HAWK AVIATION STORIES #3

BY

M.T. BASS

AN ELECTRON ALLEY PUBLICATION
MUDCAT FALLS, U.S.A.

Electron Alley Corporation
The Herald Building
732 Broadway Avenue
Lorain, OH 44052

Manufactured in the United States of America

Edited by Elizabeth N. Love

ISBN 978-1-946266-24-8 (Hardback)
ISBN 978-1-946266-23-1 (Trade Paperback)
ISBN 978-1-946266-22-4 (eBook)

www.mtbass.net

The characters and incidents contained herein are fictional. Any resemblance of persons, living or dead, may, in fact, be a violation of copyright statutes.

For

Grandpa, Uncle Wallace & Uncle Don

and

Jack Dianiska

"If everything seems under control,
you're not going fast enough."

~Mario Andretti

Prologue

It was Father Bob's idea, I guess. Of course, he's not a priest anymore—old habits die hard—just a rich, out-of-work engineer with lots and lots of time on his hands. So, he rented a hangar at Van Nuys Airport from Al McGuire and treated it all top secret, like Kelly Johnson's Burbank Skunk Works. All under lock and key. Him and Sparks. And, well, after Congo, I wasn't doing anything anyway, so when he finally let me in and showed me, I said what the hell...

~A. Gavin Byrd

~~~

Antelope Acres

I chased Scotty down the long straightaway. Three hundred feet back. A hundred feet off the ground. One hundred seventy knots.

Quick looks at the panel: *Thirty-six hundred RPM*. Look: engine oil pressure—*green*. Look: oil temperature—*green*.

All good.

Banking hard into the "pylon" at W Avenue G and Myrick Canyon Road over the desert, a shadow on the ground to my left crawled toward my British Racing Green colored wing. He had to be outside. You can't look to the right. It's just not safe. But the sun was behind us…

I lofted a bit in the eighty-degree turn—climbed twenty feet or so—then quickly dove back down to close another hundred and fifty feet on Scotty, picking up a bit of his wake turbulence.

Rolling out and down the front straightaway, I found smooth air twenty-five feet above his hot red Jensen Cassutt.

We used the crossroads, a pile of rocks, a little hump in the desert sand, and a windmill water pump to set up our three-mile oval course. I knew Scotty from Van Nuys, but the other three guys were new, from other SoCal airports. We were all on "Company Frequency," one-two-three point four-five. We joined up in a loose formation for a pace lap, then got down to business with a flying start.

Like Henry Ford said, racing began five minutes after the

second airplane was built. And that's where Father Bob came in. There were a ton of modified Cassutts out there. Anybody could buy the design for $20. But Father Bob used his engineering skills to develop and, with Sparks' help, build *White Hawk Redux,* an 85 horsepower, Continental C-85 Goodyear racer that we were pushing over two hundred miles an hour.

It was all unofficial because, after fifty years of glorious history, airplane racing fell off the face of the earth for a while in the Sixties. There were no sanctioned races around anymore, so we made up our own course, kicking up dust devils and rooster tails over the desolation of Antelope Acres. Our version of California street drags.

Of course, I didn't really know what I was doing, but I was learning fast.

Around the windmill and up to the forty-foot hump in the sand. I chased Scotty down foot by foot. I knew I could take him.

Only two laps left. It was now or never.

Banking hard into the crossroads, I juiced the power up near four thousand RPM and pulled back on the stick to take Scotty up and outside.

But dammit, I missed him—

In my peripheral vision, a Tweety-yellow racer on my right came toward me.

I flattened my wings and rolled off the power sweeping below him to keep from colliding. But I caught the tornado of his wingtip vortices and involuntarily flipped inverted.

A Joshua tree bloomed overhead in my canopy as I arced upside-down towards the ground at two-hundred-fifty feet. Gravity pulled my shoulders down against the straps of my five-point harness.

Without thinking, back pressure on the stick moved quickly forward to illogically raise the nose with a nudge of left rudder to roll level and maxing out the power.

I finally caught the blue of the horizon on the bottom of my windscreen. The engine coughed, losing the gravity feed of fuel from my tank.

A hundred feet, but now climbing.

I finally exhaled, then took a deep breath. I raised my left wing around one hundred eighty degrees until right-side-up, veering off from the pylons to the south.

The engine started purring again.

I leveled at a thousand feet, pulling the throttle back to two thousand, and looked over my shoulder at the rat pack flying away down the straightaway. Scotty battled off the Tweety-bird racer, cutting tight and low around the windmill water pump.

My day was done, so I headed southwest towards the San Fernando Reservoir on my way back to Van Nuys Airport.

Images in the windscreen nibbled at my brain, but I quickly distracted myself with calling tower, the landing checklist, then lining up for One-Six Left and greasing it down on the pavement.

I mindlessly taxied to our hangar.

Sparks stood out front with his hands on his hips. He saw it on my face.

I pulled the mixture back and the propeller spun down to a stop. I opened the canopy.

"What the hell happened?" Sparks asked.

"What do you mean?"

Sparks wiped his hands on his khaki overalls as he slowly marched around the airplane giving it his careful eye, no doubt looking for popped rivets or gnarled fabric. "I know that look."

Father Bob wandered out and leaned his wiry frame against the inside of the main door.

I undid my harness, pulled myself up and out of the tight cockpit onto the seat, then stepped down onto the asphalt. "I, ah, got a little sideways on the course."

"Sideways?" Sparks scowled at me.

"Yeah, just two laps to go. I was trying to pass Scotty and, well, got turned upside down. I just didn't see the other guy on my wing, so I pulled out."

Sparks exhaled loudly. He shook his head. *"Upside down?"*

I looked off towards the runways, eyes hidden behind my Ray-Bans. "It was nothing."

"How high were you?" Father Bob asked calmly.

"A couple hundred feet or so. Maybe more."

Father Bob made the sign of the cross over his chest.

"Did you bend anything?" Sparks demanded.

"I don't think so."

"Better not, *damn it.*"

Father Bob scratched the back of his head and went back into the hangar.

"Well, we'll just see about that," Sparks said. *"Idiot!"*

Sparks yammered on, but I didn't hear any more of what he said as I jammed my fists into my pants pockets and wandered away towards the runways, replaying the five or maybe ten seconds of unintentional desert aerobatics over and over and over again in my head.

The Joshua tree…growing bigger and bigger.

You know, at the time, your life really doesn't flash before your eyes. But it sure did now.

~~~

The Wing Walker

I walked to the end of the taxiway and watched the airplanes pivot around the airport in the traffic pattern. Some landing, then taxiing off the runway. Some skidding along doing crash-and-goes.

Scotty's red Jensen Cassutt turned base-to-final for Runway One-Six Left. Twenty minutes later, he stepped up beside me and watched the planes, too.

"What the hell happened to you? I thought you were going to take me," Scotty said.

"Got tangled up a bit with the guy in yellow. I forgot to keep the blue side up."

"Upside down? At two hundred feet? And you're still here?"

"Yeah, I cheated the Grim Reaper again."

"How many lives do you have, anyway?" Scotty asked.

"I lose count."

We watched a black-and-red colored Stearman 75 biplane enter downwind.

"So, did you hold off the Tweety Bird?" I asked as we watched the Stearman arc left onto the base leg.

"He came at me like a bat out of hell on that last lap and beat me to the line."

"Really? Who is he?"

"I got no clue, but he's got some serious mojo behind his prop."

"Hmmm…"

The Stearman crabbed down to the numbers on final, then kicked out the fuselage and eased onto the centerline.

"That's a nice old ride," I said. "I haven't been in a PT-17 since the Army taught me to fly."

"Come on, their hangar's three down from mine. I'll introduce you."

I followed Scotty back to the rows of hangars. "Who is it?"

"Well, it's either Doug or his sister, Allison."

"Allison?"

"Yeah, she flies, too," Scotty said. "Actually, they do a wing walking act for air shows."

"And you never told me about her?"

"Yeah, well, you might as well give it a try yourself." Scotty nervously brushed the top of his flattop. "I crashed and burned and died hard. Maybe you can use up one of your lives on her."

We walked up the opposite side of the taxiway between the long, low rows of hangars, stopping in front of Scotty's open door as the Stearman wove up from the other side. The tail arced around. Moments later the radial engine coughed and died, then the prop blade shuddered to a stop. We walked over towards the plane.

The pilot's head was buried in the cockpit as we came over. Standing up, it was obvious from the tight-fitting flight suit that this was Allison, not Doug.

I smiled.

She pulled off her goggles, opened the chin strap on her canvas helmet, then pulled it off, shaking out dishwater blond hair to her shoulders.

I took my sunglasses off for a better look.

Racing the Dream

Scotty must have noticed me smiling like a goofball teenager. He jammed his shoulder into my back. "She'd make a bulldog bite his chain."

"Might be worth burning a couple-three lives on," I said.

"Hey, Scotty…" She climbed down out of the cockpit, hopped off the wing, and walked our way. "Who's your friend?"

"Him? Oh, just Hawk. He's got a green Goodyear racer over in the D hangars."

"Yeah. I've seen it." Allison came over. I'm only five-eight which put me in a fighter pilot's slot, so her dark emerald eyes met me eyeball-to-eyeball. She held out her hand. "I'm Allison. Nice to meet you."

"Pleasure's all mine," I said, taking her hand, trying hard not to crack a lecherous smile. I looked over at her plane. "This is a nice-looking ride. Really clean, too."

"Have to keep up appearances for the crowds," she said.

"Yeah, Scotty was telling me. So, who does the wing walking? You or Doug?"

She gave me a coy smile. "That would be me. No one wants to see my stupid brother risking life and limb, now, would they?"

"You know what they say about skydivers: fools jumping out of perfectly good airplanes. And here you are climbing out on the wing without a chute."

"It's a living."

"I was telling Scotty, I haven't been in one of these since primary training."

She looked me up one side and down the other. "You don't look so old."

"Ouch!" Scotty shook his head and covered his eyes. "That's got to burn a bit."

"What a maroon." I glared at him. "I've got a few hours on the engine, but I'm nowhere near TBO."

"I mean—" Allison sputtered. "I—ah…"

"Come on, he's ancient." Scotty grabbed my shoulder and squeezed. "Damn near an aviation fossil. How many Fokker's did you shoot down in the War—*World War One*, that is?"

She hung her head and blushed a bit. "Hey, I'm sorry."

"No worries. Just take me for a ride sometime," I said.

"Sure." Allison looked up and smiled. "I'd like that."

"Good. Let's get your plane back in the hangar."

Scotty and I went back and grabbed the tail to push it inside.

"You dog, you," Scotty muttered at me.

"More like a cat," I said, "with nine lives."

"Whatever…"

~~~

Tweety Bird

When I got back to our hangar, the bright yellow racer was parked outside and the pilot was walking around his airplane talking with Father Bob. He stood ramrod straight—at least six feet tall—with his hands clasped behind his back, nodding and gesturing with a quick wave of his left hand or a pointed finger here and there in answer to Father Bob's questions. Tall, blonde, and square-faced, he looked Nordic or German.

In the hangar, Sparks watched the two closely, standing guard at the cowling of *White Hawk Redux* with his arms crossed.

"Hey, I know you, don't I?" I asked walking up to the yellow bird.

"Antelope Acres?"

I nodded.

Head held back, cold blue eyes looked down the ridge of his nose at me.

"Hawk."

"Ax." We shook hands. "Well, I am very sorry about, you know, flipping you inverted out there." He looked over at my plane. He nodded at Sparks who simply stared back.

Father Bob winced a bit.

"No worries. Just keep the blue side up, right?" I said.

"Right. Well, I am good that you are still alive."

"Scotty says you've got some serious juice in that cowling."

"He's got the red Cassutt, right? He sure can move along."

"I could have taken him."

Ax gazed off to the west. "Yes, yes…again, sorry."

He said it, but I didn't feel it. "Where are you based?"

"Ax, here, flies out of Lockheed," said Father Bob.

"With all the movie stars?" I winked at him.

"It keeps the scenery…*scenic*. You know?"

"Your accent…"

"I am German." Ax put his hands on his hips. I swear he took a deep breath and declared, "I fly for Lufthansa. Seven-Oh-Sevens."

"My, my…lucky you."

"And yourself?"

"Just the second-best pilot there ever was."

"What does that mean?"

"Nothing, really. I'm just an airport gigolo."

Ax furrowed his brow. He looked at Father Bob. "Gigolo?"

"He is hilarious, isn't he?" Father Bob waved his hand at the Tweety-yellow plane. "A Shoestring design, but Ax made some special modifications. He cut back the horizontal stabilizer and did some work there around the intakes, too."

"Interesting." I nodded my head.

"I studied aeronautical engineering in Munich."

"Oh, yeah? Munich? I've been there a few times…but never landed."

Ax gave me a half-smile and nodded. "A few years before my time, then."

What the hell? Why is everybody giving me a hard time about my age?

"Yes, well, I should head back to Lockheed."

"Thanks for stopping by," Father Bob shook Ax's hand.

"I am glad you are okay," Ax extended his hand.

We shook. "Next time. Okay?"

"Yes. Next time."

"I'll get the prop," I said.

Ax squeezed his six-foot frame into the cockpit, buckled up, flipped some switches, then called out, "Contact."

I spun the prop blade to two o'clock, then pulled it down hard, stepping back and away as the engine coughed to life.

Ax stepped on the left brake to pivot three hundred sixty degrees, then taxied off towards the runway.

"So, what do you think?" I asked Father Bob.

"I don't know about his modifications to the tail. Speed might be a bit better, but not sure about the stability."

"What about under the hood?"

"Didn't get a chance to see."

"Scotty said the guy just blasted by him on the last lap."

"Well, I wonder if he's dumping nitrous into the carb."

"Now, that doesn't quite sound fair," I said ironically.

"Or legal," Sparks said as he walked over to us. "Don't trust him. Nope. Not this one. Not one bit."

"Who do you trust?" Father Bob asked.

"Not the Germans…and certainly not the CIA. That's for sure."

"Alfalfa?"

Sparks nodded.

"I agree."

"Hawk, step into my office." Father Bob grabbed my arm and pulled me into the back corner of the hangar where he parked his desk and an engineering drawing board. He reached into the bottom drawer and pulled out a bottle of Glenlivet, half-filling a

Paramount Studios and a Looney Tunes coffee mugs. Grinning, he handed me the one with the cartoon characters.

"So, you worried about the Tweety Bird maybe?"

"Nah. I'm sure he's fast, but no. Not much," Father Bob said, parking himself in his desk chair.

I held up my mug and we clinked. I drank, then asked, "So, what's the occasion?"

He sipped his scotch, nodded his head, and looked at my the British green racer. "I talked you into this."

"What do you mean?"

"It was all my idea and I know you're not a God-fearing man, Hawk, but—but—let me just say this, I don't want you diving into a smoking hole in the desert. Especially after Congo."

I took another long sip of scotch, not thinking about Antelope Acres, but about that one very bad day at the banana plantation. "Yeah, I've had better days."

"I just had this idea about racing planes and stuff. And I thought…"

"It's a good one."

"Look—"

"You know, there's an edge," I said. "A hard red line out there."

"Yeah. And you crossed it today."

"But I came back."

Father Bob shook his head. "You should not have crossed it in the first place."

"What? Do you think I want to drag cattle back and forth over the ocean in the front office of a big Boeing jet…like Ax? Yeah, I don't think so."

"But you wouldn't be looking at eating sand off the desert floor."

"It happens sometimes."

"But it doesn't have to."

"No…but it does."

Father Bob gave me a quizzical look.

"That red line is out there—whether you like it or not. And it can reach out and grab you—anytime. Anywhere."

"Like getting shot down in the jungle?"

I nodded slowly.

"I think I understand sometimes—re-living the past and the war and all—but then, again, sometimes I really don't."

"Yeah? And who saved you with your broken leg?" I kicked his left foot. "When you crossed the line and got kidnapped just for being a friendly neighborhood priest?"

"I'd say the line crossed me."

"See? It just doesn't matter."

"Yeah…I guess." He sipped his scotch.

He didn't say it, but I saw we were both thinking about Ella getting shot and killed by the Simba rebels. I looked at Bugs Bunny, Foghorn Leghorn, and Sylvester the Cat on my mug then downed the rest of my scotch.

Father Bob reached over with the bottle and poured another shot into my cup, then his. "You don't have to go out there and tempt fate."

"I'm not tempting anything. I'm just trying to go as fast as I can—as smooth as I can. There's a…oh, I don't know, a perfect precision you are seeking—but still, you are reaching. You're pushing the limits."

"Like dogfighting, maybe?"

"Grunting and bending metal and getting all you've got out of your machine? Yeah."

"I've never…"

"You are nudging the line and you just keep testing it, just a little more and a little more…but I'm not tempting fate. You've got to put it all out there." I looked at Sylvester and thought about passing beneath Ax's Tweety-yellow racer over the desert again.

"The thin red line?"

I nodded.

"You sure?"

"Yeah. I'm kind of in love with something again."

"Okay, then. Just don't screw up my beautiful airplane."

I hid my eyes behind my hand and said in my best Sylvester, Jr. voice, *"Oh, father…"*

~~~

Slow is Smooth

I took Van Nuys Boulevard into the hills to Mulholland Drive, heading back into Beverly Hills losing myself as I arced smoothly through the turns on the mostly empty road in my new red '62 Corvette.

I shouldn't have done it, but it was just easier to move into the casita out back behind my brother's mansion. Elaine said it would be okay to move into the big house with her—of course, there's plenty of room—but I wanted to be on my own and it had everything I needed—a bedroom, a kitchen, and a big sitting room upfront. And privacy. Stitch used it as his studio, but I got it cleaned up and furnished for myself. There were still some of his oil paintings hung on the walls. Abstract stuff. Kind of depressing, but I couldn't take them down.

I pulled into the servants' entrance outback, went inside to grab a beer, and parked myself on the swing hung out on the front porch, closing my eyes to soak in the last of the day's sun.

I must have dozed off because I didn't hear Elaine walk up.

"Well, you don't seem any worse for the wear," she said.

I had to smile. Elaine possessed a Lauren Bacall *"you-know-how-to-whistle"* kind of voice that just melts you somewhere deep inside your chest. I lifted my head and opened my eyes. Her arms were crossed over her bosom. I think it was her deep blue, soulful eyes that got me at first. She was still beautiful in spite of the scarring and the slight facial palsy that Stitch's surgeon hands couldn't completely fix to save her acting career after the car wreck so long ago. "Don't you have a movie to make or something?"

"Story conferences. *Ugh!* Writers. What a bunch of whiny brats."

"Didn't you feed them? It helps take the edge off."

"Yes, I did, but it didn't matter." She put her hand over her heart, throwing her head back dramatically. *"Oh, my words. Oh, my art. How could you? How dare you?"*

"So, how was your day, dear?"

She put her hands on her hips and gave me an actor's studio glare. "Don't you get cranky on me."

"Well, then, feed me."

"Writers…and now pilots, too, huh?" She smiled a bit crookedly. "Come on, I'll have Andre cook up some steaks."

"I'm in for that." I swallowed the last of my warm beer and put the bottle down on the porch.

"Hey, this isn't a fraternity house."

"Who's cranky now?"

She just pointed at the bottle, so I picked it up and carried it with me to the big house. I put my arm around her and gave Elaine a kiss on the temple.

She rested her head against my chest. "I'm glad you're here."

"Yeah. Me, too."

"So, what's with the little guy?" she asked.

"Who? Father Bob?"

"Yeah. He gets himself a little worked up about things. About you."

"Eh, just trying to bring a wayward sheep back into the flock. Why, did he call you?"

"He's always calling me, but that's okay. He's funny and does seem to care. So, don't make him mad—just like you always do with everyone else."

"Sparks still likes me."

She looked up and scowled at me. "I don't believe that one bit."

I sighed. "It was worth a shot. Okay? I'll get to work on that right away."

She grabbed my forearm with both of her hands and twisted them to give me an Indian burn.

"Hey!"

"Yeah. *You do that.*"

"Alright, already. Geeze. So, what's your movie about?"

"They don't think I can do it."

"Do what?" I asked.

"A suspense thriller. With a female lead. But, no. Everybody's got to be all Hitchcock-like for crying out loud."

"They don't really know you, do they?"

"No. They don't. But they'll find out. That's for sure."

"I feel sorry for them."

"*What?*" She punched me hard in my upper arm.

"Hey, that hurt."

"What did I say about making people mad at you?"

"But you're still going to feed me, right?"

"I suppose."

"Good."

~~~

I got *White Hawk Redux* out of Van Nuys before the boys got to the hangar the next morning and headed back out to Antelope Acres to work on my technique.

Slow is smooth. Smooth is fast.

I rolled back the RPM as I came over the mountains and banked to the west to dogleg onto the back straightaway. I passed down through a thousand feet, arced around W Avenue G, rolling out to cross our pretend start-finish line at two hundred feet. I took a deep breath, let it out slowly, clicked my stopwatch, and juiced the power back up to twenty-five hundred.

In your mind, you see your line before you fly it, and the trick is finding the right pressure on the controls—like pulling a trigger—to hit your perfect apogee around the pylons. As close as you can without cutting the pylon. But *smooth.*

I banked left, pushing myself into the seat with two or three Gs, watching the string of yarn on my cowling and adjusting my left rudder to keep it straight—no skidding, no slipping. But I started too late and drifted too far outside. Too little bank. Too long of a line. Losing time. I banked ten degrees more around the windmill water pump to get back on track.

Ease off the stick pressure down the back straightaway—check the panel.

Oil pressure: green. Oil temperature: green. Down to a hundred feet. Three...two...one...stick left and back to hold altitude clipping the pile-of-rocks pylon.

Close, but still outside.

Roll out. Bank again hard around the intersection to the start-finish line: one minute, forty-five seconds on the stopwatch.

Power to three thousand.

Banking now sooner...Smoother...Cutting tight over the

hump in the desert…Trying not to cut the pylon. Earlier into the back straight. Down to fifty feet, kicking up rooster tails in the sand behind me. Cutting the rock pile closer, then arcing around the intersection, and across the line.

And around again…and again…

It wasn't so hot yet, but I was sweating.

Three thousand five hundred on the tach.

And again…

Ten laps later, I crossed the finish line at one minute, ten seconds. About one-hundred eighty-five miles per hour.

I eased back on the throttle and climbed east, closing my eyes for just a minute and wiping the sweat off my forehead. I swear I must have worn a couple of buttonholes in the seat upholstery.

Traffic at two o'clock and three miles. It looked vaguely familiar: a black-and-red biplane.

I turned right and climbed above their altitude by five hundred feet and came up on them from behind, on the right.

And there she was, standing out on the top wing.

Jesus! Just insane.

I gave the Stearman a wide berth, then cut down across their flight path with a couple of rolls, just to be sure Allison saw me.

Then I headed back home.

✳✳✳~ ~ ~✳✳✳

Reno

I greased the racer down on One-Six Left, then taxied to the fuel pumps. Popping the canopy, even the warm Santa Ana breeze felt good on my face and neck. I took off my ball cap and ran my hand back through my sweat-soaked hair.

"Looks like you had a pretty good workout," Al McGuire said as he strolled out of the airport's main offices and over to the pumps with his hands buried deep in his pants pockets. He was my age, but somehow looked younger, a wavy toe-head with a big, toothy grin on his face. He always dressed like a PGA pro—probably because he was inevitably heading to or coming back from the links at the Los Angeles Country Club. He claimed to handle most of his real estate business there—along with managing my finances. He made us both rich in the fifties investing in orange groves down south that morphed into subdivisions.

"A minute, ten," I said stepping out of the cockpit.

"What's that? A hundred and ninety?"

"There about. One-eighty-five." I walked over and shook his hand.

"Sweet. Can you break two?"

"Yeah…with a little more practice. And maybe a bit more of Father Bob's engineering magic." I grabbed the avgas nozzle and started filling the tank.

"So are you serious about racing this thing? For real?"

"Why do you ask?"

"Met with a rancher named Stead from up north around Reno. He wants to put together some races there."

"You think he's legit?"

"Well, he's a pilot and used to race speedboats. I think he's serious about it. You want in?"

"To race?" I capped the tank. "Sure."

"And maybe get a little side hustle going."

"Mmm, I don't know."

"What else are you going to do with all your money?" Al's voice jumped into excited little kid mode. "Come on…*it'll be fun.*"

I pushed the plane away from the pump by the propeller. "Okay, I guess. Check the guy out and let me know for sure."

Al pointed at my plane. "And get that thing over two hundred to win some races."

"I'm working on it, okay?"

"I know. I know." Al winked and shot me a big grin.

I hopped back into the cockpit. "Pull my prop, will ya?"

"No problem."

The engine fired up and I taxied over to my hangar, thinking about getting into a real race.

Sparks wandered out of the big open door, polishing one of his wrenches, and squinted my way. When I popped the top, he came over and asked, "Well?"

"One eighty-five."

He scratched the back of his head with the wrench. "Huh. Should do better."

"I kept it under thirty-five hundred on the tach. I didn't want to go crazy on the engine. Do you think it will do two hundred?"

"Full rich?"

I nodded.

"Should. Get out of there and let me check the plugs and the mags to see if they're running hot."

I climbed out and we pushed the plane back into the hangar.

Outside, Father Bob pulled up on his Norton Atlas 750.

"Look at him." Sparks scowled. "His feet don't even touch the ground on that damn thing."

"Lovely morning, boys," Father Bob said. He pointed at *White Hawk Redux.* "You been out?"

I nodded.

"One eighty-five," Sparks said, twisting the screws open on the cowling.

"Huh. Should do better than that." Father Bob slid off the bike and pulled it up on the stand. He took off his helmet, stepped over to me, and whispered, "You're not losing your touch now, are you, son?"

I looked down on the former priest. "Cut it out, now."

He poked me in the ribs and grinned. "It can't be the mechanic. And it surely can't be the design."

Sparks chuckled as he lifted the cowling.

"What are you looking at?" I asked Father Bob as he scanned my head.

"I don't see any grey hairs yet."

"You guys are hilarious. Seriously, do you think this thing will turn two hundred?"

"Not a problem," Father Bob said. "Why do you ask?"

"Some guys are talking about putting together races up in Reno."

"We'll get you there." Father Bob patted me on the back.

"Hey, fly-boy," Allison called out as she walked up behind us.

"Saw you showing off this morning."

"And this would be…" Father Bob gave me a *sinners beware* look with a raised eyebrow.

"Allison," she said. "I've got the Stearman over by Scotty's hangar."

Father Bob gracefully accepted her extended hand. "I'm Bob. And that there is Sparks."

Sparks just ignored her, wrenching on a spark plug.

"Don't mind him." Father Bob smiled. "It is a pleasure to meet you."

"Scotty introduced us the other day," I said.

"So, what's wrong with your plane?" Allison asked.

"Nothing. Nothing at all," Sparks called out. He held a spark plug up close to his right eye to examine the gap. "This one looks just fine."

"Hawk and I were just discussing the whole man-versus-machine conundrum on how to get the most speed out of the plane." Father Bob put his hand on my shoulder. "If you know what I mean."

"Oh, you mean the age thing?" Allison looked over and smiled my way.

"Hey—"

She gently looped her arm around my elbow. "Oh, get over it already."

I looked at Father Bob and shrugged.

He scratched his chin and chuckled.

"Nice to meet you guys." She pulled me away from Father Bob, heading towards the main office. "Come on, I'll buy you a cup of coffee."

"You're not buying me machine coffee, are you?"

"What if I was? Would it make a difference?"

I shuffled along for a few steps. "No…I guess not."

"You hungry? I worked up an appetite out on the wing this morning."

"Your treat?"

Allison skipped ahead for a few steps, then turned around to face me. "You know, my mother tried to warn me about boys like you."

"Boys?"

"Yeah. *Boys.*" She winked at me and took my arm again.

"Come on, I'll drive," I said, steering her to my red Corvette in the parking lot.

"Yours?"

I nodded.

"I approve," Allison said as I held the door open for her.

"Well, she likes the car—that's a start." I got behind the wheel and put the top down. "Let's go to Norms. For flapjacks."

"You're the Pilot-In-Command."

Ten minutes later we were sitting in a booth looking out on Sherman Way. Doris came over and filled my coffee mug without asking. She held the pot up for Allison, who turned over her mug.

"I already know what *he* wants," Doris said. "How's about you?"

"I think I need a minute." Doris walked away and Allison opened the menu. "It's almost like you had this all planned out."

"Plan your flight…"

"And fly your plan, right?" She scanned the breakfast items, then closed her menu. "And what, exactly, is your plan?"

I could only smile.

Allison mirrored my grin.

Doris came back and asked. "What'll you have, hon?"

"A western omelet with cheddar cheese, please. And a large orange juice," Allison answered, still smiling at me.

Doris wrote as she said to me, "Pancakes, sausage patties, a large milk, and extra butter, right, Ace?"

I nodded.

She looked at me, then at Allison, and muttered as she turned for the kitchen. "Yeah. I thought so."

"So, how do you know Scotty?" Allison asked.

"The racing thing. Father Bob met him while he was working on the plane and introduced us."

"He's a funny guy."

"Funny—ha, ha? Or funny interesting?"

"No. *You* are the one who is interesting."

I scratched the back of my head. "Not quite sure how to take that."

"Well, I've always been *interested* in *interesting* people."

"Hmmm…"

"I walk wings for a living. What about you?"

"I flew Mustangs in the Big One—but you knew that from Scotty. Worked as a movie stunt pilot with Paul Mantz. Owned a bush pilot operation in Alaska for a while and I recently retired from the Congolese Air Force. So, I'm between gigs right now."

"That all must pay very, very well." She pointed at my Corvette parked out front.

"It's a living—sort of."

Doris served our breakfast and topped off our coffee. She laid our check by me.

"And what possessed you to venture out on the wing of an airplane?"

"I'm an Air Force brat. Dad flew out at Edwards and taught me and my twin brother Doug how to fly when we were seventeen. And to be honest, I didn't want to work for a living, so it seemed like the lesser of two evils."

I munched on my flapjacks. "So, tell me, what is your plan?"

Allison took a couple long gulps of orange juice, then asked, "How is your breakfast?"

"It's good."

She reached over and slid the check next to her plate. "Well, that's a start."

~~~

Beautiful Downtown Burbank

Coming back from Norms, I dropped Allison off at the airport and lingered a bit, watching as she headed to her hangar. Looking back, she gave me a friendly wave goodbye, then disappeared between the low steel buildings.

"And how does it feel to only have eight lives left, *Señor Cat?*" Scotty walked up from behind and leaned on the driver's door. "I feel for you, man."

"You know, I think I'm good."

"No, really?"

"She bought me breakfast."

"Get out of town. Tell me more."

"What are you doing right now?" I asked.

"Nothing."

"Hop in. Let's take a ride."

"Why not? But you have to give me the full scoop." Scotty came around and got in beside me. "I need to know everything."

I pulled out and headed east on Sherman Way.

"Come on. Spill it."

"I was out over the desert this morning and saw her and Doug out practicing their act, so I flew by. She stopped by my hangar afterwards and offered to buy me a cup of coffee. So we went to Norms. No big deal."

"No big deal." Scotty looked at the passing storefronts and

shook his head. "No big deal, he says. So, where are we going anyway?"

"Lockheed. You know the guy in that yellow Shoestring? That's where he's based."

"How do you know?"

"He stopped by our hangar yesterday to say hello."

"Good. I'd like to take a closer look at what he's got."

I parked in the northwest corner of the lot by the FBOs. We walked inside to ask where Ax's hangar was.

Scotty tugged at my sleeve. "Hawk—Hawk—*Hawk!*"

I stopped and looked back at him. "What?"

"Look." He pointed at a young blonde woman sitting by the windows, paging through a *LIFE* magazine.

"Yeah? So?"

"It's Kim Novak. Man, she's gorgeous."

"Do ten push-ups and it'll go away."

"You have no class," Scotty scolded me. "None whatsoever."

"Come on."

I thanked the receptionist who told us Ax's T-hangar was on the north end. I headed out the door, dragging Scotty behind me by his arm.

"She was in that Hitchcock film with Jimmy Stewart."

"*Vertigo,*" I said as we headed north.

"Yeah. That's it." He looked back over his shoulder at the FBO. "Oh, man, I think I'm in love."

"You've got about as much chance with her as with Allison."

"You're killing me—a dagger to my heart."

"Look. There's the Field Marshall." I pointed up ahead.

"Man, he's tall."

Dressed in his Lufthansa uniform, Ax was standing at near-attention outside the main door with his hands clasped behind his back barking out some kind of orders in German. Inside were a pair of mechanics in coveralls standing on either side of the open cowling of the yellow racer. The inside of the hangar was way too clean and spotless.

Ax noticed Scotty and me as we walked up and stopped himself in mid-sentence.

"Ax, I was in the neighborhood and thought I'd bring Scotty by to introduce him," I said.

"So, you're the guy, huh?" Scotty extended his hand. "I've been wondering who you were."

"Yes. Likewise, I am sure," Ax said. "And you have the red Cassutt design. Correct?"

"That's definitely me."

"We're not interrupting are we?" I asked.

"Oh, no. Of course not." He waved to the mechanics. "These fellows are my cousins. Peter is a machinist apprentice at Lockheed over there. Manfred is studying to be an airplane mechanic."

"Hey, guys," I said.

They gave us a feeble wave back.

Scotty eyeballed the yellow racer closely. He started walking over to the plane.

Ax intercepted Scotty with an outstretched arm and turned him back towards the parking lot. "As you can see, I must be heading to LAX for my flight to Frankfurt."

"Oh, yeah. Your day job." I nodded.

"And Peter and Manfred were getting ready to close up, now, you know."

The cousins gave each other confused looks.

"So, we will have to visit with you another time." Ax rattled off some German and the cousins covered the cowling and began to put their tools away. "Come. Come, let's walk together to my car."

Scotty gave Ax a sly look.

"How do you stay awake on those flights?" I asked. "Flying a long straight line seems kind of boring."

"There are always many things to be done. Especially navigating to stay on your proper course."

"You've made some modifications to your design," Scotty said.

"Yes, and we can talk all about that next time." Ax stepped up next to a Mercedes 300SL Coupe. "And here I am."

"Hey, look, Scotty. It matches his airplane."

"I will see you soon, then, yes?" Ax lifted the gullwing door and stepped inside.

"Yeah, hurry back. I think we'd like a rematch." I smiled.

"Yes. Of course." Ax gave a two-fingered salute and pulled the door shut. We watched him drive away.

"See anything interesting?" I asked Scotty.

"He seems kind of secretive about things. I guess it makes sense him being here at the Skunk Works."

"It's not the machine, my friend." I put my arm around Scotty's shoulders. "It's the man in the machine."

~~~

Hangar Talk

When Scotty and I got back to my hangar at Van Nuys, Sparks was inside wrenching on the engine, and Father Bob lay out front in a lawn chair wearing shorts with his Hawaiin shirt draped over the back, soaking in the rays. His short, wiry body was sprawled out with his legs spread apart. He held a couple of small polished aluminum wing panels up to his neck as sun reflectors.

"I can't believe you ever left this place." Father Bob squinted at me out of the side of his eye. "To go to Alaska? Seriously?"

"I had my reasons."

"I suppose," he said closing his eyes tightly again. "I never got sunshine like this in Congo."

"It was a jungle. With a triple canopy and constant rainstorms."

"I think Bob's got a point," Scotty said. "Moving to the Great White North is a bit looney in my book, too. You've got the sun. You've got the beach. You've got the ocean. You've got the girls…ah, the girls—hey, we saw Kim Novak over at Lockheed Airport."

That got Father Bob's attention. He glanced over at Scotty. "Does she look as good as she does on the screen?"

"Ab-So-Lutely." Scotty pulled a stool out of the hangar and sat down beside Father Bob. "She'd make a puppy pull a freight train."

"She was in that Hitchcock movie."

"Yeah. *Vertigo.* With Jimmy Stewart," Scotty said. "I've seen it. A couple of times or so."

Sparks stood up and put his hands on his hips. He shook his head slowly. "Women—turn the lights off and stand 'em on their heads…"

Father Bob, Scotty, and I all looked curiously at Sparks.

"They all look alike." Sparks stuck his head back into the cowling.

Father Bob sat up. "So, did you talk to Miss Novak?"

"I wanted to, but, *noooo.* I didn't get a chance." Scotty pointed at me with his thumb. "Somebody had more important things to do."

I went in the back to the refrigerator by the desk and grabbed four beers and passed them out. "Here, Scotty, drown your sorrows."

"Sure. You've got a girl, now."

"I don't got no one," I said.

"Are you talking about Allison? She stopped by here earlier." Father Bob looked at me and winked. "I suppose Hawk might be considered moderately handsome to some women."

"Moderately?" I asked.

"Moderately—*schmoderately.*" Scotty looked back at me. "What's he got that I ain't got?"

Father Bob and I looked at each other and chuckled.

"Well, my boy," Father Bob said, "I mean no offense, but if you didn't look so much like Eddie Haskell…there might be some hope for you with Allison."

"That's not fair!" Scotty got up and walked into the hangar and stood on the other side of the plane from Sparks, looking down on the engine.

Sparks stood up straight. He calmly slapped his wrench in his open palm and cleared his throat.

"What?" Scotty asked looking up.

Sparks cleared his throat again.

"Oh, alright." Scotty shuffled back out of the hangar and pulled his stool away from Father Bob in the lawn chair. After a long pull of beer, he declared. "Say what you want. Ken Osmond is a legitimate television star."

"Of course, he is," Father Bob said kindly. He looked up at me. "So, I take it you went over to visit our friend, Ax."

"Just trying to be neighborly," I said.

"And what did you learn?"

"That he's more secretive than Kelly Johnson," Scotty said. "What's he hiding, anyway?"

"There are no secrets about the world of science and nature," Father Bob said. "Only about the thoughts and intentions of men. We have nothing to hide."

I shook my head. "Like I said, does it really matter?"

"I'm just curious, you know?" Scotty said.

"Well, I'm sure if they put together the races in Reno, he'll have to pass technical inspections. So, there's really nothing to worry about," Father Bob said. "If he enters."

"I'm sure he'll be in the lineup," I said.

"Reno?" Scotty asked.

"All talk right now. Al McGuire's been in touch with the guy trying to put it together and thinks he's on the up-and-up," I said.

"I'm in, too," Scotty said. "Bring it on."

"Yeah, well, I would have taken you the other day, if I didn't get spun around by Ax."

"Yeah…right…so you say."

"I do say," I said.

"And so do I." Father Bob grinned. "Can you do two hundred, Scotty?"

"Ah, pretty sure."

"Well, Hawk can."

"Told you so," I said.

"We'll see…" Scotty rubbed his chin. "We'll see…*on the course.*"

"Yup." I finished off my beer. "Cause that's where it counts."

Father Bob stood up and put on his Hawaiian shirt. "Yes, yes, that's all well and good, but I think you're missing the most important thing of all."

"What's that?" Scotty asked.

"Allison." Father Bob walked over to me and looked up into my eyes. "Well, are you?"

"Am I what?" I asked.

"Oh, for crying out loud! Take off your stupid hat, already," Sparks hollered out from the garage. "Are you going to ask her out on a date or not?"

"A date?"

"Yes, quite typically that would be the normal thing for a man to do," Father Bob said.

"Well, I, ah…"

"Holy, mackerel," Scotty said, burying his face in his hands. "Maybe Hawk gets vertigo around pretty girls."

"Now, son…" Father Bob put his hand on my shoulder. "Do we need to talk about this?"

I sighed heavily.

"Not my pasture," Sparks muttered. "Not my bull crap."

~~~

The Albatross Hotel

Just out of spite for Father Bob and Scotty, I waited a few days before I called Allison.

"God, *finally!*" she said. "What took you so long?"

"I've been busy."

"Busy? I thought you were between gigs?"

She was definitely going to make this hard on me. "Look, do you want to go out or not?"

"You're not real good at this, are you?"

I hemmed and hawed a bit. "It's been a while."

A rather long silence on the line.

"In your red car?"

"Yes. In my Corvette."

"Well…okay—your treat this time, right?"

Turnabout is fair play, so I figured a little silence on my end was in order.

Finally, I heard a heavy sigh.

"Well…okay," I said.

"And no Tail O' the Pup hot dog funny business. A real restaurant. With a real menu. And drinks, too."

"I suppose."

So, when I stopped by to pick Allison up at her West Hollywood apartment at six o'clock on Friday, she was waiting for me out front dressed in a tight, black sheath dress and wobbling a bit on her high heels.

"What are you smiling at?" she asked.

"You dress up real nice."

"This old thing?"

"Did you do that for me?"

Allison just smiled and said, "Well, are you going to get the door or what?"

"Yeah, yeah. Of course." I got out, went around, and opened the passenger door for her.

She slid herself into the seat and immediately kicked off her shoes. "Ah, so much better."

Chuckling to myself, I got in and pulled out west on Sunset heading towards the coast.

"Now, remember, you promised me a real restaurant with real food—or why would I bother to get dressed up like this?"

"And why do you think I wore this sports jacket?"

"Okay, then."

"You do look nice, by the way."

"Thanks."

"You don't mind taking the scenic route, do you?" I asked.

"Where to?"

"Malibu."

She smiled. "No. Not at all."

"Al McGuire from the airport told me about this place. You should like it. It's got a real menu."

"And drinks?"

"Yes. And drinks."

"Good." She smiled.

We wove through Pacific Palisades and dead-ended into State Route 1 at Sunset Beach. The 340 horsepower V-8 roared nicely when I turned north and accelerated through the gears up the Pacific Coast Highway. Allison lay her head back on the seat and let her hair blow freely in the wind.

I wound back and forth around the curves along the coastline, drinking in the ocean air, watching the sun sinking toward the horizon, and glancing admiringly at Allison's fine looks. We finally got to Malibu and I pulled into the Albatross Hotel.

"Here?" Allison sat up and looked over at me. "So, does Al think you're going to get lucky tonight?"

"What? Lucky, how?"

"You boys are all alike, aren't you. Don't you remember the movie, *Strangers When We Met?* With Kirk Douglas and Kim Novak?"

"What is it with that woman?"

"Who? Kim Novak?"

"It's like she's haunting me."

"Wow! You have some funny kinds of nightmares, being spooked by a gorgeous movie star."

"No. Scotty saw her waiting at the FBO over at Lockheed while we were there."

Allison flipped the ends of her beachy blonde hair. "And is tonight just another bad dream for you, too?"

I shook my head. "No. No, it's not. It's just—oh, never mind. So, what about this movie with her and Kirk Douglas?"

"They had a torrid, passionate love affair. But he was married to someone else."

"Here? At the Albatross?"

"Oh, please, this place is well-known for that kind of thing in the movie business. Is that why Al told you about it?"

"Honest, I just asked him for a nice, quiet place to eat."

"Yeah, *nice and quiet*. Well, I'm sorry. It's not going to happen."

"Okay. Okay. But we can still eat here, right? I even made a reservation."

"You're darn right." She slipped on her shoes and fussed with her hair after the ride up with the top down.

I quickly got out and held the door open for her.

She stood up and looked me directly in the eye. "First, we eat. Then…then, we will see what happens."

"So, there's hope?"

"We'll see." She took my hand and led me inside. "We'll see."

I used Al's name like he said when I made the reservation and they sat us by windows looking out on Santa Monica Bay.

The waiter brought her Chardonnay and my gin and tonic. Allison ordered abalone. I asked for the Parmesan-crusted halibut.

"I really developed a taste for it up north," I said.

She smiled, sipped her wine, and watched the waves roll up the beach to the north. "This is nice. Thanks."

"Of course."

"So, I have to ask, were you really in the Congolese Air Force? That sounded kind of made up."

"They really didn't have much of an Air Force."

"Well, not with the likes of you in it." Allison reached over and patted my arm.

"Ha-ha. It was a spur-of-the-moment kind of thing—I had to get out of Alaska and the equator sounded like a good change of pace." I swirled the ice cubes in my gin and tonic. "I actually worked for the CIA flying T-6 Texans with a bunch of Cuban ex-patriots from the Bay of Pigs invasion. It was an interesting bunch of folks."

"From what I could find out, it sounded pretty brutal."

I shrugged my shoulders. "It was war."

"But, why?"

"I couldn't just climb back into a Mustang, but it was the closest I could get at the time."

She nodded. "I understand."

"Your dad?"

"Yeah. I guess it kind of runs in our family, too. Instead of being doomed to repeat the past, you were actually trying to relive it."

"That sounds kind of…philosophical."

"Santayana. And that's all I've got after four years at Stanford."

"Stanford? You don't really strike me as the dusty old librarian, bookworm-type of girl."

"Which is why I make a living standing on the top wing of a biplane."

"Really? Philosophy?"

"And history."

I shook my head as the waiter served our dinners.

"Could we get a bottle of that, please?" I asked pointing at Allison's wine glass. "Okay?"

She nodded.

We took a few bites until the waiter returned and went through the ritual sommelier opening and serving of the wine.

"I take it dinner meets your expectations?"

"It does indeed. Thank you." Allison slowly chewed a bite of abalone. "So, why did you *retire* from the Congo Air Force?"

"Well…" I took a sip of Chardonnay. "…I kind of got shot down."

"Kind of? That's like *kind of* being pregnant."

"It was a lucky shot. Funny story, though, the villagers who caught me thought I killed their chickens."

"Chickens? In Africa?"

"Sure. Why not?" I asked. "They were going to cut my hands off, but Alfalfa kind of saved the day."

"Who's Alfalfa?"

"Some guy who worked for the CIA. He was sometimes helpful like that."

"Anything else?"

"Huh?"

"Like a girl? A doctor?"

I sighed.

"I talked to Father Bob and he told me that the rebels killed her. I just wanted to know."

"There was nothing between us." I looked out at the ocean. "Could have been, but no. Nothing."

"I'm sorry."

"It was a very bad day."

"But you saved Bob."

"Yeah. And so now I'm back in LA."

"Well, I'm glad." She reached over and took my hand.

We polished off the last of the wine and headed out.

"Come on, Let's go walk on the beach." Allison pulled on my arm towards the water.

I shrugged. "Why not?"

Allison kicked off her shoes and dropped them in the car. I stripped off my jacket and left it, then we wound our way around the Albatross to the waterfront where she skipped ahead and waded into the surf.

Staring out to sea, she took a deep breath. "You've got to love it. It's the law."

"Well, I'm kind of a desperado."

Allison spun around to kick water at me, then started walking north.

I followed along just outside the retreating waves.

"Sure, sure—*a desperado.* Well, don't make me walk out here all by myself."

"But—"

"But nothing."

So I slipped off my shoes and socks, then rolled up my pants legs. She didn't stop. "Hey, wait for me."

Allison ran ahead, stopped, then turned to face me.

"I'm beginning to think that you're the one who's an outlaw," I said walking up to her. "A real Black Rebel."

"Maybe…"

"So, what are you rebelling against?" I asked.

"Whadda ya got?"

I looked her in the eyes and smiled.

"Well, then, don't wait too long."

I leaned in and we kissed, softly. Then more passionately as I took her in my arms.

"Mmmm…" she moaned sweetly, then put her head against my chest. "Come on."

She took my hand and we walked north through the moonlit surf.

I watched her looking out to sea. "What are you doing?"

"Oh, nothing," she sighed. "Just counting waves."

"Why?"

"Force of habit. It's what you do in the lineup."

"The lineup?" I asked.

"Uh-huh. When you're surfing."

"Oh, no. Don't tell me you're a surfer girl."

Allison began to sing The Beach Boys song: *"Do you love me, do you, surfer girl? Surfer girl surfer girl."*

"Seriously?"

I stopped walking, but she pulled me along. "Everything's a song."

"Aye-Yi-Yi," I moaned.

"And, you know, it does make sense—considering my job and all."

I thought about it a bit. "Yeah…I suppose. A surfboard is kind of like a wing. And how long have you been doing that?"

"Before I started flying. I learned in Hawaii when Dad was based at Hickam. I think I might have been twelve. And, of course, there are great waves up north when I went to Stanford. It gets in your blood. You're not fighting gravity, you know? You are riding a wall of green that some storm has thrown at you from way out at sea. And some of them get pretty big and mean and, man, you are racing for your life with the wind blasting in your face as the wave crests over your head. You're scared, but your juices are flowing like crazy, too."

"Sounds wild."

"Yeah. Yeah, it is. Some say it's better than sex."

"You?"

She smiled at me. "Haven't decided, yet."

*"Right…*and you surf here?"

"Up north past the Malibu pier, at Surf Rider Beach. And Zuma Beach and County Line."

"Well, what do you know: flying, philosophy, and surfing."

"I do lead a full life."

I looked out at the waves, then back at her. "So you do."

We walked another half-mile north, then turned back south

towards the Albatross, got in the car, and drove back to Hollywood.

When I walked her to her apartment door, we kissed again.

"Don't wait so long to call, again," Allison said as she slipped inside. Before she closed the door, she looked back at me. "Who knows, one of these days you just might get lucky."

"Yup. Got it."

~~~

$100 Hamburgers

"Van Nuys Tower, Experimental One-Four-Echo, flight of two, ready at One-Six Left, northbound departure," I radioed after Scotty and I finished our run-up.

"One-Four-Echo, taxi into position and hold. Departing traffic on the right," replied the female controller. "Hey, there Scotty."

Scotty clicked his transmit button twice as we turned ninety degrees onto the numbers.

I looked back at him at my four o'clock and smiled, but he stared straight down the runway.

We watched a DC-3 roll down One-Six Right, until the tail wheel rose, and it arced lazily up into the blue.

"One-Four-Echo, cleared for take-off. Left turn approved."

"We're rolling. One-Four-Echo."

I advanced the throttle, followed by Scotty. We lifted off a third of the way down the runway, climbed to five hundred feet, and banked left to follow State Route 7 north. We leveled off at three thousand five hundred feet.

A few minutes later, the controller advised, "Departing the Van Nuys traffic area. Good day."

"Thanks, Kate. One-Four-Echo."

We veered right to follow SR 14, passing north of Magic Mountain heading to Antelope Acres.

"You want the lead?" I asked Scotty.

"You take it."

I descended to three hundred feet and banked west onto our track with Scotty sliding behind me. I arced east around W Avenue G with the red Cassutt in trail, settling in at twenty-five hundred RPM.

It's more than just finding the right line around the course. We race on a three-dimensional chessboard in a way, because we're not just flying around on a flat track. If you simply pass on the outside, you're making the oval longer for yourself, which means chewing up more time and falling further behind. You've got to use the vertical plane, too. And that's what we were working on.

I found a solid groove around the pylons, letting Scotty chase me down until he passed me overhead crossing the start-finish line, then it was my turn to chase down the red Cassutt.

He banked hard around the desert hump towards the windmill. I lofted a bit on his outside wing to trade altitude for speed.

I held my position as we arced around the windmill onto the back straightaway. Releasing back pressure on the stick, I gained on Scotty a bit and slid into his five o'clock position.

Scotty cut his bank early at the pile of rocks and wrapped tightly around the west end of our oval. He dove down close to the ground, kicking up a rooster tail of sand.

I held my line, then rounding W Avenue G, I traded a hundred feet of altitude for speed and slid out with my left wing crawling up from his four o'clock position.

Around the desert pile, wingtip-to-wingtip. We were on the same line. Scotty flew at fifty feet. I pivoted above him as we rolled out on the back straightaway.

He had nowhere to go and I slowly wound down my altitude,

creeping ahead.

Sixty degrees of bank into the west part of the oval, pulling us down into our seats.

Scotty lagged a bit in his turn.

I rounded the intersection clipping around his red wing and dove down quickly to thirty feet to pull ahead.

And then it was Scotty's turn to catch me, again.

We traded back and forth seven or eight times, until Scotty veered right off the course at the start-finish line, heading west.

"Whew," he radioed. "I think I'm done."

I made a more leisurely turn around the windmill and climbed into the center of the course. "Had enough?"

"Yeah, right. I'm hungry. Let's go to the Waypoint."

"I'll join up on you," I radioed, banking to the west to follow Scotty to Camarillo Airport.

We landed and parked on the tarmac out front. Inside we grabbed a booth by the window.

"Hi, guys. The usual?" Tiffani, the waitress, asked.

"I am starving, man," Scotty said. "We sure worked up an appetite. Give me a Red Baron. No cheese. Extra pickles. And a chocolate milkshake."

"Could I have the same, but with cheese and all the accouterments. And a Pepsi, please?" I asked.

"No shake?"

"I'm watching my figure."

"Right." Tiffani shook her head and headed to the kitchen.

"I saw you fellows come in," said a slender black man who walked over to the table. He stood ramrod straight, nattily dressed in an argyle sweater. "Nice looking airplanes. Did you build those yourselves?"

"I built the red one. It's a Cassutt design originally—but I've made some *special modifications*, if you know what I mean," Scotty whispered conspiratorially. "I reworked the intakes, clipped the wings just a tad and, you know, sleeked things down a bit."

"She looks hot. By the way, my name is Harold."

"I'm Hawk and this is Scotty," I said as we shook hands all around. "Pleased to meet you,"

"I don't recognize the design of your green model," he said.

"Well, to be honest, I just drive the darn thing," I said. "Had nothing to do with the design or the build. A friend of mine is kind of an engineering savant, so it's really his baby all the way. And I've got an ace mechanic who built it and keeps it running just fine."

"I like the sculpted wings. Looks like it moves along nicely."

"Yeah, it does. Just ask this guy here."

"He ain't got nothin' on me," Scotty said.

I just snickered.

"Looks like a lot of fun," Harold said. "I flew some myself. In Italy."

"A Red Tail?"

Harold nodded.

"Awesome. We heard a lot about you guys," I said. "I was in the 357th Fighter Group out of Yoxford. Flew in forty-four and forty-five."

"With Anderson and Yeager?"

"Yeah, Yeager and I both ended up with eleven-and-a-half kills," I said. "Hey, why don't you grab a seat and we'll bore Scotty to death with old war stories."

"I'd love to, but..." Harold looked over his shoulder. "I'm here with the missus."

"Understood. Well, we're based over at Van Nuys. If you're in the neighborhood stop by and meet Father Bob and Sparks."

"Will do," Harold said. "Great talking with you."

As we watched him walk back to his table, Scotty asked, "A Red Tail?"

"Tuskegee Airman. They got the job done."

Tiffani served our burgers and we plowed into them.

"So…" Scotty said slurping on his milkshake.

"So, what?"

"Come on. How was it?"

"It?"

"Your date. With Allison."

"Oh, that…It went fine."

"Fine?" Scotty asked. "Just fine?"

"You know, she's a surfer girl."

Scotty closed his eyes. "Yeah. Blonde and—well, you know. Yeah, I can see it. You dog you."

I grinned.

"So, will there be a second date?"

"I do believe there will be."

"I hate you. I really do."

"I get that a lot," I said. "So, what about you and Kate in the tower? She seems kind of sweet on you."

"She's kind of bossy."

"*Of course*. She's an air traffic controller for crying out loud. What a maroon."

"I don't know."

"Pay a visit to the tower and at least say hello."

"I suppose."

We finished our burgers and debriefed our flight over Antelope

Acres, spinning our palms in left-hand turns around the salt and pepper shakers for an hour or so, before we headed home.

~~~

Angels in the Outfield

Van Nuys was a ghost town by the time we got back later that afternoon. I taxied to my hangar, but Father Bob and Sparks were nowhere around, so I parked in front and pulled *White Hawk Redux* inside by the tail.

Wondering if Allison might be around, I wandered over that way, but both Scotty's and Allison's hangar doors were pulled shut and locked up. Maybe Scotty went to see Kate in the tower, but I seriously doubted it. Back at my place, I pulled the three doors closed, pinned them down, and snapped the padlock shut.

"Hey, Hawk," Al McGuire called out as I headed to the parking lot. "What are you doing right now? I got tickets to the Angels. Wanna go?"

"Today?"

"Five-oh-seven. We'll scarf down some dogs and throw back a couple of beers." Al grinned. "They're playing the White Sox."

He knew my weak spot, being from Chicago originally and hating the Cubs. "What can I say? I'm in."

"Come on. I'll drive."

We walked over to his new black El Dorado convertible.

"Are we going to a ball game or a funeral?" I teased Al.

"Don't you scoff. It'll put down your 'Vette."

"Not dragging around five thousand pounds of steel, it won't."

"One of these days, we'll just see about that out on One-Six Left."

"Bring it on. Any time," I said getting into the passenger seat.

Al just cranked the ignition and revv'ed up the engine. He squinted his eyes, looking my way. "Plus, I have room in the trunk for my golf clubs—*and* I can fill all of these seats with pretty girls. Try that in your little toy car."

Al squealed the tires as he pulled out of the lot. It was a pretty quick trip down to the Ventura freeway east, heading to Dodger's stadium where the Angels played. As we merged south on Interstate 5, he cranked up "Act Naturally" by Buck Owens and the Buckaroos on the radio.

I rolled my eyes back. "Really?"

"None of that Nashville Sound here, son. This is the real deal." Al stretched his right arm out across the seats and looked into my eyes with his infamous *trust-me-with-investing-your-money* smile. "So…how was your date with Allison?"

"You did that on purpose, right? The Albatross Hotel?"

"It does have a certain charm among the Hollywood in-crowd—*if you know what I mean*," he snickered. "So, did you get lucky?"

"She was on to you. Right from the start."

"Oh, well, I did my part for love."

"It worked out all right."

Al parked and led me inside to box seats just off to the first base side of home plate.

"Nice view," I said. "To what do I owe this honor?"

"Gene Autry's office hooked me up. I'm working a deal with them in Orange County."

"It's good having friends in high places."

"Speaking of which, it looks like those Reno races might just happen after all. Something to do with the one-hundredth anniversary of Nevada becoming a state or something."

"That sounds good."

"I threw some of our money his way, so now you're an investor."

"But I can race right?"

"Don't be silly. Of course."

We stood for the National Anthem, then watched the Angels warm-up on the field before the opening pitch and actually heard the home plate umpire cry out, *"Play ball!"*

Al snagged us a couple of beers and we watched the White Sox score three runs in the top of the first inning.

"I like the way this game is going," I said.

"There's still eight-and-a-half innings to go." Al took a swig of beer. "You know, you are going to have to get some real racing in before Reno next year."

"Yeah. Yeah, I know."

"Spinning around over the desert is sandlot stuff. You need to get into the game. Against some pros." Al pointed at the Major League players on the field.

"Where at?"

"Maybe Ft. Wayne, or down in Texas, and Cleveland. I hear they're having races there again, like the good old days."

"I'll check with Scotty. He knows some of those guys."

"Do it."

We got some hot dogs and another beer in the fifth inning, as the White Sox went up seven to two. Then crunched on a couple of boxes of Cracker Jack during the seventh-inning stretch. The Angels went down swinging in the bottom of the ninth with

Al grumbling the whole drive back to the airport to get my car.

I whistled the melody line to "Act Naturally" just to aggravate him.

Heading home to Beverly Hills, I found that my refrigerator was in dire need of beer, so I went inside Stitch's house to grab a few from Elaine.

I strolled into the kitchen and there, in a light blue terry cloth bathrobe, digging through her Frigidaire, was Father Bob.

He stood up, crunching on a piece of celery, and looked my way. "Oh, hey there, Hawk."

"Father Bob?"

"Ah, well, you can call me that, but you know it's just not true anymore. After Africa and all."

"What are you doing here?"

He put his left hand on his hip and looked back into the refrigerator. "You know me. I love my snacks."

"But…"

Father Bob's hand struck out cobra-like into the fridge and he popped a grape in his mouth. "Mmm, maybe some of these and chunks of cheese. You want some?"

"And in a bathrobe?"

"Well…"

"He's my guest," Elaine said. She leaned against the kitchen door frame, a slinky black nightgown clinging tight to her still gorgeous curves. It was over a long time ago between us, but *Father Bob?*

"Oh…I, ah…um…" I sought absolution in Father Bob's eyes.

But he just winked at me and shrugged his shoulders.

"Is there a problem?" she asked.

"No. Nope. Not at all. Nothing to see here." I looked at her, then at him, then back at Elaine.

"He makes me laugh."

I smiled at her. "Yeah. He does that. I was just looking for a beer."

Father Bob reached inside, pulled out four Olympia long-necks, and held them out my way. "Will this do?"

"Yup. All good." I looked at Elaine and nodded. I grabbed the beers from Father Bob and headed out back to my casita.

I didn't want to park out front on my porch in the Adirondack, staring at Stitch's mansion, so I popped a beer and sat inside, trying to figure out the abstract paintings hanging on my walls—and how Father Bob got lucky, but I didn't.

~~~

Woodies and Kaydets

Tired of boring holes in my bedroom ceiling with my eyes, I got up in the dark, showered, then headed to the airport—but, of course, I went around the front of Stitch's mansion and saw Father Bob's motorcycle parked on the circular driveway…which gave me something to think about on the drive in.

As I sat in the airport parking lot watching the sunrise, still pondering my predicament, an old Ford Woodie with a surfboard strapped on top pulled in next to me. Allison looked my way, smiled, then came around and leaned down with her elbows on my door.

"You're up awful early," she said, pulling her hair behind her ear. "You seem more like a crack-of-noon kind of guy."

"You are funny." She melted my heart a bit. I scanned her ride. "Nice car."

"Goes with the lifestyle. It's real, you know. Wood, that is."

"Are you going surfing later?"

"Maybe. Maybe I am." She reached over and pulled my head her way, giving me a kiss on the cheek. "I had a good time up in Malibu."

"Yeah. Me, too."

"You know, I promised you a ride. So, how about now?"

"In the Stearman? *Absolutely.*"

"Come on." She stood up and opened my car door. "Let's do this thing."

I got out and she grabbed my hand as we walked to her hangar. "It's been a while since I've been in one."

"Come on. It's like riding a bike," she said.

"Yeah, I know. It takes off at seventy knots. It cruises at seventy knots. And it lands at seventy knots."

"Yup. You've got it."

We opened the hangar doors and pulled the Kaydet out by the struts. I pointed at the tangle of wires holding the wing walking strut down on the top airfoil. "You really go out there on that?"

"Don't be such a wuss," she said pulling her hair back into a ponytail.

"Yeah…you're nuts."

I followed Allison as she did her walk around, checking the ailerons, the brakes, the forward struts, the bracing wires on the wings, and the engine. Hijacking the melody to "Oh My Darling, Clementine" she sang, "*Check the cotter pins, check the cotter pins, check the cotter pins on the plane*—see? Everything's a song."

Shaking my head, I helped her pull the prop through to clear the oil in the cylinders of the huge radial engine, then she primed it seven times.

Back behind the cockpit, She opened the lid of the luggage compartment and handed me a leather helmet with goggles and a headset.

"Well, shall we?" Allison asked, then climbed up on the left side of the wing to the front cockpit. She hopped on the seat and checked the fuel tank. "We're full."

I pulled on the helmet and followed her up, stepping onto the back seat, then sliding on down. I adjusted the seat down an inch or so, then strapped myself in with the five-point harness.

Racing the Dream

I flipped the levers on the rudder pedals to push them out a bit and locked them up. Unlike my racer, the cockpit seems huge with plenty of room to stretch about. Sitting inside the Stearman, scanning the instruments brought a huge grin to my face as memories of basic training at Randolph Air Force Base in San Antonio flooded into my mind.

I read the placard at the bottom of the panel, "Don't do nothin' dumb!"

"That's for my brother, Doug. You know, just to remind him," she said.

Allison went through the start-up checklist and I watched the mixture and throttle controls on the left move into position: full rich and one inch open. Gas valve on.

Allison looked around outside and cried out, "CLEAR!"

Magnetos on both. The starter switch went on.

And there it was—that whine of the starter spinning the Continental R-670 radial. I closed my eyes as the cylinders coughed and coughed and finally began to fire. I caught the smell of smoke and felt the wind from the prop rise in my ears as the engine roared into life.

My eyes went to the tach: 700 RPM.

Oil pressure rising.

The earphones crackled as the intercom came on.

"Ready, ace?" she asked, releasing the brakes.

I looked up in the mirror mounted to the wing and saw her beaming at me. "Do it."

And we rolled forward heading to the runway, Allison's head swiveling left and right clearing the wingtips as we taxied slowly out onto the apron. She gently S-turned us to the runup area where she checked the controls, instruments, fuel, and trim. The radial wound up to 1400 RPM and she confirmed the left and right magnetos operational. Engine back to 700.

"Stearman Five-Two-One-Delta-Mike, ready at One-Six Left. Departing north," Allison radioed.

"One-Delta-Mike cleared for take-off."

Allison taxied onto the runway. She locked the tail wheel and raised her hands above her head. "It's your airplane. Take me for a ride, Hawk."

I forgot how thick the control stick is on a Stearman—like a baseball bat, but it felt good. "I've got it."

I gripped the throttle in my left hand a couple of times, then pushed it forward. The engine roared and the wind sang in my ears as we rolled south until I just flew the plane off the ground like a P-51. I climbed to eight hundred feet, turned crosswind, then banked again to climb out on downwind.

"You know the way, right? Allison asked.

"I'm on it," I said.

North along the highway. I arced close around Magic Mountain, then northeast out over the desert. It was severe clear with a deep blue sky.

"This is awesome," I said. "I soloed in one of these."

Allison turned her head back and grinned. "Good times…good times."

I dove down on the back side of the mountains and skimmed at a hundred feet or so over the desert floor, then climbed to the west. Two thousand feet AGL, I did a couple of sixty-degree turns, left and right, then dove, banking thirty degrees and pulling the nose up to Chandelle back to the east.

"Is that all you've got?" Allison taunted me. "Show me some of that fancy fighter pilot flying stuff."

I laughed, then dove to pick up speed, confirmed 110 knots, then pulled the nose up thirty degrees for aileron rolls, left, then right.

I rolled inverted, then did a half loop down to the east, finding W Avenue G. I arced north, then west again over the road, pushing the airspeed to 125, working the throttle back to keep the RPM below 2100.

Full throttle. Pull up along the road, pushing us down in the seats with four Gs. Eyes on the left wing when the horizon went behind the nose. Thirty degrees over, looking front to catch the W Avenue G again right under the nose where it should be to the top of the loop—weightless. Over and back on the stick to follow it down to the bottom of the loop, pushing our butts back into the seats.

I banked hard left, dove, leveled off, verified my airspeed, then pulled us up again, this time rolling level at the top in a half loop, flying inverted to the north. Engine to idle, right ninety degrees, then I arced down in a sixty-degree bank, around and around, heading west again, and rolled out in a shallow dive west and cranked the engine to full throttle, heading perpendicular to a north-south road.

I verified 140 knots, then pulled back in a vertical climb, dropping airspeed until we almost seemed to freeze in mid-air, then kicked the right rudder over in a hammerhead before the stall and headed straight down at the desert floor.

"So…what do you think?" I asked as I pulled us up and out of the bottom of the dive.

"Not bad. Not bad at all," Allison said over the intercom. "Okay. Try just a little straight and level. Think you can do that for just a minute or two?"

"Getting dizzy are we?"

So I throttled back heading west, level at four thousand feet—and before I realized what was happening, Allison grabbed the handholds on the upper wing and stood up on her seat. She planted her foot on the windshield right in front of my face and pushed herself up through the support wires and around the struts on the top wing. Her feet slid into the step holds. She strapped into the wing walking support and lifted her arms in the air.

Holy crap—she's really doing it. Right now!

I caught us diving from her weight being out in front of the forward cockpit. I added power and trimmed up.

She gave me a thumbs up, then made a looping motion with her right hand.

I hesitated.

Allison grinned at me over her shoulder and raised her palms up as if to say, *what are you waiting for?*

I aligned with an east-west road, throttled up and dove five hundred feet, verified the airspeed, then pulled back arcing up until we were inverted. As I transitioned forward I glanced down and saw Allison waving her arms around.

I followed the road as we dove on the back side of the loop, the G-forces pulling her arms back down as we leveled off.

Allison signaled for a hammerhead.

Nose down, holding 2,100 RPM, I hit 140, then climbed straight up to a stall, then kicked the right rudder full over to pivot around into a dive. I pulled out to the east.

Rolls left, then right. Another hammerhead back to the west followed by another loop.

Racing the Dream

Allison held her palm level in the wind. She looked back at me and I gave her a thumbs up and maintained four thousand feet again.

She unbuckled and climbed down off the upper wing. She worked back my way on the lower wing, holding on to the wall of the cockpit. She pointed out to the end of the left wing.

She hollered, "Going out to the end. Make sure you keep the wings level."

I nodded.

Allison climbed her way out between the bracing wires to the far strut.

I eased the stick to the right to hold her weight.

She waved back at me, then turned, sat backward on the wing, and clutched her legs around the far strut. Letting go with her hands, she lowered herself upside down into the airstream, waving her arms around her head.

I really don't know how long we flew along like that—we were frozen in time.

It seems like maybe five minutes later, she pulled herself back up to sit on the wing facing backward, and gave me a thumbs up.

Allison stood and carefully wound her way back to the cockpit moving slowly from wire to wire. She climbed into her seat, strapping herself in and putting her helmet with the headsets back on. Grinning at me in the mirror, she said breathlessly, "You did great!"

"You really trusted me like that?"

"Of course, silly—wow, I'm beat. That's definitely a workout." She closed her eyes behind her goggles and rested her head back in the seat. "Why don't you take us back home."

Her wing walking done now, all I could do was shake my head in disbelief as I banked southwest towards the San Fernando Reservoir.

Brother Doug

"One-Delta-Mike cleared to land."

"You got this?" Allison asked.

"I'm on it," I said pulling the throttle back to a thousand as we passed abeam the numbers on downwind.

We glided down three hundred feet, then banked left for the base leg, maintaining 70 knots. Turn to final.

It was a perfectly calm day. A little power to carry me over the fence. Raising the nose above the runway numbers slowly and touching down perfectly on three wheels.

Allison was right: just like riding a bike.

"One-Delta-Mike clear of One-Six Left," I radioed.

"Taxi to the D hangars. Monitor ground, point seven. Good day."

"Point seven. One-Delta-Mike."

"I'll taxi us in," Allison said, raising her seat up and taking the controls.

"It's your airplane." Feet on the floor, I released the stick and held my right hand out flat, flying in the prop wash. "Thanks. That was a blast."

"Anytime."

As we approached her hangar, Scotty was standing out front talking to Allison's brother, I guessed.

They backed off, watching with hands on hips as Allison stood on the left brake and spun us around.

Throttle to 700. Mixture to idle cutoff and a few moments later the engine died and the prop spun down to a stop. Mags off.

I took off my goggles and helmet and stepped out on the left wing. "I can't believe you went out there on the wing like that."

"It's what I do." Allison got out and yanked her ponytail free, shaking her hair out.

As I jumped down off the wing, Allison put her arms around my neck and hopped, piggy-back on me, wrapping her legs around my waist. "Take me for a ride, Hawk."

I put out my arms and flew her around the tail of the plane.

"So, you guys are up early gallivanting around," Scotty said.

Allison hopped off my back and said, "Hawk, this is my brother, Doug."

I reached out to shake his hand.

"You've got the green Goodyear racer, right?" he asked.

"That's me." We shook hands. Doug was a couple of inches shorter than Allison with dark brown, curly hair. I looked at Allison, then at Doug, and back to Allison again. "Twins?"

"Fraternal," she said. "Not identical."

"You can tell because I got all the good looks," Doug said.

"Yeah…otherwise, it might be creepy," Scotty said.

"Is this the guy that took you to the Albatross?" Doug asked. Allison nodded.

Doug looked at me. "And you shut him down, right?"

All I could think about was Father Bob and Elaine.

"He was a gentleman," Allison said. "Honest."

"I find that hard to believe." Scotty winked my way.

I held my palms up in surrender.

"And how did it feel, yanking the controls around on that

old biplane?"

"Great," I answered, then turned to Doug, "I learned to fly in one of these."

"And he flew Mustangs during the war—like Dad."

"Ouch," Scotty moaned.

"But Dad was way, way older, you know?"Allison said. "Like thirty or something back then."

I rolled my eyes.

Doug eyeballed Allison. "Him?"

She punched Doug hard in the arm.

"Hey! That hurt."

Allison raised her fist again.

"Now, kids…" Scotty warned.

Doug looked up at me, snake-eyed.

"Who wants flapjacks?" I asked. "My treat."

"We need to practice for Bakersfield," Doug said to Allison. "Before it gets too rough up there."

"Well…"

"Well, what?"

Allison looked my way. "I vote for flapjacks."

"Me, too—especially if Hawk is paying," Scotty rubbed his belly with his palm.

"You were out there? With this guy?"

"Wing walking?" Scotty asked. "That's certifiable."

"It was just some fun," Allison gave me a coy grin. "I had to show him."

Doug scowled at me.

"Real butter," I said. "And lots of maple syrup."

"Come on, I'll drive." Allison pulled Doug by the arm towards the plane.

So we pushed the Stearman into the hangar, piled into Allison's Woodie, and headed to Norms.

Allison pulled me into the booth beside her. She stuck out her tongue and gave Doug a big raspberry, as he sat down next to Scotty who was already studying the menu.

"What do I want? What do I want?" Scotty asked himself. "You're buying, right?"

"Knock yourself out. Get whatever you desire." I asked Doug, "Are you doing the wing walking act full time?"

"I instruct at Van Nuys and Burbank. Independently, trying to build my hours to get on with an airliner."

"We know a guy you should meet. Right, Scotty?"

"Huh? What?"

"He flies for Lufthansa," I said. "Seven-Oh-Sevens."

"I want to get on with United or Trans World." Doug looked up from his menu. "I know a few of the guys at LAX who are going to help me out."

"And what about her?" I pointed at Allison.

"Come on, Hawk," she said. "You know those Airline Transport guys only work six or seven days a month. A real grind."

"You're back again with him?" Doris asked Allison as she came over to the table with her order pad out. "Some people never learn."

"Well, this time it's his treat."

"Mr. Big-time Spender, eh?" Doris took a deep breath and let her shoulders sag when she exhaled. "Okay. What'd ya want?"

"I'll have the usual," Allison said.

"Western omelet with cheddar cheese and juice." Doris shook her head and ignored me. Pointing at Scotty, "Don't even start with me, ace. What about you?"

"I don't know." Scotty shook his head. "Come back to me."

"Two eggs, over medium, bacon, and wheat toast," Doug said.

Doris pointed her pen at Scotty. "You, back there. You're up."

"Steak and scrambled eggs, dry. Medium on the sirloin. Hash browns, crisp—extra crisp. Okay? And a short stack with lots of butter and extra syrup. A side of sausage links. And a side of bacon. Orange juice, a large milk, and some coffee." He winked at Allison. "I'm watching my girlish figure."

"Now that guy is getting his money's worth," Doris muttered at me. "Coffee, everyone?"

We all nodded.

"Al says we need to get some real racing under our belts before Reno," I said to Scotty.

"And you're sure *White Hawk Redux* will pass inspection—the G ratings and all?"

"Father Bob's on top of all that I'm sure."

"Who is Father Bob?" Doug asked.

"I met him in Congo. He devoted himself to God in a local village there for a little while—coming off an ugly divorce, I guess. Before that, he was a brainiac engineer who invented some gizmos for diesel engines and built up a business on it. At any rate, he's a technical wizard."

"What happened to God?" Doug asked.

"Father Bob got kidnapped by Simba rebels...but we rescued him and he found his true path back to the slide rule."

"And he designed Hawk's plane from scratch," Allison said.

"It's a good airplane, I guess." Scotty scratched the back of his head. "But I beat him last time."

"Thanks only to Ax."

"Doesn't matter—a win is a win."

Doris came back, served our breakfast, then topped off our coffee.

"And what were you doing in the Congo?" Doug asked.

"You were some kind of mercenary, right?" Scotty eyeballed his steak and eggs and hash browns and sausage and bacon and flapjacks.

"Why, no. That would have been illegal for a U.S. citizen. I flew T-6s, but I didn't get paid. How's that?" I asked Scotty, "So, where can we get into some real racing?"

"Boy, I don't know. I don't think anyone's been racing Goodyears since fifty-nine." Scotty chewed on a huge hunk of sirloin. "But there's a guy I know in Pasadena—an old Army pilot who might have something going on."

Doug pointed his fork at Allison. "You know, we do need to practice."

Allison waved him off. "*Mañana…Mañana.*"

"Now you sound like a real *Makasi*," I said.

"What's that?" she asked.

"It's Bantu—African. That's what they called the Bay of Pigs pilots I flew with in Congo. That was their attitude, too: *Mañana.*"

"Yeah, well, today I'm surfing." She shrugged her shoulders at Doug, then asked me, "You want to come?"

With a mouthful of flapjacks, I could only nod.

And it looked to me like Scotty was eating his liver out over it.

✳✳✳~~~✳✳✳

Hodadding

"So, where are you taking me?" I asked Allison after we dropped Scotty and Doug off at the airport.

"We'll go back up to Malibu. Surfrider Beach."

"Sounds good, I guess." I leaned sideways against the passenger door. It creaked a bit, but gave me a good view of Allison, smiling with her hair blowing in the wind. I definitely liked what I saw. "Of course, I don't know anything about it. Surfing, that is."

"Yeah. I can tell your tan comes from your convertible or through the canopy on your racer—all arms, neck, and face."

"Not much of a beach guy."

"Who knows. Try it and maybe you'll like it."

"I take it you're not going to surf in your flight suit, are you?" I really wanted to see her in a swimsuit.

She shook her head impatiently. "No. My wet suit is in the back."

"Cold out there?"

"Can be."

"Okay, so what do you do? Paddle out into the surf and hop up?"

She sighed heavily, pulling north onto Highway 1. The Woodie slowly accelerated. "It's all about form and timing, you know."

"Like wing walking?"

"Yeah. Kind of. You have to find the right spot—outside the breaks and wait for a green wave. When you see one you want to catch, you turn with it and paddle, arching your back with your head up, keeping your board up out of the water, and looking back, trying to match its speed. Then when the wave lifts you up, you climb on top, center yourself on the board, and away you go. If you wait too long, you'll get tossed over the back."

"Sounds easy enough."

"Yeah…right. You want to try it, ace?"

"Nah, I'll just ride my wings."

"Smart move."

Allison turned around in the Malibu Lagoon lot, then parked on the road by the beach. She went to the back and got her wet suit.

"You want I should wait here?"

"I'll be right back," she said as she headed for the changing rooms.

I leaned against the grill of the Woodie and watched the surfers already out on the water. There were a ton of them and, frankly, it looked like kind of a big mess of surfers paddling out over the crashing waves, but somehow avoiding the ones standing on their boards riding in. Meanwhile, there were floaters out past the breaks, riding over the incoming waves like a flock of seagulls. It was a constant flurry of activity.

Allison came back dressed in a black wet suit with bright red shoulders and arms. It wasn't a swimsuit, but close enough for government work. I wanted to take off my Ray-Bans, but that would have been too obvious. I just nodded. "You look ready."

She gave me the hairy eyeball as she tossed her clothes into the rear seat.

I followed her around to the back of the Woodie. "You want some help with your board?"

"Sure. I think I'll use the short board."

"Which one is that?"

Allison looked at me like I was wearing a dunce cap. "It would be the one that's shorter than the others…" She tapped on the end of the middle board with the squared tail.

"Are these all yours? Why do you have so many?"

"Different boards. Different kinds of surfing," she said. "You could never wing walk on your little racer. I connected with Dale Velzy and talked him into getting me a board that's a couple feet shorter than usual. So he got a core from Grubby Clark and he made it with a strong rocker and sharp rails, so it's quick and agile."

"Who's Dale Velzy…and Grubby Clark? And what are rockers and rails?"

"Dale is a shaper from way back. Used to have a shop in Manhattan Beach. They're kind of like Father Bob is to you. Technical types."

"Technical types?"

"Never mind. Just help me get it down."

I opened the rear door, stepped up, and unstrapped the front. She climbed up on the back bumper to pull it down.

"Looks kind of crazy out there—you know, like a big dogfight with people going every which way and all. How do you keep from crashing into one another?"

Allison lifted her board under her arm and turned towards the beach. "We usually look out for one another. You know, don't drop in on someone and give way to the guy at the peak. Surfer etiquette and all. Of course, there are always some Barney wave hogs out there, but it's usually pretty cool."

"Okay…"

"You can watch from the beach, here. But maybe check out the view from the pier, too." Allison stepped off onto the sand. She stopped and turned back to me. "You going to be okay—I mean, just sitting and watching like a hodad?

"What's that?"

"Oh, you know, a looky-loo."

"I'll be just fine. Go play and have some fun."

"Okay. Remember, look for my red arms and shoulders." She held her arm out.

"Got it."

Allison hopped onto the sand and jogged for the surf. She turned and waved one last time before she threw herself on top of the board in the water and paddled through a crash of white waves.

She was out beyond the breakers bobbing in the waves with a group of other surfers. Two or three waves passed her by, but then she turned abruptly and started paddling towards the shore. Behind her, a wave caught up with her and before I knew it—just like that morning when she climbed up on the wing of the Stearman—Allison was standing on her board and the wave broke with white water. She curled to the left in front of the crest, riding it down until it looked like she might lose it and get tossed into the water, but she pivoted back into the top of the wave and quickly spun around heading left again.

And before I knew it, she was done. Maybe thirty seconds or so on the surf, then she coasted in and stepped off into the water. Allison grabbed her surfboard. She looked over and waved my way.

I gave her a salute.

She dove in again and paddled back out.

Racing the Dream

I waited, watching the crazy dogfight among the surfers, then watched her sail in again, cutting back and forth along the front of the wave.

I looked over at the long wooden pier reaching out into the ocean and decided to wander down that way and check it out. When she came up out of the surf, I pointed that way.

She gave me a thumbs up.

I strolled down the parked cars along the beach and out the long walkway to the end of the pier. And it just so happened that I stumbled upon the Malibu Sports Club, which had a very fine selection of beer items, so I ordered up an Olympia and found a table and chairs on the north side facing the waves. And I sat…and watched…and enjoyed a few more beers, soaking up the sunshine and actually enjoying the surfing exhibition.

When Allison found me later that afternoon, my feet were propped up on a chair and, I don't know, maybe it was a restless night of sleep thinking about Elaine and Father Bob or getting to the airport before dawn or doing aerobatics with Allison or a belly full of flapjacks, but the fact is, I had nodded off at the table.

"So, did you learn anything about surfing, ace?"

"Huh—What?"

Allison sat down across from me and deliberately counted up my afternoon. "Eight?"

"Maybe I was learning how to enjoy the beach." I pulled my Ray-Bans off and rubbed my eyes. "What happened to your wet suit?"

"I changed. You know, you should have put on some sunscreen. You are going to be hurting, I think."

"I'll be all right."

"Can you make it back to the car?"

"Don't be a smart alec. Okay?"

She grabbed my arm and helped me up.

"Oh…okay, then."

We shuffled back slowly to her Woodie.

"You know, that seems like an awful lot of effort for, what, a thirty- or forty-five-second ride in on the waves," I said.

"Yeah, well, it's just you and your board against the sea."

"Seemed like some pretty tall waves—especially out there at the end."

"Third point seems pretty good for my board. We had some gnarly waves today."

"Gnarly?"

"Big and curly and knot-like."

"Whatever you say."

Inside the Woodie, I leaned back against the creaking door. Allison pulled away and I just nodded my head up and down as she went into serious details about her different runs on the surf. I looked west at the orange glow of the setting sun. I tried to pay attention but drifted off again.

As we got close to the airport, she shook me awake again. "So, where do you live?"

"Live? Why?"

"You don't think I'm going to let you drive, do you?"

"I'll be fine. I'll be fine."

"Nope. Not a chance I'd put you behind the wheel of that gorgeous Corvette. Now, which way?"

"But my car…"

"We'll get it in the morning. Which way?"

"Van Nuys to Mulholland."

"And then?"

"Beverly Hills. My brother's house."

"Well, this should be interesting."

I gave her the directions to the mansion. She lazily drifted through the corners, chasing her headlights around the curves through the mountains on Mulholland Drive.

When we got to the house, she slowed down to a crawl out front. "Wow. Nice place."

"Yeah. I live out back."

"So, who lives in the big house?"

I moaned just a bit, thinking about Father Bob.

"You know what? Never mind. It's none of my business."

I pointed to the servants' entrance. She pulled in and parked.

"Coming in?" I asked.

"Can I trust you?"

"What do you think?"

"A perfect gentleman?"

I just nodded wearily and we went inside. "It's not much, but it's home."

"I like it." Allison wandered around the living room looking at Stitch's paintings. "These are kind of interesting."

"My brother did those. Kind of his hobby. He was actually a plastic surgeon."

"So, he lives up front?"

I shook my head. "No. Stitch was murdered a long time ago. I inherited this place, but I couldn't move in. That's when I went to Alaska with Sparks."

"Oh, I didn't know." Allison stepped around the couch and sat down.

I stood there, vaguely looking around at the pictures, but not really focusing on them.

"Come on. Sit down. You look beat."

"I kind of am." I plopped down at the other end of the sofa.

"I don't think I told you, but I had fun this morning."

"This morning?"

"Yeah. Out over the desert. Flying with you."

"Oh, yeah. That was a blast."

"I wasn't scared at all."

I looked over at Allison, scratching my temple. "Huh?"

She smiled, reached out, and pulled my shoulder over until I was laying out with my head on her lap. "I think you're better than Doug."

"Oh, yeah. *Don't do anything dumb.*"

"He's good…but a little too mechanical. You—you've got the touch, the feel."

I nodded my head against her thighs. "Right now, I feel tired."

She stroked my hair and I drifted off again.

When I woke the next morning, my head was on a pillow and I was covered with a blanket. And Allison was gone.

~~~

Big Donut

I sat up on the couch rubbing the ache out of my temples. There was a knock on the front door.

"Yeah? Who is it?"

"Let me in. My hands are full."

Elaine. I got up and opened the door. She carried in a tray with a pot of coffee and mugs. She set it on the kitchen counter, while I dropped myself back down on the couch.

"You alone?"

"Yeah. I guess."

Elaine poured us mugs of coffee. She handed me mine and sat down on the coffee table, facing me. "Andre's special blend."

"As long as it's black, hot, and full of caffeine, I'm good."

"You look a bit ragged."

"Top of the morning to you, too."

Elaine sipped her coffee. "So…who was she? We saw you guys come in last night. Kind of noisy."

"*We?*"

"You know. Me and Bob."

I just nodded. "He knows her. She's another pilot at the airport. Allison. Flies an old Stearman."

"Serious?"

"I don't know. Maybe…or maybe not." I looked around my living room. "You don't see her around, do you?"

"You never know…"

"Woman's intuition?"

"Call it what you want."

I took a gulp of coffee. "What about you and Father Bob? Serious?"

"I don't know. What if I said it might be? Is that a problem?"

"It's been a long, long time. Hasn't it? There never was anyone else, besides Stitch, right?"

She shook her head. "No, just my work, really."

"Then, good." I smiled at Elaine. "If it's right, it's right. You'll know."

Elaine reached out and rubbed the top of my thigh. She nodded.

"I hope so—for you and for Father Bob."

"You know, he's not really a priest."

I grinned. "Old habits…"

Outside, a car door slammed shut. Moments later, Allison bounded in through the front door, carrying a box of donuts. Her hair was pulled back in a ponytail and she wore just my number eighteen Rams jersey and flip-flops.

"I went to the drive-through at Big Donut down by LAX. Didn't know what you like, but I figured you'd need the sugar…" She froze when she saw us. "Oh…I…ah…sorry—"

"Allison, this is Elaine. She's the one who lives in the big house up front," I said.

Elaine stood up and stepped towards her. "We're old, old friends. Hawk's brother helped me out a long time ago." She looked back at me. "That's all."

"Oh, okay."

"I brought down some coffee." Elaine motioned towards the tray on the kitchen counter.

"Nice to meet you," Allison said.

"And I should be getting back to my house guest." Elaine winked my way. She stepped around Allison heading towards the door and patted her lightly on the shoulder "It was very nice to meet you, too—and good luck with *him*." She cocked her thumb over her shoulder at me.

"Did you get any apple fritters?" I asked after Elaine left.

"I got one of each kind they had."

"You look good in that jersey—a lot better than Roman Gabriel ever did. "

"I hope you don't mind. After you fell asleep—*again*—I went and slept in your bed."

"No problem. I'm glad you stayed."

"Well, I promised to take you back to get your 'Vette. And I always keep my promises."

We looked at each other awkwardly. I got up, walked around, and took the box of donuts from her.

"I guess at least I was a gentleman last night—thanks to the Olympia Brewing Company," I said.

"Well, you know…" She pulled out her ponytail and her hair fell about her shoulders. "…sometimes that's not always what a girl wants."

It gave me pause. So, I set the box of donuts down on the coffee table, then reached out to take hold of Allison by the hips and pulled her to me.

She held my gaze.

I wrapped my arms around her back.

Like I told Elaine, if it's right, it's right. *And I knew it for sure.*

I kissed her.

She ran her fingers up through my hair and drew me closer.

I could feel her melt into my arms.

I kissed her cheek gently, then found her ear lobe, then kissed her neck. "You taste salty."

"Mmm…that's very nice."

I wrapped my arm around her waist and headed toward the bedroom.

"But what about the donuts?" she asked.

"They will still be here."

"*Okay…*"

~~~

Barney's Beanery

Later—much later, like almost noonish—we sat against the headboard with the box of donuts on our laps. Allison had the sheet wrapped around her naked body. I had finished off the apple fritter and we taste-tested the other selections, taking alternating bites out of the Glazed Old Fashion, the Raspberry Jelly-Filled, and the Chocolate Long John's with Creme. We were working our way into the second half of the dozen, washing the bites down with milk.

"So, what did Elaine mean when she said your brother helped her out a long time ago?"

"Just after the war, Elaine was an eighteen-year-old rising movie starlet. She was…well, gorgeous—"

"She looks good now."

"Good, yeah. But, honestly, she was like Grace Kelly back then—until some no-name actor wrapped his Porsche Spyder around a telephone pole."

"Ouch."

"He walked away. But her time in front of the camera was all over. Stitch was a Beverly Hills plastic surgeon who did—I don't know, nine or ten surgeries on her, all for free. And paid some of the hospital bills, too."

"Were they involved?"

I took a bite of the Chocolate Iced Cruller and passed it to

Allison. "No. It didn't really work out."

"You?"

"Honestly, I fell for her hard."

"Even after…"

I nodded. "But she was really only interested in Stitch."

"But you let her live in the mansion here?"

"I couldn't move in, but I didn't want to sell the place either. So it worked out good for everybody."

"But your brother, what happened?"

I looked at one of Stitch's paintings hanging on the wall. "It was a long, long time ago. You know?"

Allison started to say something but stopped herself. I felt her hand rub my leg.

I grabbed the Glazed Crondy, took a bite, then handed it to her.

"Eh, I can't go on." Allison looked at the donut, then dropped it back into the box. She nuzzled into my neck. "Anyway, now I'm glad it didn't work out between you and Elaine."

"Yeah, well, funny, though. Elaine and Father Bob are…you know…"

"Hmm. Well, that seems okay. Do you think so?"

"I do."

"Then everybody's happy now."

"So it seems."

"Even you?"

I rolled Allison over on her back and unraveled the sheets from around her body. "Especially me."

"Good. I am too."

She kissed me and we made love again.

Afterward, we took a long, hot shower together and she drove me to the airport.

Racing the Dream

As I walked Allison back to her hangar, Scotty saw us and headed over our way. "Where the hell have you been? I saw your car, but…"

"Hi, Scotty," said Allison.

He scowled at us, then turned and paced back toward his hangar, muttering to himself, "Oh…my…*God*…"

"Is it that obvious?" I asked.

Allison looked down at my hand holding hers. "You know what? I don't care."

"Good morning, Scotty," I called out.

"Morning? *Morning*?" He marched back our way. "It's four o'clock in the afternoon."

"I guess I lost track of time." I elbowed Allison lightly in the side.

"You know…you know, if I—I could really, really hate you sometimes."

"Comes with the territory."

"So, I've been looking for you, because we have a meeting today," Scotty said.

"Yeah? With who?"

"Jack over at JPL"

"The Jet Propulsion Labs?" Allison asked. "And who's Jack?"

"An engineer, I guess. He works on the Ranger Program, trying to get pictures of the moon or something—but that's not important. In his spare time, he's organizing some Goodyear races again."

"Oh yeah? Where at?" I asked.

"Bakersfield, Waco, Ft. Wayne, and Cleveland. And maybe a couple of other sites this year."

"Real racing?"

"Sounds like it. He's building a Cassatt in his garage, but he's tired of just waiting around, like everybody else. And he's got a crew of guys to help him out."

"And he wants to meet with us?"

"Today at five. In Pasadena."

"Okay," I said. "You want me to drive?"

"Well, *duh!*"

"Guess I gotta go, then," I said to Allison.

"Call me later."

I gave Allison a kiss.

"Oh, get a room," Scotty moaned.

"Didn't need to."

"Come on. Come on." He headed towards my car. "Oh…my….*God!*"

"He ain't gonna help."

"Not me. You."

I pulled out of the parking lot. We drove in silence south on Balboa to the 101 east. It was a test of wills. I whistled the melody to "Act Naturally."

Finally, Scotty said, "Well, I'm not going to ask."

"And I'm not going to tell you…but I know you want to know."

"Dammit."

"*Cause all I got to do is…act naturally.*"

"I think I do hate you."

"So, where are we going?" I asked.

"Barney's Beanery."

"On Colorado?"

"It's Jack's favorite place."

"I'm good with that."

Scotty looked at me expectantly, eyebrows arced like a pair of McDonald's arches.

"I'm still not going to tell you."

"*Dammit!*"

So we drove on into Pasadena in silence, with me smiling and Scotty scowling. I found a parking spot on North Raymond and we headed inside.

"There he is, back there," Scotty said, pointing to a booth near the pool table. He led me that way. "Hi, Jack. This here is Hawk, one of my racing buddies."

"Good to meet you," Jack said in a low, slightly gravelly voice, worthy of an airline captain. "Sit down. Pull up a bench. You hungry?"

"Actually, I did work up an appetite earlier," I said, staring at Scotty sitting next to me.

He bared his teeth and growled back a bit.

Jack gave Scotty the hairy eyeball, then looked at me like, *what's up with him?*

"Girl problems." I shrugged.

"Whatever." Jack waved over the waitress. "I'll have the usual."

"Yup. Classic chili," she said.

"Best in town."

"A Juicy Lucy with Sweet potato fries," Scotty said.

"A Pastrami Rueben—and throw some onion rings on the side."

"No chili?" Jack shook his head. "It's your funeral."

I sized Jack up, then asked, "Where'd you learn to fly? Army or Navy?"

"Army. Flew H-13s into MASH units in Korea."

"Wow," Scotty said. "No pucker factor there."

Jack shrugged it off. "Grew up in Cleveland and rode my bike down to the Air Races. I saw them all—Jimmy Doolittle, Wiley Post, Jimmy Wedell, Roscoe Turner—all the greats. I guess it gets in your soul."

"Awesome."

Jack asked me, "You?"

"Mustangs with the 357th out of Yoxford. Did some movie stuff with Paul Mantz after, ran a bush pilot operation in Alaska, then flew T-6s in Congo."

"Well, I know Scotty's got a Cassatt. What about your ride?"

"Custom design. My buddy is an engineering savant. Studied a bunch of different models out there and came up with his own special creation."

"It's pretty fast," Scotty said. "If I do say so myself."

"And I know you hate admitting it. Anyway, Scotty says you're building a Cassatt, too?"

"*Miss Pasadena.* A couple of guys are helping me out from the NAARA."

"What's that?" I asked.

"North American Air Racing Association."

"So this is for real, then."

"Already filed with the state. And we've got four dates set."

"Like I told you," Scotty said. "They're going to race Goodyears at Bakersfield, Waco, Ft. Wayne, and Cleveland in the fall."

"We are calling them Formula Ones," Jack said. "And we've worked it out using six pylons on a three-mile course. Got it spread out so the bank angles shouldn't be more than sixty degrees. Should be pretty safe."

"We've been using four up in Antelope Acres."

"Yeah. I heard about that little adventure. You know Art Chester killed himself on a four-pylon course in San Diego."

I shrugged my shoulders at Scotty. "What about the guy up in Reno?"

"Stead? He's got something going for late September next year with the Nevada Centennial or something. But you've got to have more than one race a year. That's what we're doing. So, you guys in?"

"What's involved?" I asked.

"A hundred dollar membership fee and if your planes pass inspection, you go race."

"What about the pilots?"

"We're all adults here. I'm assuming you have FAA tickets and medicals. As long as you've logged ten hours in type and sign a hold harmless agreement with us, you are good to go."

"Not a problem. I guess I'm in." I reached into my pants pocket and pulled out my money clip. I slid two hundred dollars toward Jack for Scotty and my memberships.

"Welcome aboard."

"When is Bakersfield?"

"Next month, so you better practice up."

The waitress served Jack his chili and our sandwiches.

"You don't know what you're missing," he said as he dug in a tortilla chip.

~~~

Fear of Falling

I dropped Scotty off at the airport and headed home. Turning into the back entrance, I saw Allison's Woodie parked around the side.

Now that's a nice surprise, I thought, pulling in behind it.

I hopped out and came around front to find Allison and Elaine camped out on my front porch, sipping wine.

"*Uh-oh…*" I muttered under my breath. My right foot froze on the bottom step. "So, am I interrupting anything?"

"Hey!" Allison called out. "You never told me that Elaine was a movie director. I loved *Fear of Falling*."

"One of my best," said Elaine.

I shrugged. "Sometimes falling feels like flying…*for a little while*."

Allison pointed her wine glass my way and said to Elaine, "Funny guy."

"He is hilarious."

"And how was your meeting?"

"Well, I guess I am now an *official* airplane racing pilot. Scotty and I joined the North American Air Racing Association."

"That's a real thing?" Allison asked.

"Seems like it. The first race is in Bakersfield next month."

"Seriously? At the air show? Doug and I are one of the acts up there."

"That should be fun, huh?" Elaine said.

"You'll get to see our show."

"Excellent."

Elaine took a long, slow sip of wine.

I smiled. "And what did I miss out on here?"

"Just a little girl talk," Allison said.

"Oh, yeah? How much girl talk?"

Elaine waved at the two bottles of Cabernet Sauvignon on the floor between their Adirondack chairs. She picked one up and eyeballed the contents. "Looks like a little over a bottle and a half. Want some?"

"I think I'm good."

"It's your loss." She split the rest of the wine between their two glasses.

"Where's Bob?"

"I think he's working on *your* airplane," Elaine huffed.

"Idle hands are—"

"Yeah, yeah, yeah, the devil's workshop," said Elaine.

"No, *playground*. The devil's not exactly a hard worker, if you know what I mean."

"And who taught you that?"

"Maybe Father Bob?"

Elaine rolled her eyes back in her head.

"Anyway, I hope you don't mind I stopped by," said Allison.

"Honey, you are always welcome around here." Elaine gave me a one-eyed look. "Right?"

I sat down on the top step, leaning against the side post. "You heard her—remember she lives in the big house up front."

Allison and Elaine clinked their glasses and drank.

"So, Hawk…" Elaine said.

"So, what?"

"What are your intentions here?"

"Here?"

"With her." Elaine tipped her glass at Allison.

I looked her way.

"I, ah, Elaine—really…"

"I like her. A lot," Elaine scolded me.

"Well, good. Me, too."

Elaine and I gave each other the *High Noon* squinty-eyed, showdown look.

"I think I can handle this myself, thank you." Allison closed her eyes and leaned her head back against the chair. "*Really.*"

"Watch yourself, Hawk."

"Okay, then."

"All right, already."

"And that's that."

Just then we heard a motorcycle pull up front.

Elaine grinned. "I believe I must be going." She poured her wine into Allison's glass, then tousled my hair as she stepped down from the porch. "You kids be good."

We watched Elaine sashay up to the big house.

"Hey, Hawk, I'm sorry, I—"

"You know, it's funny."

"Funny? What's that?"

"She took your side. Usually…Elaine looks out for me."

"So…she does like me."

"So it seems." I gazed back at Allison.

"I like that look on your face."

"What look?"

"That big grin. You look like a happy little kid." She took a gulp of wine.

"Well, I am happy."

She took another sip, then peered down into the wine. "So…*us*. We're alright, aren't we?"

"Alright?"

She looked my way. "You know, your intentions."

I pointed to the smile on my face. "All good."

Allison stood up and wobbled a bit on her feet. She blinked her eyes slowly a couple of times. "Ooo, maybe too much."

"Too much vino?"

"Maybe." She took a deep breath and slowly set her wine glass down on the table between the Adirondacks. "Maybe I should head home."

"And risk turning your Woodie into kindling? Yeah, I don't think so. Just make yourself at home."

She shuffled over my way and plopped down on the porch beside me. "Really?"

"Sure."

She leaned up against me. "Okay."

I put my arm around her shoulders and kissed her on the top of the head. "I am happy."

"Yeah. Me, too."

A minute later, she snored softly in my ear.

~~~

Father Bob

Early the next morning, I heard Father Bob's Norton fire up. After idling for a minute or two, he revv'ed the engine a few times and pulled away.

"What was that?" Allison asked sleepily.

"Elaine's house guest."

"Father Bob? Where is he off to so early?"

"My hangar, I guess."

"He works way too hard. How much do you pay him—not nearly enough, I think."

"He loves it. Honest."

"Still…" Allison yawned and rolled over to look at me. "You know, this is getting to be kind of a habit with us."

"Fine by me." I lay on my back with my head against the pillow and my eyes closed.

She leaned over and kissed my cheek. "I do have to meet Doug to practice for Bakersfield and I should probably head home to change. So, where did you put my clothes?"

All I could do was grin.

"Oh, you'll pay for that."

"Oh, yeah? How?"

"I don't know I'll think of something." She scampered off to the bathroom.

I got up and put water on the stove for instant coffee. I stared at the pot, waiting for it to boil.

Allison came out of the bathroom all dressed. "What are you doing?"

"Making instant coffee."

"That's as bad as machine coffee."

"I think it is machine coffee."

"We really need to get you some appliances."

"It's all I got."

"I think I'll pass." She gave me another kiss on the cheek. "All good?"

I took her in my arms. "All good."

We kissed more passionately, then she left.

I made myself a cup of Nescafe and sat in the Adirondack chair out front.

Sipping the brew, I thought, *She's right. I really need some appliances.*

~~~

When I got to my hangar, Sparks was doping up some fabric on what looked to be elevator parts.

"What's this all about?" I asked.

He pointed over his shoulder at Father Bob's workspace in the back corner. "His idea. He claims it might help get a few more knots out of the thing."

"Think it will work?"

"I just build 'em and fix 'em." Sparks squinted my way. "I don't noodle out the designs and I don't fly 'em."

"Fair enough." I headed back. "Hey, Bob."

Father Bob spun on his work stool to face me. "Hawk, my boy. Good to see you here...so early."

"Yeah, Scotty and I are going up."

"Well, I want to show you a few *special modifications* I have in mind."

"You mean like the elevators Sparks is working on."

"Yes, yes. And a couple of others, too."

"Sure thing."

He took a sip of coffee. "Well, I—"

"Where did you get that?"

"What? The coffee?" He held up his cup. "I made it."

"Is it real? Or instant?"

"I would never drink instant coffee. *Ever.* I shudder to even consider it. Not even in the jungle."

"Yeah? Then how did you make it?"

Father Bob pointed to a scientific-looking laboratory beaker-type contraption next to his hot plate. "It's a Cona. It boils the water from the bottom vessel up to the coffee in the top and when it cools, it flows back down for you to pour. Quite tasty."

"That looks complicated."

"Then just get a percolator—and why are you asking about making coffee anyway—oh, oh, oh, I believe I know: *Allison.*"

"Forget about it."

"I'll bet Andre could help you out."

"I don't need anyone's help."

"My boy, you do." Father Bob stared me straight in the eyes from beneath his bushy brows. "You really do."

"Anyway, we're racing in Bakersfield next month."

"Racing? Like...for real?"

"Scotty and I joined the North American Air Racing Association. That's their first event."

"Hmmm...next month?" Father Bob rubbed his chin. "Well,

I guess we have some work to do."

"Like what?"

"Besides my special modifications, we definitely need to get a trailer."

"What for?"

He waved his arms around the hangar. "You can't expect Sparks to work on the plane in Bakersfield without any tools, do you?"

"Guess I didn't think about that."

"And spare parts? And we'll need some way to pull it there. Are there other races?"

"Waco, Ft. Wayne, and Cleveland."

"Hmm, this is all very interesting. You'll be able to fly up to Bakersfield, but Ft. Wayne and Cleveland? We'll definitely have to trailer the plane to those races."

"Really?"

"It would take you forever to get to Cleveland with the tiny fuel tank in the darn thing. Stopping every hundred miles or so." Father Bob scratched his temple. "What about technical specs?"

"Jack said something about passing a seven-G test. He's supposed to send me all that info."

"Well, the sooner the quicker. Of course, we won't have any problems with that, I'm sure." Father Bob stood up and we walked outside the hangar. "This is real racing, right?"

"Part of the air show up there. Three days' worth."

"Let's see, what else do we need? Just a month. Wow, not much time."

While Father Bob pondered our needs, I heard a radial engine go to full throttle. Looking down between the rows of hangars, I followed along as Allison and Doug took off, then turn to the north.

Father Bob looked up at the biplane, then at me, and patted me gently on the shoulder. "You really should talk to Andre."

"Wow! You must be taking this air racing thing serious-like," Scotty said, walking up behind us. "Up before the crack of noon and everything."

"Are you racing, too?" Father Bob asked.

"Wouldn't miss it for the world." Scotty shaded his eyes and watched as the radial engine faded away. "You are hopeless, you know that?"

"What a way to go," I snickered.

"Whatever. Hey, so you really don't mind me asking, do you?"

"Huh?"

"You know…" Scotty pointed at Sparks in the hangar. "Like we talked about in the car."

"Sure. It's a free country," I said. "But I warned you."

"Yeah…whatever." Scotty slid between me and Father Bob and headed into the hangar. "Hey, Sparks."

"What's that all about?" Father Bob asked.

"Scotty's going to ask Sparks to be his part-time mechanic, too."

"He'll never go for that."

"I tried to tell him, but…"

We couldn't hear the conversation, but Sparks listened, then scowled my way.

Scotty flapped his arms around like a wounded duck, making his case, but he was obviously going down hard.

Sparks put his fists against his hips, leaned in squinting Scotty's way, and shook his head.

Father Bob and I could read his lips as he clearly said, "Nope."

Scotty made one last attempt, but Sparks cut him off, then turned back to doping the elevators.

"He just wouldn't listen," I whispered to Father Bob.

Scotty shuffled back out of the hangar. "You were right."

"I figured."

"He said it wouldn't be fair to try to split his time being a mechanic on both of our planes. He might get distracted and miss something." Scotty sighed. "Now I have to find somebody to help me."

"Talk to Al McGuire. He might know somebody around the airport. Or the EAA chapter. Those guys are always working on their own planes."

"Yeah, I guess."

"You'll be fine," I said. "Come on, let's go fly."

"I'll meet you out there." Scotty headed back to his hangar.

I walked over and grabbed *White Hawk Redux* by the propeller to pull it out of the hangar. I started my walk around.

Sparks walked over. "You knew?"

I nodded. "He did ask me yesterday."

"Well, I guess you've got to let the man say his piece. It's okay, but I can't do it." Sparks scratched his back with a thirty-inch breaker bar. "He's got to find his own guy, you know? That's just how it's got to work."

I worked the elevators and rudder back and forth, checking the hinges were secure. "Thanks, Sparks. I appreciate it."

"You want to race around in circles like a crazy fool, that's your business, but, I'll tell you this, you ain't going down because of me. That's for damn sure. Got it?"

"Got it."

"Good." Sparks marched back into the hangar. "*Idiots.*"

I grinned as I checked the oil level and drained the fuel tank.

"You got to love him," Father Bob said.

"Yup. You do." I stepped around front to make sure the propeller wasn't nicked up and the air intakes were clear. "So, you and me, we good?"

"Ah, er, you mean with me and Elaine?"

"Jesus, no. With, you know…" I waved at the plane. "I mean with all this work here."

"You do recall that this was my idea."

I walked down and around the left wing, checking the aileron. "Yeah, but—"

"Count your blessings, my son. As do I. You don't think I really want to go back and work for a living, do you?"

I shook my head as I pulled the seat harnesses back in the cockpit.

"I don't need the money. Never did. And neither do you, right?"

"Nope."

"I want to see you break two-hundred in *my* design. And I want to see you win."

"Fair enough." I stepped into the cockpit and strapped myself in.

"Besides, I'm having a blast." Father Bob gave me a huge grin.

"Then, fire me up, okay? I gotta go race."

~~~

Barnstorming in Bakersfield

Scotty and I spent the next month chasing each other around and around Antelope Acres. Sometimes we had company, which made it as real of a race as we could have. Most times it was him against me. Father Bob squeezed a few more knots out of my Formula One racer, so I think I came out on top more often than not as we debriefed ourselves again and again at the Waypoint Diner at Camarillo Airport.

Allison and Doug flew nearly every other morning polishing up their wing walking routine. Her arms and legs were bruised from banging into the flying wires on the Stearman, especially after mornings with a little more turbulence in the air, but she shook it off. It was just part of the job for her. On off-days, she worked out to keep in shape. In the afternoons, she dragged me to hodaddy at Malibu, Newport Beach, Huntington, Laguna Beach, and Rincon Point in Santa Barbara, while she chased and caught the waves. I steered clear of the brews and spent my time reading old Raymond Chandler mysteries, Mickey Spillane's Mike Hammer novels, and Elmore Leonard westerns—and I worked a bit on my beach tan. I was starting to look like a real Californian. One night I took Allison back to the Albatross Hotel where we had dinner again and spent the night, just to have the last laugh on Al McGuire.

Allison made good on her plans to equip my kitchen with all

manner of appliances—a coffee percolator, a toaster, an Oster blender, and a weirdly green KitchenAid Mixer—not to mention pots, pans, mixing bowls, measuring cups, sharp knives, and a myriad of utensils—all of which she used with reckless abandon and skill. She was a great cook. At least as good as Father Bob. Maybe better.

We were out front on my porch one evening drinking wine, trying to decide what to have for dinner when Father Bob pulled in back piloting a twenty-foot long aluminum, kind of bus-like vehicle, honking his horn, and waving out the driver's window. He parked alongside my 'Vette and Allison's Woodie.

"What do you think?" he hollered out.

"What in the world is that?" Allison asked as we stepped down off the porch.

"It's a Dodge-Mahal." Father Bob grinned. "My buddy, Ray Frank, makes them up in Michigan. It's built on a Dodge truck chassis with a V-8 engine and a TorqueFlight automatic transmission. It will do ninety miles an hour. It just came in today."

We came up next to the driver's window. I looked down the length of the vehicle. "This is like a house on wheels."

"That's exactly Ray's big idea. He calls them motor homes. Come on in and check it out."

We circled around front and Father Bob waved at us through the huge windshield, then disappeared inside. Moments later, he held open the side door for us. I followed Allison in.

"Look, there's even a kitchen," Allison said.

"Plus three beds—one for each of us. You, me, and Sparks." Father Bob pointed at a day bed on the right and a pair of bunk beds to the left, then walked to the back, opening a narrow door showing us a commode. "And a bathroom back here with a shower. We are going to be living in style."

"What are you talking about?" I asked.

"Bakersfield, Waco, Ft. Wayne, and Cleveland—and then, Reno, right? And whatever else comes down the road after that."

"For racing?"

"Look—there's a stove and a refrigerator, too." Allison started rummaging through the cabinets.

"He's a bit slow, huh?" Father Bob asked her.

"What? Hawk? He's like a Neanderthal in the kitchen."

"True enough." Father Bob nodded. "True enough."

"But you don't have any pots or pans or utensils or dishes or anything," Allison said.

"And I got a brand new trailer for hauling *White Hawk Redux*, spare parts, and Sparks's tools." Father Bob looked around and grinned. "What do you think?"

"I think you are crazy."

"Crazy like a fox." Father Bob pointed at his temple.

I could only shake my head as I stepped back outside. Inside they were still yakking away.

"Come on, we should go down to Montgomery Ward and get you set up in the kitchen," Allison said.

"Right now?" he asked.

"Well, yeah. The race is next week. Why wait?"

I stood back, looking up and down the motor home shaking my head.

"What is this thing all about?" Elaine asked as she came up from the big house.

"Bob's idea. For going to the races. It's like an apartment inside there."

"He *is* a big thinker."

"Yeah. That he is."

Allison pulled Father Bob out the door. "We're going shopping."

"Right this minute?" I asked. "But what about dinner?"

"Later." She held out her hand to me. "Come on. Let's see some greenbacks. After all, Father Bob bought this thing."

I reached into my pocket and pulled out my money clip. I started peeling off bills, but just gave up and handed it to Allison.

"Thanks." She gave me a kiss on the cheek. "Come on, Bob. Let's go."

"She seems to like it," Father Bob said as he followed Allison to her Woodie.

Elaine and I watched them drive off.

"Careful, Hawk. She's going to domesticate you."

I could only sigh. "I'm kind of afraid of that, too."

~~~

Wednesday before the Bakersfield races, I met up with Allison at the airport to fly to the air show, her in the Stearman and me in *White Hawk Redux*.

Father Bob and Sparks left the day before in the motor home, towing the trailer, and Doug would follow on Thursday after his flight instruction lessons.

When I heard her Continental rotary fire up, I pulled the prop to start, then climbed in to taxi out behind her for departure. After our run-ups, she pulled into position on the runway. She gave me a big smile, then pushed the throttle forward and I watched her rumble down One-Six and slowly lift off. At eight hundred feet she banked to the north. Tower cleared me for departure and I followed her path towards Bakersfield. When I caught up with her, I throttled way back and tucked myself into formation on her wing.

This is definitely something new, I thought, *following my girlfriend in another airplane.*

I liked it.

We picked up I-5 on the other side of Santa Clarita and followed it west of Castaic Lake, then up to six thousand five hundred feet to clear the mountains through Tejon Pass and back down over the greening farms in the Central Valley. Allison picked up Shafter VOR and I followed her north to Meadows Field airport.

She radioed me to land first and waved as I sped up and called the tower. They had me cross mid-field for a right-hand downwind to Three-Zero Right. As I lined up on final, I noticed some of Jack's crew setting up pylons on the south side of the runway. Father Bob's motor home was parked on the tarmac by a hangar which would be the pits for the Formula One racers. I landed and requested from ground control to taxi that way. Allison landed right behind me and headed for the show plane parking.

Scotty came out of the hangar waving as I throttled down and cut the mixture on the engine. He was shadowed by a heavy-set man in a Dodgers baseball cap. They looked a bit like Laurel and Hardy.

I popped the canopy. "Fancy meeting you here."

"Your pit is over this way," Scotty said, walking up to my plane.

Loosening my safety belts, I stepped out of the plane. "And who is this?"

"This is Ed, my crew chief guy. Ed, this is my buddy, Hawk."

"Good to meet you." Ed leaned around Scotty to shake my hand.

"Likewise, I'm sure."

"He's building a Baby Ace at Van Nuys. Al McGuire hooked us up," Scotty said.

I coyly eyeballed Ed's waistline considering the size of a Baby Ace cockpit and smiled.

"And…" Scotty nodded back over his shoulder. "…you'll never guess who else is here."

"Let's see, I'm thinking the *Reichsminister of Aviation?*"

"Who's that?" Ed asked.

"Mr. Lufthansa himself." Scotty pointed into the open door of the huge hangar where I saw Ax's canary yellow Shoestring.

"Well, this should be fun, then."

Scotty folded his arms across his chest. "Just like old times, eh?"

"We'll see about that."

"Come on. I'll help pull you in."

Scotty and I grabbed the tail and pulled the plane into the hangar.

Sparks stood in the middle of my space with his hands on his hips. "Yeah, 'bout time you showed your ugly mug around here."

"Where's Bob?" I asked.

"Making lunch." Sparks stepped aside as we set the tail down.

"Wow. That's great. What are we having?" Scotty asked.

Sparks growled. He stepped over to his toolbox and yanked open the top drawer, pulling out a screwdriver.

I counted about eight or nine planes already parked inside, maybe four or five I remembered chasing around Antelope Acres. Didn't know any of the pilots, but I recognized the paint jobs.

Colorful—like a broken bag of Halloween candy spilled on the hangar floor.

"Jack's Technical Director will be by with a G-meter to test your plane," Scotty said. "We'll get some time on the course tomorrow. Friday we do time trials, then we race Saturday and Sunday."

"It is very good to see you now in Bakersfield, my friends." Ax came over and held out his hand. "We will have some fun here then. No?"

"I'm looking forward to it." I grinned and grabbed his hand.

"And you, too, Mr. Scotty."

"You all ready to race?" Scotty asked.

"Yes, yes. Peter and Manfred have my airplane in top-notch shape. Ready to go. So we will meet you out on the course, then. No?"

I noticed Sparks' eyes boring holes through Ax. He shook his head slowly. Ed stood back and just watched.

"You bet," I said.

"So, who's your new friend?" Allison asked walking up from behind and putting her hand on my shoulder.

"I am Axel. I am a racing pilot here."

"Of course. Nice to meet you."

"It is certainly my pleasure." Ax clasped his hands behind his back. He bowed a bit and winked at Allison. He nodded at Scotty, then slowly smiled at me. "Until tomorrow, then."

I flashed my pearly whites back his way. "You got it, ace."

Ax turned and marched back to his pits.

"He's the one who flipped you over the desert, right?" Sparks asked, popping the turnlock fasteners on the cowling to pull it off.

"He is," I said. "The Red Baron, himself."

"Just don't like him. Surely don't."

"Well, we never get to choose who our competitors will be."

"And damn sure don't trust him, neither."

"Of course, we don't trust him. Never do. And never should."

"Yeah, well, I don't like him either," Allison agreed. "Just something about him."

"I just need to beat him on the course. That's all."

"You do that. Okay?" Allison rubbed my back gently.

I nodded as I watched Ax step back into his pit and bark orders at Peter and Manfred. "Yup. That's the plan."

"*Idiots*," Sparks mumbled.

~~~

The next morning, Jack's Technical Director came by with the G-meter, so I went out and pulled some aggressive loops without tearing the wings off to pass their aircraft inspection.

We got some practice time on the course just after lunch. It was a bit different than Antelope Acres. With three-and-a-half miles around, the six pylons rounded out the course and flattened my turns a bit. I wound the engine up to three thousand, then thirty-five hundred. I didn't want to press it to the limit—not in practice anyway—but it ran smooth and sweet. It took a while until I found my groove at seventy-five feet around the pylons, with fifty feet being the minimum altitude. I felt like I was pulling two or three Gs in the corners, cutting them closer and closer, gaming the wind in and around the turns.

After twenty laps or so, I pulled up out of the course and circled at three thousand feet overhead to cool the engine. Below, the racers out on the course looked like parrots whirling over the jungle canopy in Congo.

"Well?" Father Bob asked when I landed and taxied back to the pits. "How is she running?"

"You done good. You done real good," I said, smiling up from the cockpit.

Father Bob beamed. "Excellent."

~~~

Friday afternoon, we all qualified, just me against the clock on the course and the best of my two laps was one eighty-six. I was disappointed to end up fourth fastest. Scotty beamed at me in the hangar, actually finishing a second or two ahead of me while Ax ended up in sixth place. Back in the pits, he seemed to be sharing some angry thoughts with Peter and Manfred. I sure didn't envy them. But we all would be racing together in the first heat on Saturday.

I killed some time comparing notes with Father Bob and Sparks, then meandered around talking to the other pilots. I wandered down to the grandstands joining the sparse crowd to finally catch Allison and Doug's act as they ran through their routine.

It was one thing sitting behind her in the cockpit when she climbed out on the wing over Antelope Acres. I was surprised then, but I had my hands full wrestling the Stearman around the air. Now, sitting as a spectator watching her out there in the braces, with Doug rolling at two or three hundred feet—then arcing overhead in barrel rolls, a pair of back-to-back Cuban eights, pulling up in loops, hammerheads, and Immelmans with the wind tearing at Allison's hair and her flight suit—*and so close to the ground*—we were at four or five thousand feet over the desert. The crowd oohed and aahed every time they passed show center, but it took my breath away seeing Allison battling the airstream on the wing twenty or thirty feet off the runway.

Doug climbed and Allison crawled down from the top brace. I knew she banged her way through the wing wires to the right, but from down on the stands, she moved slowly and gracefully. Allison laid out against the javelin strut in the middle of the wings, stretching her arms out as Doug flew by like she was Superman leaping a tall building.

The Stearman circled to come in from the left at a hundred feet. Allison climbed down and wrapped her legs around the strut, lowering herself below the wing and holding her arms beneath her head. Turbulence yanked her down as she passed show center. It caught my breath—but Doug quickly brought the wings back level. Crazily, Allison just kept doing her wacky upside-down Rose Bowl float parade waves to the crowd.

At the end of the show line, Doug rolled around quickly to enter a downwind. Allison quickly worked her way back to the cockpit and climbed inside. Doug cut in on a short base leg, then made a short-field landing in front of the grandstands, and as he rolled out, Allison climbed up on the top wing and waved at the grandstands as the Stearman taxied by. The crowd clapped and some even gave her a standing ovation.

I sighed, closed my eyes, and leaned against the back of the grandstands, finally letting myself take a deep breath. I headed down to the tarmac and found my way to the show planes.

"Hey, Hawk! I saw you sitting down there," Allison called out to me climbing down from the Stearman. "What did you think?"

I pulled my Ray-Bans off. "I don't know…to tell you the truth, it made me nervous watching you out there."

"Oh, now you sound just like my mother!"

Squinting her way, I chuckled, "Guilty as charged."

"Anyway, flying like that always gives me some grum-bellies and Father Bob is making chili."

I put my specs back on and reached out my hand. "Well, then, shall we?"

"How did the time trials go?"

"Fourth," I muttered.

"Not bad."

"But—do you believe it—Scotty beat me."

"What about Axel?"

"Sixth."

Allison took my hand and pulled me towards our motor home. "*Good.*"

~~~

Late Saturday morning, Jack briefed us at the far end of the hangar. He had folding chairs set up in five or six orderly rows and stood in front of an aerial photo of the three-and-a-half mile race track set up along runway Three-Zero Right. I brought Father Bob and Sparks. Scotty had Ed sitting next to him, but Ax sat by himself in the back row, leaving Peter and Manfred in his pit.

"Severe clear. Winds forecast to be two-nine-zero at twelve. So weather will be absolutely no problem this afternoon," Jack lectured us calmly, like it was a World War Two pilot briefing—the only thing missing was a long pointer in his hands. "Our start time for the first heat is one-thirty. *One-thirty.* Everybody's got to be out on the runway, in position, and we'll get your engines started then. Remember, to the promoters we are just another act in the show. If you're not there, you will be DQed. Got it?"

Jack looked around the room. Everybody nodded.

"Remember the rules," Jack continued. "Maximum altitude is two-hundred fifty feet. Minimum is fifty feet. That means your head inside the cockpit needs to stay above the tops of the pylons. We'll have judges out there to monitor the turns." He pointed to the six pylons forming the curves of the track oval. "If you cut a pylon it is a two-second penalty per lap. No inside passing. Outside or above. And keep your victims in sight. Got it? You'll be DQed unless the other guy is so far off the course that it's impracticable. But that's the judges' call. And no blocking if you're being overtaken.

"On the runway, red flag goes up, you start your engines for warm-up. You'll get five minutes. When it comes down the pit crews leave. Green goes up, you've got one minute. It comes down, brake release and you're off. Fly one lap for oil warm-up—and, of course, you are free to position yourself on the startup lap—but timing begins when the lead pilot crosses the start/finish pylon the first time. Then you race to the checkered. Eight laps. If there's an emergency, you climb inside the course and do not—*DO NOT* cross the show line over the spectators in the bleachers by the tower on the tarmac. Any questions?"

We all shook our heads.

"Okay. Fly low…Fly fast…and turn left."

The group stood and scattered back to their pits.

"Sounds easy enough," I said to Father Bob and Sparks as we walked back to *White Hawk Redux*.

"You sure about the prop?" Sparks looked at Father Bob.

"I think so," he said.

Racing the Dream

"You think so?" I scratched my head and looked down at Father Bob.

"You're inside on the second row. The prop pitch will get you up and ahead at the start, giving you an advantage…I think. It's different with a standing start to the race. Over Antelope Acres you guys have been doing flying starts. Everyone's already at altitude, at full power, so you just want the speed. Now, you've got to climb and get in front as quick as possible. I think position is everything."

"Okay. You're the boss," I said.

"So, Hawk, are you ready? First real race ever," Allison called out when we got back to our pit. She was leaning on the wing of my plane.

"Hey, *you*, I had that plane all polished up and now you're trying to slow us down putting fingerprints on the damn wing." Sparks peered out from under his baseball cap, pointing his index finger at Allison.

She quickly pulled off the wing. "Oh—I'm sorry—I, ah…"

Sparks gave her a half grin as he stepped over, pulling a rag from his back pocket to polish where her hand and butt prints might have been on the wing—if you could see them.

"You're not here to distract my pilot, now are you?" Father Bob asked.

"I just came by to wish him luck. Boy, you guys are just crab apples this morning."

"Women weaken legs." Father Bob shook his finger at me. "You'll need to be on those rudder pedals during the entire race."

"I think I can handle it."

"Good to see you, Allison." Father Bob winked her way.

I took her hand and led her outside the hangar. "Come on,

let's get rid of those losers."

"Are you nervous?"

I thought for a moment. "I don't think so."

"Well, you don't look it, anyway."

"You and Doug go on after us, right?"

"At two-forty-five."

"So, what about you?"

"I can't wait. I get excited, but I'm not nervous. You know, like paddling to catch a really big wave and riding it in. It gets the adrenaline pumping."

"Whatever you say."

Allison stopped and turned me back towards her. She zipped up the front of my flying suit. "Just have fun, okay?"

"Yeah, I don't know if I can do that." I grinned at her.

"Oh, you'll be all right."

"I might not be."

"And come in first, too." She kissed me and walked back towards the show planes.

"That I can do."

~~~

One-thirty. On the runway, I tightened my belts, pulled the canopy down, and locked it.

Scotty stood beside his Cassutt. He looked back my way with a huge 'How-are-you-today-Mrs.-Cleaver' grin on his Eddie Haskell-looking face. He spun his index finger in the air.

I gave him a crisp salute and muttered to myself, "Bring it on, Scotty. Bring it on. Let's do this thing."

He climbed into his cockpit.

Racing the Dream

At the front of the pack, the red flag went up. I primed the engine, flipped on the master, and switched the ignition to both magnetos, then signaled to Sparks, who pulled the prop through and backed away. The engine coughed and quickly caught. I settled the RPM to a thousand. Oil pressure green. Temperature rising. Now I wait.

Sparks came around the right wing, next to Father Bob. I nodded.

Father Bob gave me a thumbs up.

Allison is right. It isn't nerves. But there's an excitement building inside, like waiting in the queue to take off from a grassy field at Yoxford and escort B-17s into Germany. You want to be in the air, heading into injun country. Not idling on the ground burning avgas and getting nowhere fast.

Come on already. Let's get going.

I took a few slow, easy breaths.

There were two of us in the second row. I was on the inside. Ahead were three more racers with Scotty's red Cassutt on the outside. Three more were behind me. Back over my left shoulder somewhere was Ax's Tweety Bird.

I checked the gauges. Engine oil temp was up in the green.

Good. Anytime, now. Anytime…

The red flag came down.

I looked at Father Bob and Sparks, giving them the Churchill victory sign, then they turned and headed off the runway.

I ran the engine up to seventeen hundred, checked the left and right magnetos, the carb heat, then pulled it back to idle.

Well, that's definitely been the longest five minutes of my life.

I grabbed the stick and exercised the ailerons, the elevators, and the rudder. My hand gripped the throttle as I watched the flag man to the left side of the runway.

He raised the green flag.

I throttled up. The RPM was pushing thirty-five hundred. I pulled the mixture back until the RPM dropped a bit, then enriched the fuel flow to best power.

The green flag came down. I released the brakes and rolled a bit ahead of the racer in my row on the right.

Five hundred feet down the runway, the lead aircraft lifted off.

I was right behind, climbing faster than the pole position guy as we headed towards the first pylon.

A hundred feet. The front row flew a tight echelon into the turn.

I was already above the middle of the pack. I rolled outside a bit, passed around the outside of the middle plane, and into first place, heading around the second and third pylons. I extended my lead down to the end of the oval and back around across the start/finish line and the timers started.

The race was on.

I pulled in harder to get back on my line down around the first turn—G-forces built, yanking me down in the seat. I grabbed a lung full of air and clenched my throat to keep the blood in my head—they call it an M1 anti-G straining maneuver. I lofted up seventy-five feet. Rolling out, I took a deep breath and eased off the back pressure, trading altitude for speed down the back straightaway.

I looked down for the shadows and saw I had opened up more of a lead on the pack. Being first is definitely a good thing. Smooth air. No prop wash.

Turning into the fourth pylon, the tailwind out of the west pushed me outside my line. I banked around the turn, holding seventy-five feet, trying to catch my groove again. I passed the start/finish pylon in just under a minute and ten seconds. One ninety-two.

Around the northwest corner and down the back straightaway pushing two hundred miles per hour. I anticipated the tailwind and turned earlier on the fourth pylon, but I still looped outside my line by more than fifteen feet—and the shadows showed a tight string of the pack catching up. I roared down the front straight and around again.

Needing the speed, I pressed the RPM up to thirty-eight hundred going into the third lap, but coming down the front straight again, I got detonation in the engine. The oil temperature spiked, so I enriched the mixture to cool the cylinders and I eased back on the throttle.

Father Bob made it clear that this is a marathon, not an eight-lap sprint.

"Make sure the engine makes it through three days of racing," he lectured me in the pits, with Sparks nodding behind him. "You have to be running on the last lap on Sunday to win."

As my speed ebbed, the pole sitter, then Scotty's red Cassutt passed me coming down the front straightaway. All I could do was hold my low line, as they climbed on my wing then dove down in front of me. I started wrestling the stick from their wake turbulence, costing me a bit more speed.

I held my line as best as I could searching for smooth air to hold my position on Scotty in third place around the course again.

Radio traffic is minimal during the race—as everybody is busy concentrating on hitting our marks and maintaining our groove.

"One-four, three o'clock. Passing high."

Ax's voice, calling my number.

It's called uncooperative formation flying. Yeah, we're in an echelon, but nobody's really trying to get along.

And up above, Ax's yellow Shoestring eased over me at two o'clock at one hundred fifty feet.

He seemed to be slowly reeling in the leaders. On the sixth lap, Ax caught and passed Scotty, like he mysteriously found an extra ten knots of speed in his engine.

Ax passed the leader crossing the start/finish, taking the white flag for the last lap. On the back straightaway, he held his line and pulled away to win.

I followed Scotty across the line in fourth again. Easing back on the throttle, I pulled back on the stick to climb up to three thousand feet, cooling the engine, wondering how Ax did it.

How did he suddenly find the extra speed?

~~~

I landed and taxied back to the pits, goosed the engine, and stood on the right brake, spinning ninety degrees, then stopping. Mixture to idle-cutoff. The engine choked off and the prop locked up.

"Dammit!"

Ignition *off*. Master switch *off*.

Father Bob and Sparks walked out of the hangar and over to *White Hawk Redux*.

Pulling my belts off, I popped open the canopy and climbed out.

"Well, that was…um, not what I expected." Father Bob scratched the back of his head. "You got out front right away, but fell off there in the middle."

"The oil temp spiked and the engine started running rough, so I went a little rich and cut back the revs a bit." I walked back to the tail of the plane. "Come on. Help me get inside."

Sparks came around to pull the plane back to my pit. "If you hadn't rolled off the engine, don't you know, it'd have been curtains, for sure."

"Yeah, well…fourth, again."

As we set the plane down, Scotty came over with Ed in tow.

"It's like he just came out of nowhere." Scotty put his hands on his hips and looked over at Ax being congratulated by a couple of the other pilots. "How did he do that?"

"Black magic, I guess." I shrugged my shoulders.

"Very odd…very odd…" Father Bob came up to us. "He was clocking at one eighty-nine, but he ran fifth behind you until the last three laps and then…like you said, black magic."

"Well, come on, Scotty. Let's go over there and eat our livers out."

Scotty and I walked over to Ax's pit, leaving Ed behind to debrief with Father Bob and Sparks.

Ax grinned as we came over. "We raced quite well today, didn't we?"

"You had a good run," I said, reaching out to shake his hand. "Congrats."

"Thank you."

I kicked Scotty in the shin and he finally held out his hand.

"Yeah. You got me this time. But, tomorrow, we'll see. We'll see."

"Yes. We shall see, will we not?"

As they talked, I wandered around Ax's plane and checked out the cockpit. Peter and Manfred eyeballed me suspiciously until I felt Ax's hand on my shoulder.

"I meant to ask you," Ax said, turning me away from his plane, "how did you pick your racing number?"

"Fourteen? It's A.J. Foyt's number—he won the Indy 500 in sixty-one."

"Indy 500?"

"Kind of a famous car race."

Ax nodded slowly. "Interesting."

"Yeah…interesting."

"So good of you to come by to congratulate me. Thank you."

I looked up at Ax and grinned.

"What is it?"

"Nothing. Nothing at all. I'm gonna head back to my pit. So, we'll see you again tomorrow."

"Tomorrow. Yes, yes. I will be in the pole position."

"Yeah. I know."

~~~

I was in the same starting spot the next day—second row inside. Scotty was on the outside again, but now Ax was in the pole position.

I stared at his canary-yellow bird as my engine warmed up until a knock came on my windscreen.

I looked over and saw Father Bob grinning down at me. He shook his head and waved his index finger back and forth my way.

I knew what he meant: *just fly my race.*

The red flag came down. Father Bob backed off slowly and left the runway with Sparks.

A quick run-up. Flip the controls and take a deep breath.

The green flag went up and so did my RPMs. When it came down I released the brakes and rolled quickly towards Ax. I was off the ground first, making up half the distance between us. A great start.

Scotty was off to a poor start, and into the first pylon, I climbed on Ax's wing until reaching two hundred feet coming out the back straightaway in the lead. I angled down direct towards the fourth pylon, quickly building my airspeed to two hundred miles per hour.

I banked hard at seventy-five feet, raising the nose, spinning close in the corner, holding my breath, and clenching my neck muscles against the Gs.

I arced down to the start/finish line beginning the race in first again today.

Leading into pylon one, I wrapped in tight, twenty feet or so inside. Lofted twenty feet, then rolled out and dove down the back straightaway, paralleling runway One-Two Right. No shadows yet on my tail.

Just fly my race…

Timed my left turn early for the tailwind. Rolled out a bit to keep clear of cutting the pylon, losing a second or two…maybe. Flattening out on the front straight, I pushed the throttle up three hundred and gave the mixture a half-turn inward.

Around the first turn again, checked the oil temperature. Higher, but still green.

A shadow appeared on my tail. From the slab wing, I bet it was Scotty's red Cassutt.

I held level.

Picked up my mark at the third centerline on Runway Three-Zero Right and into the turn right where I wanted to be.

Quickly caught the windsock—still northwest. I stayed level just a second more before my turn into pylon four.

Scotty narrowed on my lead, but he was being chased, too.

Across the start/finish line and around the first turn. I picked up some rough air as I caught up with the last man in the pack. Climbed twenty-five feet and reeled him in, holding high on his right wing into the turn.

I went by quick on the front straight, hoping it would slow Scotty down a bit, too.

Timed my turn. Held my line at seventy-five feet, eating up the clear air reeling in the next plane to lap.

A bit faster, but I still had at least ten miles per hour on him. He rose in the turn, forcing me higher and a bit more outside than I wanted, pushing me out on a longer track. Scotty passed the lapped traffic, chased close by the third-place plane running a higher line.

I chased my traffic in a high echelon into the first turn and passed him on the back, diving down for every mile per hour I could wring out of the engine.

Oil temperature was pushing the yellow. I gave it a bit more fuel on the mixture but held the RPM at thirty-eight hundred. It was the last day of racing and I needed it to hold off Scotty as his shadow crawled slowly up my tail.

Into the fourth pylon, he was forty feet off my tail, but being chased hard himself by the third-place plane ten feet off his tail and flying a higher line.

I rolled out and throttled up to four thousand. Oil temperature pushed into the yellow—the engine backfired going into the first turn, then again around pylon three, so I turned the mixture in another half turn.

Scotty got passed on the high side as he was closing above me in the far corner.

Racing the Dream

I rolled level and began a shallow dive—suddenly the propeller shook violently—engine backfired repeatedly—I pulled the throttle back and immediately arced up, turning inside the course—away from the show line. My energy quickly carried me up to pattern altitude.

I looked over my left shoulder to see a line of smoke chasing my plane. No smoke in the cockpit—*yet*.

I cut the engine to idle and put myself on a right downwind for Runway One-Two—a downwind landing, but it seemed a safer bet than limping around to final on Three-Zero.

"Mayday, one-four for One-Two," I radioed.

The engine shook the front end a little less, but I couldn't shut the engine down if I needed power to make the runway. A bit high—that's okay.

I smoothly banked a continuous turn around base to final—and once on the centerline, I dropped my left wing and pushed the right rudder to dump altitude in a crab.

Sure I had the runway, I cut the mixture off completely, turned off the fuel, and killed the magnetos.

Over the numbers, I popped the canopy and raised the nose to drift slowly down to the asphalt.

Hold it off…hold it off…hold it off…

The main wheels touched down. I rolled, then braked hard and turned off at taxiway Foxtrot, then stopped on Alpha.

The emergency trucks rolled up.

I pushed the canopy up, unstrapped, and got myself out of the plane as quick as I could. Rescue workers surrounded me aiming fire extinguishers at the plane.

"It's okay—it's okay," I said, backing away from my plane to bend over and grab my knees.

"Are you all right?"

I took a deep breath. "Fine. I'm doing just fine."

A pickup truck parked twenty-five feet back. Father Bob and Sparks hopped out of the bed and ran over.

"Hawk—Are you okay?" Father Bob put his arm around my shoulders.

"All good," I sighed. "All good."

Sparks stared at *White Hawk Redux* and shook his head. He looked my way and nodded his head at me.

I just nodded back so he knew I was okay.

"Well…now you've done it, for sure," he grumbled. *"Idiot."*

"Thanks, Sparks. Good to see you, too."

~~~

After Sparks opened the cowling and the rescue guys confirmed there was no engine fire, they hooked the tail of *White Hawk Redux* to the trailer hitch on the pickup truck and pulled it back to the pits.

Father Bob, Sparks, and I shuffled behind it like we were in a New Orleans funeral—only without the Dixieland band. No one spoke.

Up overhead, Allison and Doug began their routine, but I had little interest at the moment.

I missed Ax and Scotty up on the podium after the race, shaking up the champagne bottles to squirt each other, then pumping their trophies in the air. I'd catch up with Scotty later to congratulate him.

Father Bob and Sparks unhooked the plane and pulled it into the hangar.

Racing the Dream

I just kept walking, not sure exactly where I was going at the moment, but I didn't need to talk to anyone right now.

I replayed the last lap again and again: rolling out—four thousand—mixture up—backfires—the rumble, then shake of the propeller—pulling up and out of the course. DNF—*Did Not Finish*…

I ended up down where Allison's Stearman usually parked, pulled up a milk crate against the front of the hangar, then sat, closed my eyes, and waited for them to land.

~~~

DNF

The Stearman radial engine rumbled louder and louder as it taxied up. I opened my eyes, watching from my milk crate as they spun into their tie-down spot and Doug shut down the engine.

I stood up.

Allison was out of the cockpit before the prop wound down. She ran over to me.

"We saw the smoke. What happened?" Allison asked. "Was that you?"

"DNF. I popped the engine."

"Are you okay?"

"We'll, I'm still vertical and not room temperature…*yet*."

She wrapped her arms around me in a bear hug.

I grabbed her back. "So, I don't think we'll be flying back home in formation."

"Don't care, as long as you're okay." She kissed me on the neck.

"I'm okay. Honest." I looked over at the PT-17. Doug seemed to be wandering around the plane aimlessly with a weird, anxious look on his face, but I just dismissed it. I kissed Allison on the forehead. "Come on, let's go see what kind of damage I've done."

"I'm sure it's not so bad."

"Yeah, well, you know Sparks. I'm sure I'll get a boatload of grief from him."

"Oh, come on, he's really just a big marshmallow inside—you know that, right?"

"You've met him, haven't you? About this tall?" I held my hand up at six-foot-two inches high. "Kind of curmudgeonly with a scurvy look in his eye, malice dripping off his lips, and usually some kind of large wrench in his fist?"

"How long have you actually known him?"

"It's been a while. Met him at Van Nuys back in the Fifties. He was a mechanic for Al McGuire at Sundance Aviation. He actually worked on my MG back then. Put a Chevy engine in it."

"And, let's see, he followed you to Alaska when you went up there, right? Then to the Congo. And back here, again."

"Yeah, well…"

"Aw, kind of sounds kind of like puppy-love to me." Allison poked me in the ribs.

"You have no clue—honest to God."

"Right…right…"

We stepped through the open hangar door into the pits. A couple of racer pilots came up and asked how I was doing and what happened in the race. I just pointed at my plane and said I'd probably find out soon enough from my crew chief.

"Hey, man, what happened to you out there?" Scotty asked as we walked by his Cassutt. "Saw the smoke. You didn't catch on fire, did you?"

"Shake, rattle, and roll." I stopped and shrugged my shoulders. "Guess I'll find out soon enough from Sparks."

"Boy, I don't envy you there, pal."

"Hey, good finish today. Second place. Sorry I missed you up on the podium."

"I think you might have held us off."

"Doesn't really matter now, though." I looked over at Ax's pit where he held court for a crowd surrounding him and his racer.

He looked my way and waved.

"*Wa—co,*" I moved my lips silently.

Ax grinned and gave me a thumbs-up.

"Come on. Just forget about him." Allison pulled my arm towards my pit.

Sparks lay on a crawler underneath the front end, reaching up into the engine. Father Bob squatted beside him.

We stood silently behind them as they mumbled to one another like a pair of embalmers staring at a mangled corpse.

Allison cleared her throat. Then again, louder.

Father Bob turned around.

"Any hope for it?" I asked.

"Sure. I don't think it's really so bad," he said.

"What do you think, Sparks?"

"Well, you damn near shook this thing off its mounts. Good thing you got the cables to hold it to the firewall."

"That I already knew. I was sitting right behind the engine when it all happened, remember?"

Sparks rolled out from under the engine, sat up, and squinted my way, gripping a wrench in his right hand. "You were indeed. Yes, you were."

"So?"

"Not sure, exactly. Plugs were good. Magnetos were good. You got good compression on the cylinders. I suspect some kind of contamination blocked the fuel into one of the cylinders. So, you had three pistons running full bore and one not producing any power."

"I had some backfiring just before everything turned to crap,"

I said.

Sparks nodded. "Sounds about right. Then, the shaking broke loose an oil line onto the exhaust and that's what caused the smoke."

"But fuel contamination?"

"Best guess. I'll know more after I tear the damn thing down back home."

"Nothing you could have done about bad avgas," Father Bob said. "At least you didn't throw a rod and crack the engine block."

"What about Waco?" I asked.

Sparks slapped the wrench into his palm. "I'll have her ready. Don't you worry."

"See? That wasn't so bad, now, was it?" Allison smiled at me, then at Father Bob, then at Sparks.

Sparks gritted his teeth.

"I told you he was just a big marshmallow."

Sparks growled lowly.

~~~

We took the wings off *White Hawk Redux* and rolled it into the trailer. I rode home in the Dodge-Mahal with Father Bob and Sparks, lounging in back on the day bed with my eyes closed, trying to ignore their conversation upfront about movie stars—which, of course, led back to Kim Novak.

"Was she real pretty, Hawk, when you saw her over at Lockheed?" Father Bob asked.

"I guess so."

"He says he guesses so," Father Bob said to Sparks. "I don't believe him. Do you?"

Racing the Dream

"Oh, he's just ass deep to a tall Indian with that wing walker girl of his," Sparks muttered. "Yanking petals off a damn daisy all day long."

Father Bob laughed. "She loves me…She loves me not…"

I covered my eyes with my arms and replayed my last lap on Sunday yet again.

We dropped the trailer off at our hangar at Van Nuys. Sparks headed home in his pickup truck and Father Bob took me back to Beverly Hills.

I expected to see Allison at my place when I got home, but I guess she was resting and recuperating from the air show.

After another day of radio silence, I called a couple of times during the day and in the evening, but the phone just rang and rang and rang. I checked in with Scotty the next morning at the airport, but he hadn't seen her hangar open since he got back to Van Nuys on Sunday, so I decided to drive out to her apartment in West Hollywood. No answer at the door.

I was a bit worried but figured there was only one other place she could be, so I headed down Sunset and turned north on the Pacific Coast Highway to Malibu.

I parked and headed out onto the pier, looking north. It took a while to pick her out of the pack of surfers, but I finally saw her black wet suit with bright red shoulders cutting in across a pretty big wave.

I watched her roll up on the beach, then pick up her board to turn around and paddle back out into the lineup beyond the breaking waves.

Allison came in again, then threw herself down on the board and headed into the ocean right away.

Now I just had to find her Woodie.

I came off the pier and wandered along the cars parked by the highway until I found it. There was nothing to do but wait, so I hopped up on the hood, leaned back against the windshield, crossed my legs, and closed my eyes.

The sun warmed me up like a muffin and I guess the waves rolling against the beach lulled me into a nap.

"Hey."

I rolled my head towards the ocean. Allison stood just off on the beach, holding up her board. "Hey."

She kicked at the sand.

"Radio silence…" I sat up and swung my feet down over the fender. "What's up?"

She looked south down the highway towards the pier, then back down at her feet. "It's over."

"*Over?* What do you mean, over? You and me?"

"Oh, no—God, no. It's my stupid brother. He's the one."

I hopped down off the Woodie. "What's going on?"

"The wing walking. That's what's over. He got a slot with United Airlines and he's heading to Denver for training."

Now it made sense back at Bakersfield, why Doug was wandering around aimlessly, not looking at me, but at Allison. He was waiting to tell her then.

She laid her board on the sand and sat down facing the waves. "We were just starting to get booked at air shows. We've got one in a few weeks in San Diego, then one in Phoenix, then Santa Barbara. Now…I got nothing anymore."

I sat down beside her.

"So, what am I going to do?"

"Well, I don't know. I'm sure that Philosophy degree from Stanford will move you right to the top of the resume stack for a career in the food service or hospitality industries."

"Oh, great. Slinging hash at Norms?"

"Or you could find another pilot."

"What do you mean?"

"I know it was just my first time, but I thought we did okay out over Antelope Acres."

"You?" She pulled away and looked at me.

"You said I did great."

"You did, but…"

"But what?"

"You would do that with me?"

"Well, I don't have an airplane to fly right at the moment—I believe you know what happened with my racer up in Bakersfield…"

Allison grabbed me, pulled me down into the sand, rolled me onto my back, and sat across my hips. "You would do that for me? For real?"

I just nodded my head.

She gave me a huge hug.

"Hey, you're getting me all wet."

"Shut up and kiss me."

"Okay."

~~~

Laughing Gas

I got back to Van Nuys close to dinner time and headed to my hangar. There were three guys hunkered over my engine. Two of them, of course, were Father Bob and Sparks.

"So, what's going on?" I asked.

Jack from the North American Air Racers Association stood up and looked over at me. "There he is. Hey, Hawk."

"What are you doing here?"

"Came by to check in on you and your plane. You did a hell of a job up there in Bakersfield when you popped the engine. Hell of a job."

"Thanks, I guess."

"I was sorry to see you pull out. I thought you might've held them off to cross the line first." Jack came over and shook my hand. "Sparks, here, says you got some bad avgas."

"My tanks were clean and clear." Sparks was still hunched over the engine. "Maybe we need to bring our own fuel next time."

"Some guys do," Jack said. "It's your call."

I looked at Father Bob.

"Not sure about that," he said. "We'll see."

"I was just telling the guys how back in thirty-seven when I was twelve, I rode my bike down to the Cleveland Air Races and saw Lee Miles lose his wing."

"What happened?" I asked.

"He was out practicing and when he came around the pylon, the wing on his Miles-Atwood racer just snapped off and he went down right over the park by the airport. I hopped back on my bike and rode over that way 'cause that was by my house. There's a steep cliff there that goes down into the Rocky River below—maybe a hundred feet steep or so—but I knew where a trail was to get down, so I was the first one there—until some cop came along and tried to throw me out. I pulled out my camera and got some photos. His plane was wrecked up pretty bad, hanging upside down from a tree. He actually looked okay through the windscreen, but he was definitely dead."

"Jack's got a ton of stories from back then," said Father Bob. "Fascinating stuff. You know, real, old-time racing tales with all the great pilots. He actually met Jimmy Doolittle in Cleveland and got to look inside his Gee-Bee."

"Anyways that brings me to why I'm really here. Official racing business, don't you know. Do you know that pilot, Ax?"

"I tangled with him once before over Antelope Acres."

"He flipped Hawk upside down," Father Bob said.

"I just got careless. But after that, Scotty and I went over to his hangar at Lockheed."

"And they saw Kim Novak there," Father Bob added.

"Really?" Jack squinted my way. "She still look good?"

I just shook my head. "She looks great. Anyway, he flies for Lufthansa. That's about all I know. Why do you ask?"

"Something seems off. You know, it doesn't stink but it just doesn't smell right, either."

"He did seem to find a lot of extra speed on the last couple of laps," Father Bob said.

"He clocked out at one eighty-eight, eighty-nine on the first three laps. Then, one ninety-one, one ninety-six, and one ninety-seven on the last lap—ten miles an hour more at the end."

"Nitrous," Sparks said. "That's what I say."

"Yeah, but his plane passed the post-flight inspections. Didn't find any. But it sure is odd."

"He is kind of secretive about his plane," I said.

"Everybody is." Jack shook his head. "You know that, but…"

"It does give one pause," I said.

"Anyway, are you going to be ready for Waco?"

Sparks stood up and put his hands on his hips. "We will definitely be ready."

"And we will be there," Father Bob agreed.

"Good. We'll see you in Texas." Jack shook our hands and headed out to the parking lot.

"So, do you think Ax is cheating?" I asked.

"Hell, yes, he is. You don't just auto-magically find ten extra knots that you've been sitting on in your back pocket," Sparks said. "I'm on him like a chicken on a June bug."

"Then how?" Father Bob asked. "They didn't find anything on the inspections."

"Don't know. And don't care." Sparks pointed a wrench at me. "We'll get your plane running up there at two hundred without it. Guaranteed."

~~~

Family Business

I ran late getting to Norms, and when I walked in, Doug and Allison were arguing loudly in a back booth.

"*No!* You can't do this." Allison's hands lay flat on the table and she leaned in his way. "It's not fair."

"I need the money." Doug folded his arms over his chest and stared out the window. "I just do. You don't make anything instructing. You know that."

"Easy now. Easy," I said, sitting down next to Allison. "Inside voices, please."

"Oh, great—what's he doing here? This is a private conversation."

"Not really," Allison pointed her finger at me. "Hawk said he would pilot for me."

"Yeah, well, I don't think that's going to work out too good with his Goodyear racer."

"Problems?" I asked.

"He wants to sell the Stearman." Allison stared down Doug. "And he owns it."

"Look, I need the cash. That's it. It's got to go."

"That's a shame. It's a nice plane." I pulled my checkbook out from my back pocket. "So, how much?"

"What?" Allison asked. "What are you doing?"

I wrote in the date and put Doug's name on the check.

"How much?"

"You can't do this," Allison said.

"I most certainly can. That's my account." I showed her the check and pointed to my name on it. "See? Remember, I learned to fly in one of those planes. And it'd be nice to have one of my very own…How much, Doug?"

"I don't know."

I looked at Allison, then wrote out ten thousand dollars. "I talked to Al McGuire about buying a PT-17 and he threw some numbers my way. I think this is more than fair." I signed the check and pushed it across the table.

Doug picked it up and stared at it like the very first Sutters Mill gold nugget. "Seriously? You can do this?"

"Cash the check, then sign the title over to me—and get me a sales receipt. It's a write-off, you know."

"But I—ah…" He looked at Allison. "Yeah, I guess."

"A pleasure doing business with you."

Allison grinned at Doug. "Okay. Off you go then."

We watched him leave.

Allison turned to lean back against the wall. She frowned at me. "Do you even know what a write-off is?"

"I don't care. But it looks like we're in business together."

"So now what?"

"I guess we fly."

~~~

Sparks

"Why are you dragging me the hell over this way?" Sparks shuffled along behind me as I led him over towards Scotty's hangar a couple of days later.

"I need you to take a look at something for me."

"You know, I got better things to do right now. Waco is coming up fast."

"Maybe…maybe not." I looked back over my left shoulder. "Come on, already."

I opened the padlock and pushed back one of the doors on the hangar with my very own PT-17 in it. Doug had stopped by that morning with the title, a sales receipt, the maintenance logs, and the keys.

"What's this?" Sparks asked.

"It's all mine."

"What for?"

"Well, I think you know…"

"The wing walker." Sparks shook his head. *Christ-on-a-cracker.*

"Hey!"

"Hey, what? You gonna race airplanes or chauffeur around a pretty blonde?"

"I can do both—you think she's pretty?"

"You are a moron."

I pushed back the other two hangar doors. "I want you to

give it a close look over. Make sure everything is in good working order."

"Shouldn't you have done that before you bought the damn thing?"

"Exigent circumstances."

Sparks stepped into the hangar. He peered inside the cowling. "What's that mean, anyway?"

"It means I had to do it. Right away. Or the plane would have been sold to someone else. Then what?"

He pulled the prop through slowly. Again and again. "Compression seems pretty good. When was the annual done?"

"Last November."

Sparks nodded his head as he stepped around the prop and walked down along the left front wing. "How quick do you want this done?"

"I want it done right. That's the important thing and you'll do that. I gotta fly this thing, you know. Hard."

He nodded. "It'll take me a few days. Maybe a week, especially with what Bob wants me to work on."

"The sooner, the quicker. There's an air show coming up in San Diego we have to fly in and we need the practice."

"Looks pretty nice, anyway."

I watched Sparks walk all the way around the airplane, feeling the fabric, flipping the elevators, and pulling on the flying wires.

"I'll get started this afternoon," he said coming back around the right wing.

"Good. Here." I held out the maintenance logs and thought about Allison saying Sparks was just a big marshmallow inside. "So…Sparks…"

"Huh?" he asked, paging through the logbook.

"What are you doing here? In LA?"

"You didn't expect me to sweat it out in that African hellhole all by myself, did you?"

"But I thought you kind of liked Alaska."

"Well, I'm your mechanic." He looked up, squinting my way, and scowled. "And I work on your planes. What more do you need to know?"

"Nothing."

"And right now—thanks to you and Bob—I'm busier than a one-legged man in an ass-kicking contest. I need to go get my tools. So, do you mind?"

"Nope."

"Idiots."

~~~

Hieroglyphics

"When will Sparks be done?" Allison nudged my shoulder with her elbow.

I pulled the blanket over my head, as I planned on getting in a few more winks. "What time is it, anyway?"

"Six."

"Why in the world are you up at this ungodly hour?"

"I like to hit the waves early. And morning air is always calmer for practice—especially over the desert before the thermals start kicking in."

I mumbled a few choice words.

"Come on. Rise and shine."

I rolled over on my back and pulled the blanket off my face. Out of the side of my eye, I saw she wore my Roman Gabriel jersey, leaning back against the headboard next to me, sipping on a cup of coffee. "Is it going to be like this every single morning?"

"Well, I can go surf by myself, but I kind of need you to be back there in the cockpit."

"I don't remember signing up for rising and shining at o'dark thirty."

"It's the best part of the day. So, come on, what's going on with Sparks?"

"He's buttoning up the plane today. I'll take it out and give it a good shakedown. Then, I guess we fly."

"Okay, so that means you're going to have to look at this stuff." Allison picked up a manila folder full of papers that had been haunting the nightstand since I bought the Stearman at Norms. "Do you mind?"

I sat up against the headboard and rubbed my eyes. "I suppose. But is there any more coffee?"

"Sure, I'll get it." Allison handed me the folder and slid out of bed to head to the kitchen.

I flipped through Doug's papers. "This looks like a bunch of hieroglyphics."

She held out a mug of coffee as she came back in. "They're Aresti notations—you know, for aerobatic maneuvers. It's *our* act."

"Seems kind of…I don't know, rigid."

"That's what my brother was good at. You're a much better stick-and-rudder pilot, but he was pretty disciplined about the act." She hopped back into bed next to me.

"So, he will definitely be a good United pilot—that's certainly not my thing."

"We only get twenty minutes for the act, so it all has to be worked out ahead of time, move-by-move-by-move—especially positioning ourselves for the crowd."

"Yeah, I guess." I sipped the coffee and sighed.

"I already know you can fly. We just need to tighten up the maneuvers, especially the turnarounds to stay in front of the grandstands. You'll do just fine—if you apply yourself."

"Goes against my nature, though."

"Well, at least Doug let you have his notes."

"Yeah, well, what's that?" I pointed at a teardrop drawing with dots, arrows, a slash, and a dotted line.

"That's a reverse half Cuban eight. The dotted line is when

you're upside down."

I shook my head. "And this?"

"An Immelmann. See? It's all laid out in order on the cards that you can follow along, step-by-step."

"Do we have to?"

"Oh, you're just being a big baby. Now pay attention."

She took the papers from me and we went through the notations, maneuver-by-maneuver.

~~~

When we got to her hangar—*our* hangar, Sparks had all the inspection panels back in place on the PT-17. He sat on a little rolling stool, impatiently tapping his foot.

"About damn time!" he barked.

"You try dragging him out of bed in the morning," Allison punched my arm.

"Hey!"

"I don't want to hear about it—that's between you and your God." Sparks stood up. "The Stearman's all ready to go. Fabric and engine are in good shape—changed the oil and replaced the plugs while I was at it. Re-trimmed the aileron and elevator controls. Tightened up all the flying wires. Your brother kept this thing in pretty good shape."

"Thanks, Sparks." Allison smiled.

He scowled at me. "Just don't tear the wings off. You hear me?"

"I'll do my best."

"You trust him?" He pointed his wrench at Allison.

She nodded. "I think so."

"Well, it's your funeral."

"I promise to be careful." I held my hands up in surrender.

"I gotta go. Bob's waiting for me—my *real* job, don't you know."

"Thanks, Sparks."

We watched him head back to my hangar.

"Ready?" Allison asked.

"Let me take it up first."

"You don't trust Sparks?"

"I do…but let me take it up first. It's the way we work. Always."

"But—"

"It is my airplane now, you know."

"Can I come?"

"Nope. This is between him and me. Let's pull this thing out of here and I'll be back in a half hour or so."

Allison watched me do my pre-flight, then I climbed in the cockpit.

"Clear!"

Allison backed away from the plane.

The engine fired up with a cloud of smoke—it sounded good.

I contacted Ground, waved back at Allison, then headed to Runway Three-Four. After my run-up, the tower cleared me and I headed north toward Antelope Acres.

The controls were rigged just right, flying straight and true. Over the desert, I put the Stearman through some mild maneuvers—slow flight, power-off and power-on stalls, medium turns, then steeper ones, out to sixty degrees. Slow rolls, left, then right. A loop, then a hammerhead. Satisfied, I turned back towards Van Nuys.

I knew Sparks would do a good job on the plane, but you always test-fly after maintenance, just in case.

Back at our hangar, I shut the Stearman down.

"Come on down," Allison said, waving Doug's papers.

"Do we have to?"

She shook her head. *"Fighter pilots."*

We went over the routine again…and again, then headed out to Antelope Acres.

For the first time out we agreed on a two thousand-foot deck.

"Okay, let's use that crossroads down there for the show center." Allison pointed over the side of the cockpit.

"I'm on it." I passed the intersection at two thousand feet, then pulled the Stearman up into an Immelmann to reverse course and held it level.

"So, what are you waiting for?" I asked. "Isn't this where you get out?"

"Yes, but first let's nail down the routine. I'll talk you through it."

"But we went over it already."

"So now, do it." She shook her head. "Look I can fly the maneuvers myself and you can get out on the wing if you want."

"Thank you. No."

"Okay, then. Come back around and let's try this again. The Immelmann, a low pass—pretend I'm out on the wing—into the reverse half Cuban eight and a hammerhead."

"I got it. I got it."

Allison talked me through the routine, calling my turns at either end to bring us back past the intersection.

After twenty minutes, we were through and I was sweating. I pulled up, rolling level at three thousand feet.

"So?"

I saw her shoulders rise with a deep breath, then fall. "Not bad for the first time."

"I thought I did good."

"Pretty good. But you busted the deck a couple of times—you definitely can't do that down at fifty feet off the runway like in a show. You were up a little high coming out of the loop and didn't quite get the passes even across the intersection—that's the most important part. The people have to be able to see you the whole time."

"Yeah, yeah...*people*."

"Come around and let's try it again."

I grit my teeth and came east to west across the intersection at two thousand feet, pulling up into the Immelmann again.

~~~

After the first practice session, Allison headed up to Malibu to surf and I shuffled over to my hangar thinking about our flight and all my mistakes.

"There he is, *Mister* Barnstorming Air Show Pilot Extraordinaire himself," Father Bob called out waving his arms around like a circus ringmaster. "We saw you take off this morning. How'd it go out there?"

"Well, she gets kind of picky about things—you missed that turn—*you went too low—you went too high—keep the thing level.*" I saw Sparks standing by my plane grinning at me. "And what's your problem?"

He chuckled. "Not the kind of need like when your ass is hanging outside your britches."

"Look, it's not my style. You don't go into a dogfight over Germany or in Congo with a bunch of scribbles scrawled out on a page and just fly through the maneuvers one-after-another like some kind of Pavlov's dog." I held up Doug's manila folder full of aerobatic notes. "You have to react—by instinct, you know? And you have to make all the right moves against the other guy to come out on top and not end up being a smoking hole in the ground. Same thing out on the race course to end up standing at the top of the podium."

"Well, to be honest with you," Father Bob said, "if it was my butt out there on the airplane wing, I might get a little picky, too. No?"

"Yeah, well, I mean maybe…just maybe, but still…"

"Do you want to get out and crawl around out there at a hundred feet over the ground?"

"You are hilarious."

"That's why people love me."

I really wanted to wipe the grin off Father Bob's face. And he probably saw it in my eyes.

"Now, son…"

"Never mind. So what's going on over here?"

"Well, Sparks is getting the engine back in shape. There didn't seem to be any permanent damage, since you shut things down pretty quick up there over Bakersfield."

"What about the fuel contamination?"

"The engine was clean," Sparks said. "Had to have come in out of the tank…or someplace else."

"Someplace else?" I asked.

"Or someone else…" Sparks squinted at me.

"Speculation. Pure speculation. Forget about it." Father Bob stepped over to the front of the plane and ran his hand around the air intake. "What I didn't like is that you started running hot. Which means we've got to open up the flow over the engine to keep that from happening again. It's a trade-off between minimizing cooling drag and getting the most power out of the engine."

"I'll take the power."

"Of course, but aerodynamics are important, too. And I think I have some ideas about reshaping the wheel pants."

"That's going to help?"

"There's no magic answer here, Hawk. Every little change helps. It should give us an extra knot or two."

"Yeah, but when can I fly her again?"

Father Bob looked over at Sparks. "What do you think? Tomorrow?"

He scratched the back of his head. "Maybe. Or maybe the next day. No promises."

"*Whatever.* Obviously, there's nothing for me to do here."

Heading back over to the Stearman, I saw Scotty's hangar was open. He and Ed were hunched over the engine of his Cassutt.

"Hey, guys, what's going on?" I asked.

"Oh, hey, Hawk," Scotty said. "Just making a few *special modifications* for Waco."

"Yeah? Like what?"

"Nope-nope-nope. No can do. You know we're competitors now."

"Seriously?" I looked at Scotty, then at Ed.

Ed shrugged his shoulders.

"Anyway, I saw Allison's hangar is open, but I haven't seen her around this morning."

"She's off surfing. And, by the way, that's now my hangar. I bought the Stearman off of Doug."

"Really? What for?"

"He got a slot with United and I guess I'm taking over for him chauffeuring Allison around at air shows." I held up Doug's notes.

"What's that?"

"Our act." I handed Scotty the folder.

He flipped through the pages. 'Ah, Arresti notation."

"You know what that is?"

"I tried aerobatics for a bit. Flew a few competitions, too. Not as easy as it seems."

"Yeah. Whatever."

"And you're going to fly these? Down low? For an air show?"

"I guess that's what I signed up for."

"With Allison out on the wing? You're nutty as a fruit cake, too. You know it's one thing to be yanking loops and hammerheads way up high, but down low—it's a whole different thing. A real different look. Different visuals. Way different perspectives. And no margin for error."

"Yeah…I guess."

"And she trusts you behind the stick?"

"I suppose." I reluctantly took back the folder.

Scotty looked at Ed. "Wow. She must really love him, huh."

"I wouldn't know." Ed shrugged his shoulders. "So did they figure out what happened to your plane up in Bakersfield?"

"Fuel contamination."

"Really? On the last day? So out of the tanks up there?" Ed scratched at his chin. "And no one else got it?"

"That's what Sparks says. Or maybe…"

"Maybe what?" Scotty asked. "Someone spiked it? Who would do that?"

"Father Bob says it's just another one of Sparks' crazy conspiracy theories."

"Boy, I hope so."

"Well, I'll leave you two to your…" I made air quotes with my fingers. "…*special modifications.*"

"You going to be ready for Waco?"

"We'll be there."

"Good." He gave me an Eddie Haskell grin. "You'll get to see all of our changes there at the race."

Back in the Stearman hangar I tossed the folder down on the wing and paced back and forth, going over my flight that morning with Allison, grinding my teeth.

I flipped open the pages and pored over the maneuvers, then decided to go out to practice our act over Antelope Acres again.

~~~

Papa Bear

Allison and I worked the routine for the next couple of days, lowering the deck down to a thousand feet—still too high for the show, but getting closer. The horizon perspective is a much different look down low, rolling and coming down out of the loops. A lot more ground filling up your windscreen—and coming at you a lot faster, too.

Starting over again, reaching the top of the Immelmann and rolling level, Allison stood up in the front cockpit, smiled back at me, then put her foot on the windshield and climbed up on the top wing.

We're really doing this, then.

And suddenly I found myself concentrating that much more on the moves. Making tiny pressure changes on the stick and rudder. It wasn't so bad when she was on the top wing pulling through the hammerheads, the half Cuban eights, and the rolls—carrying a bit more power to overcome her resistance in the airstream. But going out to the end of the wing to ride on the javelin strut or hang down from the wing really made me work the controls to keep the plane level.

When we finished and she crawled back into the front seat, I think I finally let myself take a deep breath.

"We did good—real good," she said. "Come on, let's go home."

"I'm on it."

I turned towards the San Fernando Reservoir and we drove back in silence.

Entering downwind for One-Six Left, Allison said, "Why don't you do a short field landing. Stick it on the numbers, just like we're landing in front of the grandstands."

"Got it."

I came around, base-to-final, arced down at the runway, and stuck the wheels right on the big white one-and-six.

"Keep it straight—right on the Captain's line," she said, then quickly climbed out of her seat, up on the top wing, and into the struts, waving as if to an imaginary air show crowd.

I swear I heard the controller laughing when he told me to contact Ground off the runway.

Allison came down off the wing back into the cockpit.

I taxied to our hangar and shut the engine down.

Allison stood up on her seat. She grinned at me, "And that's how we do it."

"Bravo! Bravo!" Scotty cheered as he and Ed wandered over clapping their hands. "Quite an ending, if I do say so myself."

Allison turned his way and bowed. Standing back up, she moaned, *"Uh-oh…"*

I pulled off my helmet. "What the matter?"

She pointed toward Scotty and Ed. Behind them, I saw Doug with an older gentleman dressed in khakis, a light blue Oxford shirt, and a dark blue blazer. He stood at parade rest with his hands on his hips and glared our way from behind aviator sunglasses.

"Is that…" I started to ask.

Allison nodded. "Yup. Dear old dad."

Racing the Dream

She hopped out of the plane, ran over to him, and gave him a hug.

I made myself busy in the cockpit, double-checking the switches were all off, then triple-checking.

"Hawk, come on down," Allison stood next to the Stearman with her father and her brother.

"Ah, okay, no problem." I climbed out and stepped down off the wing. I held out my hand to shake. "Glad to meet you."

He looked at Doug and with a distinctive southern drawl simply asked, "Him?"

Doug nodded.

Her father took his sunglasses off and we stood eye-to-eye. He gave me a fighter pilot's squint, then finally took my hand. "Winston."

"Everybody calls me Hawk."

"You and I need to talk." He put his sunglasses back on.

"Ah, sure."

Winston put his hand on my shoulder and turned me towards the tail of the plane, pulling me away from everyone else. We walked down the line of hangars, stopping at the end to look out at the runways.

I waited. He was the one who wanted to talk.

We watched a few planes come and go. A Beech 18 slowly settled its wheels on the asphalt. It stirred up lots of memories for me, including long-ago flights with Elaine and, more recently, with Ella in Congo.

"Sweet," I instinctively mumbled to myself.

"Got time in them?"

"A couple thousand hours or so. Flying freight. Lots of good memories. It's a great old bird."

Winston nodded, following the Beech 18 as it taxied off One-Six. "I heard you bought Douglas's airplane."

"I gave him a fair price."

"It's not about the money."

"Maybe. But, still, it's got to be right—for me, anyway. I learned to fly in a PT-17. Maybe you did, too."

He looked at me and grinned. "Are you trying to shine me, boy?"

"Could it hurt?"

"And may I ask, then, what might be your intentions?"

I chuckled. "For the Stearman…or Allison?"

"Both."

I looked him dead in the eye. "Honorable. On all accounts."

Winston looked like he wanted to know more, but then asked, "Well, if you learned to fly in a Stearman, where did you serve?"

"The Three-sixty-third Fighter Squadron."

"Ah, *Old Crow*—Anderson's group. And Yeager, too. You were in good company."

"Chuck and I tied. Eleven-and-a-half apiece."

"Excellent. I was a deputy to Doolittle at the Eighth's HQ."

"So, you turned us loose to go after the Germans."

"That we did. That we did. And I was sincerely quite proud of all you boys." He took a deep breath and slowly exhaled. "You know, you can't tell her anything."

"Allison?"

"Not a darn thing—like this wing walking nonsense. Craziest thing I've ever heard of in my entire lifetime. And I thought Douglas getting hired on with United Airlines would put an end to the scheme and she could move on. But…well…there you go."

"It is a pretty nutty idea, but she really wants to do it."

"I do believe you." He nodded his head and repeated softly, "I do believe you."

I looked back down between the hangars at Allison talking with Doug, Scotty, and Ed by the Stearman, but looking nervously over her shoulder at us.

"Can you handle this?" Winston asked. "The flying part, I mean."

"I can—I will."

"Well, if for some reason you do not, you will certainly answer to her mama—and I don't think that conversation will be a particularly pleasant one." He looked back at Allison.

"Got it."

"My son said you have been flying a Goodyear racer."

I nodded. "You want to see it?"

"I believe I would."

"Come on. And I'll introduce you to my partners."

We strolled around the end of the line of buildings over to my hangar where Father Bob and Sparks were having a heated discussion about scoring the pistons.

"I just don't know if it's legal." Father Bob shook his head.

"I don't see nothing against anything like that in the rules. And it'll allow more oil into the cylinders to help keep the engine cool," Sparks insisted.

I cleared my throat loudly. "This here is Winston—Allison's father. That's Father Bob and Sparks, my mechanic."

They stared at him blankly, then Father Bob came over and reached out to shake his hand.

"I'm really not a priest anymore—but I am glad to meet you."

"Likewise."

Sparks stood in his spot and waved a wrench at Winston.

"You were a General, right?" I asked.

"No, son. Just a Colonel. I worked for a living."

"Well, Father Bob is the brains of this outfit. It's all his design," I said.

Winston stepped over to *White Hawk Redux* and ran his hand over the wing from front to back. "Laminar flow. Correct?"

"Hawk, your friend here is quite astute."

"Friend?"

Winston gave me a wry look. "We've been experimenting with tip sails to reduce drag."

"Tip sails?" Father Bob asked. "What's that?"

"Turn the ends of the wings up a bit to capture the tip vortex energy of the lift and direct it backwards."

"Fascinating." Father Bob rubbed his chin.

"Who is 'we'?" I asked.

"After my twenty, I intended to continue flying—instead of becoming a General trying to learn the stall recovery techniques for a Steelcase desk. So now I am a contract pilot up at Edwards and sometimes over in the Nevada desert."

"A test pilot?"

"It's a living. And I get paid to keep flying."

"Dad…what's going on here?" Allison asked walking up.

"Oh, Hawk was just showing me his racer. It's kind of small."

"It does move along," I said.

"How fast?" Winston asked.

"Two hundred." Father Bob stroked the end of the wing.

"With a C-85 engine?"

"Every bit—and then some," Sparks insisted.

"Tip sails, huh…" Father Bob scratched the back of his neck.

"Give it a thought or two." Winston put his arm around

Allison. "Come on, honey. Why don't we go corral your brother and grab us some lunch at the Sky Trails restaurant."

They started walking back to the Stearman hangar.

Winston looked back over his shoulder. "Hawk, you coming?"

"Absolutely."

~~~

San Diego

We idled in the Stearman at the end of runway Six Left at Naval Air Station Miramar, waiting to start our very first show together.

Allison made me go through our routine in my head over and over and over again—first thing getting up in the morning, sitting out on the front porch after dinner, in the hangar before we got in the plane to go practice over Antelope Acres, and yet again two hours before showtime that day. She made me play out every maneuver in real time—*the Immelmann turn after takeoff, holding level as she climbs up on the wing, banking and diving around for the low pass into a Cuban eight*—and on and on and on, going through every hand movement on the stick, and my feet on the rudders, and working the throttle—seeing in my mind the visual cues on the horizon.

Of course, I tried to resist at first, but like her dad said, *you can't tell her anything.* And so inevitably I gave in, and after a while it became a twenty-minute kind of meditation—and the routine became hard-wired into my brain.

I closed my eyes and felt the Continental seven-cylinder engine gently shake us.

Finally, the Navy F-8 Crusader finished his demonstration and landed. Tower cleared us to depart.

"You ready?" she asked.

"Hang on." I released the brakes and advanced the throttle.

The tail wheel came off the runway. The wings bit the air and we accelerated past the grandstands twenty-five feet above the centerline until I pulled up in a half loop and rolled upright. I locked the plane level, then Allison stood up on her seat and smiled at me.

And I grinned back. She was quickly up on the top wing in the struts and I moved the throttle forward. As the grandstands appeared at my four o'clock position, I rolled back the throttle, then dove down and around for the low pass at show center, while Allison smiled and waved her arms to the crowd.

Into the Cuban eight back and forth in front of the crowd rolling out at fifty feet…I verify 2,100 RPM…at 140 knots I ease back on the stick up into a hammerhead…nearly at the stall, right rudder, and over the top, down again in front of the crowd…building speed…

I worked hard—with Allison's gentle reminders during our debriefing sessions—to keep a light and steady pressure on the controls, providing as stable a platform as I could for her out on the wing.

Flying over the runway centerline…speed 125…RPM 2100…wings level against the horizon…three, two, one…full throttle…stick coming back, horizon gone, then eyes on the left wing…thirty-degrees over…eyes front looking for the runway at the top of the loop, then back on the stick through the bottom of the loop…

Allison threw her arms over her head and turned to the crowd on the right side of the plane.

Thirty-degree climbing turn to teardrop back in front of the crowd at one hundred feet… confirm 110 knots, then raise the nose up for aileron rolls…left…then right…up to the right and level again…

Allison climbed down from the top wing. I tried to hold the Stearman steady as she banged her way through the flying wires radial wound up to 1400 RPM and she confirmed the left and right magnetos operational. Engine back to 700.

"Stearman Five-Two-One-Delta-Mike, ready at One-Six Left. Departing north," Allison radioed.

"One-Delta-Mike cleared for take-off."

Allison taxied onto the runway. She locked the tail wheel and raised her hands above her head. "It's your airplane. Take me for a ride, Hawk."

I forgot how thick the control stick is on a Stearman—like a baseball bat, but it felt good. "I've got it."

I gripped the throttle in my left hand a couple of times, then pushed it forward. The engine roared and the wind sang in my ears as we rolled south until I just flew the plane off the ground like a P-51. I climbed to eight hundred feet, turned crosswind, then banked again to climb out on downwind.

"You know the way, right? Allison asked.

"I'm on it," I said.

North along the highway. I arced close around Magic Mountain, then northeast out over the desert. It was severe clear with a deep blue sky.

"This is awesome," I said. "I soloed in one of these."

Allison turned her head back and grinned. "Good times…good times."

I dove down on the back side of the mountains and skimmed at a hundred feet or so over the desert floor, then climbed to the west. Two thousand feet AGL, I did a couple of sixty-degree turns, left and right, then dove, banking thirty degrees and pulling the nose up to Chandelle back to the east.

"Is that all you've got?" Allison taunted me. "Show me some of that fancy fighter pilot flying stuff."

~ 64 ~

~~~

Racing the Dream

…ving. She wrapped herself around the javelin …uperman flying pose, and gave me a thumbs- …ed back to the crowd.

…rut…into a loop…reversing course with an …ts for rolls to the right…then level… …the javelin strut and wrapped her legs …to hang below the wing. …nst the drag of her hanging below the …r low pass by the grandstands at one

…nder her head—upside down …leveled, and Allison climbed …ckpit for one last low pass

… on Six Left, and as we …d up against the strut on …ppy, grinning like I had never seen before.

…wd.

~ 171 ~

I flipped the levers on the rudder pedals to push them out a bit and locked them up. Unlike my racer, the cockpit seems huge with plenty of room to stretch about. Sitting inside the Stearman, scanning the instruments brought a huge grin to my face as memories of basic training at Randolph Air Force Base in San Antonio flooded into my mind.

I read the placard at the bottom of the panel, "Don't do nothin' dumb!"

"T⸺ 's for my brother, Doug. You know, just to remind him,"

⸺ went through the start-up checklist and I watched the ⸺ throttle controls on the left move into position: full ⸺ ch open. Gas valve on.

⸺ d around outside and cried out, "CLEAR!"

⸺ both. The starter switch went on.

⸺ as—that whine of the starter spinning the ⸺ ial. I closed my eyes as the cylinders coughed ⸺ began to fire. I caught the smell of smoke ⸺ the prop rise in my ears as the engine

⸺ ch: 700 RPM.

⸺ s the intercom came on.

⸺ leasing the brakes.

⸺ ounted to the wing and saw her

⸺ to the runway, Allison's head ⸺ wingtips as we taxied slowly ⸺ ned us to the runup area ⸺ nents, fuel, and trim. The

Bill Stead

Three great days and our routine got better with each and every show. We sat in the Stearman all ready to leave for Van Nuys when the airport reopened for business at five after the Blue Angels finished their jet aerobatics and landed.

"You want to fly?" I asked.

"Yes, *pleeeeeease!*" And Allison grabbed the stick and pushed the throttle forward down Runway Six. She climbed to five hundred feet, then turned us north towards home.

Sometimes it's nice being chauffeured around. I got to see a lot more of what's passing by down on earth as we flew up the Pacific coastline: fishing boats, sailboats, and container ships to the west on the ocean; beaches, awesome private palaces, and marinas along the shoreline.

I noticed Allison's head kind of bouncing around in front of me then over the intercom, she sang:

> *Could it be the devil in me*
> *Or is this the way love's supposed to be*
> *Just like a heatwave…Burning in my heart…*

She looked up at me in the mirror, a huge smile plastered on her face. I don't believe I've ever been serenaded, on the ground or in the air—then she abruptly pulled the nose of the Stearman up and rolled us around the horizon, then leveled off.

I knew what he was doing when he caught my eye
Da do ron-ron-ron, da do ron-ron

All I could do was laugh and sing along with her:

Da do ron-ron-ron, da do ron-ron

~~~

We landed at Van Nuys and Allison shut down the plane in front of our hangar. I waved at Al McGuire as he and a blonde-haired fellow walked over to the Stearman.

"Heard your call sign in the pattern," Al said. "How was the Miramar show?"

"Awesome!" Allison pulled off her helmet. "This boy can wring the bolts off this thing."

"Yeah, I've heard that about him," the stranger said.

Allison stood up and stepped out of the cockpit. "And you would be…"

"This is Bill Stead. He's the one putting together the races up in Reno." Al McGuire reached out to help Allison down off the wing. He pointed at me. "And that's Hawk. He's my partner in our investment with you."

"Heard you did a hell of a job up in Bakersfield," Stead said.

I got out and hopped down. "Thanks. Kept the wings on anyway."

We shook hands.

"Still…you handled it well." Stead looked at Allison. "So,

what's your act?"

"Wing walking," said Allison.

"Oh, man, we have got to get you signed up for Reno. I'm real close in getting ABC to televise it—*The Wide World of Sports.* The thrill of victory and the agony of defeat and all that." He winked at me. "That is if you think you can pull double duty—racing and aerobatics."

"Can we do it, Hawk? *Please?*" She faked a woeful look my way.

"I'll make it work. So, you've got to have a ticket if you're working to bring back air racing."

"Soloed at sixteen."

"Did you fly in the war?" I asked.

"Now, that there is a funny story." Bill looked up over the horizon, squinting his eyes as he shook his head. "I wanted to join Chennault in the Flying Tigers to help out Chiang Kai-shek. They approved my application so I headed down to San Francisco—where I *literally* missed the slow boat heading to China. Then I got accepted into the Royal Canadian Air Force to fight in the Battle of Britain—but *no.* The draft board grabbed me up."

"Go ahead," Al McGuire chuckled. "Tell him."

"They stuck me on a set of skis in Alaska testing survival equipment. Does that make any sense to you?"

"The military mind at work," I said. "Or not."

"Well, after two years, I finally got transferred into the Air Corps and they sent me to fly search and rescue missions—in Panama. *Boring.*" Stead scratched at his temple. "Let's see…did a stint in the Air Force reserves. Then in Fifty-Two, I wanted to do the Flying Tigers kind of thing for the French in Indochina. Found a bunch of surplus Mustangs and finally—*finally* got approval out of the Pentagon to make it happen."

"And then?"

"Dien Bien Phu. The French got their butts kicked and headed home to Paris with their tails between their legs."

"I fought in Congo. Flying T-6s against the Simba rebels."

"Wasn't that kind of…against the law for a US citizen?"

"Technically, I was on the CIA's payroll, flying freight. But really, who knew."

"Lucky you. Anyway, I raced speedboats. Retired from that in Nineteen Sixty. And now I'm getting the air racing thing going again up north."

"And that's definitely going to happen?" Al McGuire asked.

"Yup. The FAA finally signed off on the waivers. *No problem.*"

"We'll be there," I said.

"Glad to have you." Stead grinned at me, then at Al. *"And your money."*

~~~

Heart of Texas Airshow

The green flag went up. I pushed the throttle in—ankles locked on the brakes, my knees started to shake.

We were lined up on Three-Five Right for the final race on Sunday. I was in the middle of the front row with Scotty on my left in the pole position. He and Ed definitely made a few *special* modifications to his red Cassutt and Scotty showed it by beating us all on Saturday. Ax sat to my right. I ignored them both to watch the flag man.

Since the wind was out of the north, we had to take off and head to the scatter pylon to reverse course for our left-hand-turn laps. Father Bob traded props on my plane, but still gave me a lower pitch for a quicker climb and initial speed. I intended to beat Scotty and Ax to the scatter pylon, take the lead, and keep it.

I checked the RPM—thirty-six hundred. Back to the flag man.

Waiting.

I saw the flagman's arm start to drop, released the brakes, and pushed the throttle all the way in—I was already a plane length ahead of Scotty. The tail came up and I started climbing to the scatter pylon.

I came around in first and dove down to return to the front straightaway picking up a few extra knots. I crossed the start/finish line, then turned left, tight around the first pylon. From the shadows, I had a great lead—five lengths at least.

It's always easier being first in the clean air. My left hand pressed the throttle in hard. It was the last day and I wanted to beat Scotty bad, but by the third lap, the shadow behind me was creeping in when I came around to the back straight. I wanted to look, but kept my eyes ahead, marking my spot, low and tight, for the fourth pylon.

Around, then down the front straightaway. Fifty feet off the ground. Staying smooth.

Fly my race…fly my race. Three…Two…One…

Stick right-right-right—back—three Gs down into the seat and around.

And then, red to the right in my peripheral vision: Scotty climbing on my right wing in an echelon.

You need five or six knots to pass.

Did he have it?

We raced down the back straight. I cut in early, very close around the pylon, but still outside—barely.

Scotty slid back a bit.

I just didn't have any more juice. I gave the mixture a quick turn-in.

Scotty crawled back up and high again into the first turn, keeping himself as tight as he could on the pylon but still outside my wing.

Down the front straight. Scotty inched ahead.

I concentrated on holding my line. As smooth as possible.

I felt a burble in my ailerons. I climbed a bit for clean air and lost position.

My prop was behind Scotty's wing. I pushed the throttle in, but there was nowhere for it to go.

Last lap. I held my line and made him arc out ten feet or so.

Racing the Dream

I eased back on the stick into pylon four. We were still side-by-side, but I couldn't gain position.

Pylon five…pylon six…level the wings…

We were locked side-by-side down the front straightaway.

Scotty crossed in first, a half-plane length ahead.

He climbed.

I throttled back a bit and followed him up around the course at three thousand feet to cool the engine.

The longest seven minutes ever.

I pulled up on Scotty's left wing. He shot me a classic Eddie Haskell smile.

I gave him a salute and we rolled onto downwind and landed.

I taxied in behind Scotty to Jack's technical inspectors. When I got out, I expected Ax to be behind me in third place, but he was out of his yellow plane, ordering Peter and Manfred to pull it into the pits.

"Wow! That was a great race." Father Bob wandered over with Sparks in tow. He patted Scotty on the shoulder. "Boy, at the end Hawk was on you like ugly on an ape—right across the line!"

"But Scotty beat me."

"First over the line!" Scotty raised his fists up over his head and grinned. "Eat my dust."

I stepped over and punched him lightly in the shoulder. Ed came up and I shook his hand. "Congratulations, guys—but just wait for Ft. Wayne."

"Sure, sure, sure." Scotty pointed at Ax. "So, what happened to him?"

"Don't know. To be honest, I was concentrating on staying ahead of you," I said.

"And how did that work out?"

"Ax fell off right after the start," Father Bob said. "He never got up to speed."

"Engine was misfiring. Probably a fouled plug. His boys, no doubt, screwed the pooch," Sparks muttered.

We watched Ax berate his mechanics, then Jack's tech guys pulled the cowling off Scotty's Cassutt.

"It's all perfectly legit," Scotty said. "You'll see."

And it was—which made for a very long, very quiet ride home through Abilene, Odessa, Pecos, El Paso, Las Cruces, Tucson, Tonopah, and Palm Springs.

~~~

Sitting on Top of the World

Evening and finally home. Sitting on the front porch of my casita in Beverly Hills sipping a beer, I attempted very unsuccessfully not to think about those seven minutes again in Waco.

Allison's Woodie chugged into the servant's driveway. She waved at me.

"Come on up," I called out. "It's good to see you."

She got out, bounded up the stairs, and sat herself in my lap. Before I could speak, she hugged me, then planted a wet one on my lips.

"Consolation prize?" I asked.

"Hey! I am *not* a lovely parting gift. You hear me?"

"Oh, no. Of course not—I mean…yeah, sorry."

She lay her head on my shoulder. "I saw Scotty at the airport earlier with Ed. He's pretty darn proud of himself. Chest all pumped up—well, you know, sort of. And he gave me a turn-by-turn account of coming from behind and winning."

"Don't want to talk about it."

"He showed me his trophy, too. You got one too, right?"

"Yeah. Congratulations—*first loser.*"

"It was just half a plane length."

I growled a bit. "Told you, I don't want to talk about it."

Allison took my longneck and helped herself to a sip of my beer.

"Anyway, I had a big idea," I said.

"Oh, no…a big idea?" She shook her head.

"The biggest."

"Well, let's hear it."

"I thought about this coming back from Waco—for our act. What about at the end—as a grand finale kind of thing—you know, we do the low pass with you hanging upside down from the wing strut, then I reverse course, roll inverted, and fly by with you sitting upright on the bottom of the wing?"

"Flying by upside down? That sounds dangerous."

"Dangerous? Are you kidding me? Your whole wing walking thing is dangerous."

"Yeah, I know, but down low like that?"

"I can do it. We'll try it out tomorrow."

"Okay…" she said but scowled with concern etched on her face.

"Trust me. I know what I'm doing."

"Yeah. Right."

~~~

Out over Antelope Acres the next morning, we practiced the routine at two thousand feet. After the last maneuver, with Allison beneath the wing, I made a teardrop turn then leveled out. I slowly rolled the wing over one hundred eighty degrees, upside down, stick pushed in for lift, watching the horizon closely to stay level.

I glanced left, but all I could see were her legs wrapped around the strut pointing towards the ground above my head. Allison sat upright on the bottom of the wing as I pretended to fly by the grandstands. At the end, I slowly rolled right side up.

Racing the Dream

Allison pulled herself upright and grabbed the strut. She grinned at me.

I gave her a thumbs up. I knew it would work.

She made a roll with her hand, so we tried the last few maneuvers over a couple more times. After the third time, Allison crawled back up on the wing and worked her way through the flying wires back to the cockpit.

She stopped at the fuselage. Her face was flushed. Her ponytail blew in the wind, then she climbed in and strapped herself into the seat. Breathlessly, she said over the intercom, "I didn't think it would work, but…I like it. I like it a lot."

"It's a one-of-a-kind show stopper."

"Let's work on it some more and we'll try it out at the Buckeye Air Fair."

"Great." I banked to the southwest and headed back to Van Nuys.

~~~

We put the Stearman away and locked up the hangar. Thankfully, Scotty's doors were closed up, too, so I didn't have to hear about how he beat me in Waco again.

"I'm going to see what Father Bob and Sparks are up to."

"Okay. Well, I'm heading north to Malibu. Catch some waves." Allison put her arms around my waist. "I like your new move."

"I've got a few more…for later, you might like."

She gave me a kiss and headed to the parking lot. "Tell the boys I said hi."

I wandered down and around the tarmac to my hangar. The doors were pulled back, but I didn't see Sparks around. Father

Bob was hunched over his drawing board in the back, twirling a pencil through his fingers like a baton.

"So, where's Sparks?" I asked.

"Hey, Hawk. He's helping out Al McGuire with an annual on one of his rentals."

"What are you up to?"

"Noodling and doodling."

I stepped up to look over Father Bob's shoulder. "Got any grand ideas?"

"One or two I think might work to yank a few more knots out of her."

"If I had them in Waco, I might have pulled it off."

"You were damn close, Hawk. Damn close."

"Close only counts in horseshoes, hand grenades, and dancing." I walked over to the plane. The wheel pants were off and the cowling was up. "When can I take her back up?"

"Couple of days and we'll have it buttoned up for you." Father Bob turned to look at me.

"What do you think Scotty and Ed did to get the extra speed out of the Cassutt?"

"They had it taped up pretty darn good. Cut the drag way down. Sparks thinks they retuned the exhaust, too. Said it sounded different to him. I don't know. He says he can tell."

"I need at least five more knots to beat him."

"Don't forget about Ax, too. That was a fluke in Waco."

"Yeah. Gee, that was too bad. Broke my heart."

"He'll be on your tail in Ft. Wayne. No doubt about it." Father Bob stepped over beside me. "Um, Elaine wanted to know if you guys would come over for dinner."

"Dinner? What are you making?"

Racing the Dream

"Come on, you know the routine."

"Right." Father Bob was a great cook, but his rules were you could never ask him what he was making. Always a surprise. "Okay, so what is Elaine's game?"

"Game? Nothing. She likes Allison. And so do I. So, don't screw it up, you goofball."

"You know…you know—oh, forget about it."

"Friday, then?"

"I don't know if this is a good idea, but I'll check with Allison."

~~~

On Friday, Allison, Elaine, and I sat around the kitchen table in the big house, watching Father Bob scurry about the kitchen like a whirling dervish.

"So, what is he making?" Allison asked.

"Don't know. And I was told never to ask." Elaine sipped her wine. "So I don't."

"You'll find out soon enough," Father Bob called out.

I shrugged. "Been like that for a long time. Ever since I met him. Of course, in the jungle you might not want to know what was in the skillet."

Father Bob pointed a spatula at me and chuckled.

Elaine poured more Cabernet into our glasses, then squinted my way. "Is he behaving himself, Allison?"

"Well, for the most part." Allison winked at me. Beneath the table, she ran her hand up and down my thigh.

"Hmmm…" Elaine kicked me in the shin.

"Ow! Hey, now—"

"That was for the other part."

Allison laughed out loud.

"I've got my eye on you, mister."

"Really. He's doing great. He's doing just fine."

I got up and limped over to the counter that ran along the kitchen, facing Father Bob as he whisked a pan over the burner on the stove. "I took the plane up today and it ran pretty good."

"No, no, no—NO!" Elaine said. "We're not talking shop tonight. No airplane stuff. Got it?"

"Yeah, well, then no movie stuff either."

Father Bob stood up, turned to me, and put his fists on his waist. "What are you doing?"

"Huh? What?"

"You know the rules. Nobody in my kitchen. Okay. Everybody out. Into the dining room. Right now," Father Bob ordered, waving his hands around madly. "Now. *Schnell, bitte. Mach schnell.*"

"Really? German?" I asked.

Father Bob pointed a wooden spoon at the doorway to the dining room. "Come on, you girls, too. I just can't work like this."

I followed Allison and Elaine into the dining room. Elaine waved for us to sit side-by-side across from her. She sat down beside Father Bob's empty place setting and put the bottle of Cabernet in the center of the table.

We just kind of stared at one another in silence.

Allison looked around the cherry table, buffet, and china cabinet, then into the living room. "This is a really, really nice place."

Elaine leaned into her arms on the table and asked me, "Do you miss it?"

"I never spent much time here. He was a pretty private kind of guy."

"Your brother?" Allison took a quick sip of wine.

I nodded.

"How long has it been?"

"Thirteen years." Elaine sat back in her chair. "If you are serious about staying here in LA, do you want to move in?"

"Nah. I'm happy where I am at out back."

"Come on. You can afford better with all the money Al McGuire made for you."

"I'm good. Honest. It sure beats my tent in the jungle."

"What about you?" Elaine asked Allison.

"Live here? Oh, it's so huge, I'd get lost for sure."

"It was pretty lonely in here—especially at first. But I got along. It's much nicer now." Elaine looked at the door back to the kitchen.

As if on cue, Father Bob called out, "What's going on over there?"

"Oh, nothing…" Elaine called out. She smiled at me. "He's good for my soul."

"I'm glad," I said. "He has that effect on people."

"You, too?"

I nodded.

Elaine mindlessly rearranged the forks, knives, and spoons at her setting. "You know, I blew it with him."

"Who? Hawk?" Allison asked.

"He was nuts for me back then. Weren't you? But…anyway. I had my eyes elsewhere—on his brother, Stitch—but it was a hopeless cause. And that's why you ended up heading for Alaska, right?"

"The Last Frontier. Besides, there was nothing keeping me in LA back then. Definitely, didn't want to go back home to

Chicago, so what the hell."

"What about you?" Elaine asked Allison. "I do have a weak spot for this old galoot—"

"I am not old."

"You are ancient. You're a fossil. I don't even know what she sees in you." Elaine winked at Allison. "So, what would your intentions be?"

"Come on. You know I'm happy," Allison said. "More than I've ever been before."

"So is he. I can see it in his eyes. Just don't blow it like I did."

Father Bob pushed through the swinging door from the kitchen with Chateaubriand laid out old school on an oak platter. He returned with potatoes au gratin, broccoli, and Béarnaise sauce. Then he sat down next to Elaine.

"So, what did I miss?" he asked.

"Oh, nothing…" we all said together.

~~~

Our next wing walking show was at the Buckeye Air Field outside of Phoenix. We packed our stuff in the Stearman and Allison taxied us out to Runway One-Six at eight on Thursday morning.

"You don't mind, do you?" she asked.

"It's all yours. Take me for a ride, why don't you."

Cleared for take-off, she throttled up and climbed east. Allison slid us between Ontario Airport and San Bernardino, then picked up Interstate 10. She crossed north of Palm Springs, then descended to 200 feet along the highway. Thermal Airport south of Indio has an elevation of minus one hundred fourteen feet.

"My dad taught us this—flying nap-of-the-earth along the

highway. You okay with it?"

"IFR."

"Yeah. *I Follow Roads.*"

"I used to clip along twenty or thirty feet over the jungle canopy in my T-6 in Congo. Had to watch for dead tree branches sticking up here and there—that could ruin your whole day—but it was a blast plowing through the mist and rousting up the parrots."

Allison climbed and descended to stay a few hundred feet over the highway and I entertained myself keeping track of our navigation by reading off the exit signs and water towers to her and pointing out the Joshua trees and Sonora cactus in the desert.

~~~

"So, are we going to do this new move?" Allison asked on Friday as we idled at the end of Three-Five the next day, waiting for clearance from the air boss for our take-off roll.

"Your call. I'm ready."

She turned around and looked back at me. "I trust you. Nice and easy coming over, okay?"

"You got it."

Allison nodded and turned facing forward.

"One-Delta-Mike, position and hold."

Eighteen hundred. Right rudder onto the runway. Stand on the brakes.

Allison took long, deep breaths. Part of getting herself ready to go up top.

I looked at the grandstands to the right. They were two-thirds full. Good for a Friday afternoon.

"One Delta-Mike cleared for departure. Have a good show."

Allison gave me a thumbs up and I pushed the throttle in slowly. The tail came up. I climbed up twenty feet and accelerated.

Allison looked at the crowd. I don't know if anyone in the stands could tell, but she smiled broadly as she waved both hands over her head.

Half a loop up to five hundred feet. Rolled level and Allison stepped up on her seat, placed her foot flat on my windscreen, then climbed up on the wing and into the strut on top.

We flew our usual routine. At the very end, we arced back around with Allison still hanging below the wing. I descended to a hundred feet, throttled in, and raised the nose slowly rolling upside down, bringing her around above me just fifty feet off the runway. Gravity pulled me into my harnesses as I eased back on the stick.

Of course, sitting behind the Continental R-670 engine, straining to hold us level, I couldn't hear the announcer read off our script that Allison was "sitting on top of the world" as she did her Rose Bowl parade queen wave to the applauding crowd.

And from the standing ovation after we taxied in with Allison back up on the wing again, it was obviously a grand finale.

~~~

Baer Field

Memorial Day came up quickly, so Allison and I were at Mather Airport in Sacramento for the California Capital Airshow. It was four days of shows in front of—I don't know—fifty or a hundred thousand people. It looked like a lot, especially from the air.

Allison did great and the new *Sitting On Top of the World* move was a hit. After Monday's afternoon performance, she was dead tired and we should have rested up before heading home, but I had to leave the next day for the races at Ft. Wayne.

"You don't mind flying back, do you? I'm beat," she said as we waited at Runway Two-Two Right for our take-off clearance.

"I got it. You just relax. Enjoy the scenery."

"One-Delta-Mike cleared for take-off."

"Cleared for take-off. One-Delta-Mike." I rolled onto the runway and pushed the throttle to the firewall. I gently pulled the Stearman off the asphalt and headed south. It wasn't ten minutes later I noticed Allison up front leaning sideways in the cockpit, her head tucked down out of the wind, asleep. It was a long four days for her out on the wing, so I found some calm air at fifty-five hundred feet over the Central Valley and took us back home to Van Nuys over Stockton, Modesto, and Bakersfield.

"It takes a lot out of you," Allison said after we landed three hours later and pushed the plane back into our hangar.

"I really didn't get it."

"Yeah, nobody does. But that's why I have to work so hard to keep in shape."

I gave her a hug and she flinched a bit.

"Sorry. Wire welts."

"I try to keep things as smooth as I can."

"I know. Nothing you can do. The air pushes me around, sometimes into the struts and flying wires. Can't do anything about it."

When we got back to Beverly Hills as she put on my Rams jersey, I saw that her sides almost looked like she had been whipped.

She climbed into bed and fell asleep in my arms.

~ ~ ~

I didn't sleep much and finally sat up wide awake at four the next morning. Allison snored softly beside me. I didn't want to go, but I was sure Father Bob was already in the Dodge Mahal finishing his final preparations for our trek to Indiana.

I gently stroked her hair and whispered "Gotta go."

"You get up early for Father Bob," she moaned, "but not for me, huh?"

"Just get some more shuteye. I'll call when we get there."

She nodded and I gave her a quick kiss.

"Just be careful."

"Always."

Outside, Father Bob was tapping his foot, waiting outside with the engine idling. "About time."

"It's quarter to five in the morning for crying out loud."

"Come on. Gotta go. A lot of ground to cover. Thirty hours

or so on the road."

"Great."

"Sparks is already inside."

"He's not on my bunk, is he?"

"Just get in."

And, no, Sparks was parked at the table under the glow of a fluorescent light with his nose pressed up against a manual of some sort. Don't know why he doesn't get reading glasses.

I tossed my duffel bag at the foot of my bed and flopped down on it. "What's so intriguing?"

He showed me the cover. "Continental C85 Engine Operators Manual—you know, that big noisemaker up front in your airplane. Also got the Maintenance Manual, the Overhaul Manual, and the Illustrated Parts Catalog."

"Snooze-ville."

"You wanna go fast or what? Somebody's got to work it."

"Knock yourself out."

Father Bob shifted into gear and pulled us out on the street towing the trailer with my plane packed up inside.

Once we hit the freeway, I closed my eyes, thinking about leaving Allison behind, and quickly dozed off. When I woke we were rolling through canyon country on our way north. Sparks had fallen asleep sitting upright at the table, staring into his manuals, so I went up front to ride in the co-pilot's seat next to Father Bob.

"Doing okay? Want I should drive?"

"I'm good. Only been five hours or so."

"Where are we?"

"Just passed through St. George."

"Utah? Man, we've got a long ways to go."

"Nice to be back on the road again. Drove over the road for a bit after Purdue. All that time with white-line fever gave me time to think about lots of stuff. And I banked the cash to pay for my inventions."

I pointed back at Sparks. "He's snoozing out at the table."

"Good. Then he can drive tonight."

We cruised along for ten miles or so, then Father Bob said, "Thanks."

"Huh? For what?"

"You know, everything."

"What do you mean? Saving you from the Simba rebels? Absolutely. But you know, Alfalfa was really the one who made it happen."

"Yeah, what would we have done without having the CIA handy to help us out—but more than that really."

"Like what?"

"Well, in the end, you got me out of the jungle and back to the States and now I'm working with my hands again. I like that."

"Don't miss the Father Christian business?"

He nervously ran his palms over the top of the steering wheel. "I was doing good…I think. Helping people, as best as I could. Maybe not as much as Dr…"

"Ella?"

"Sorry. Sore subject. There was nothing you could have done to save her."

I stared out at the rock formations on my side of the road. "I don't know if anything would have happened between us. Maybe…might have been nice to find out—of course, if it had, you might still be parked there at the mission."

"But, really, if I'm honest, I was running away, 'cause, you know, things got pretty bad for me with the ex and all. So I was hiding out in Congo, of all places." He shook his head. "What was I thinking?"

"Gee, don't know what that's like." I closed my eyes, remembering the mess I left behind in Alaska. I looked down Interstate 15. "Sometimes a change of scenery is nice."

"From Alaska to the equator? That's one heck of a game of hide-and-seek."

"And here we are—you and me out in the middle of nowhere looking at rocks and craters—we might as well be driving on the dark side of the moon."

"But you're back home now, right?"

"I suppose."

"Doing what you want, right?"

I nodded.

"With who you want, right?"

"You mean Allison. Not you two airport gigolos, right?"

Father Bob laughed out loud. "Well, I like what I'm doing now. Working with you, and Sparks on the plane. Solving problems on paper, then making it happen in the real world. And the racing is fun, too. Exciting, you know?"

"Not to mention Elaine, too, right?"

Father Bob grinned at me. "Is that okay with you? I know about, you know, before with you guys."

"Water under the bridge, downstream, and through the dam. She's family. Really, like a sister, now."

"And I never would have met her if you hadn't dragged me back to LA. Ever. Like I said before, thanks."

"So I guess you're not ever going back to rejoin the Pope's minions?"

"I think he's on his own for now." Father Bob grinned at me. "He's a big boy. He'll get over it."

~~~

I took the wheel when we got to Richfield, Utah and drove through Colorado, then switched off with Sparks at Cheyenne for the drive through Nebraska and Iowa. Father Bob took over for Illinois and Indiana and got us to Baer Field the next evening. We got our passes and parked by the hangar for the pits. We were all pretty road-worn, so we pulled the shades down to crash in the Dodge Mahal.

What the hell?

I was still sleeping pretty soundly when I heard a hollow clattering outside. It was dark-dark in the motor home and my watch read midnight Pacific time, which meant it was two o'clock in the morning in Indiana.

I looked around and didn't see Father Bob or Sparks in their bunks. I pulled on my pants and a sweatshirt to head outside.

"What are you guys doing?" I asked. "It's the middle of the night for crying out loud!"

They had pulled the wings out of the trailer and were inside unstrapping the fuselage.

"We got to get this thing out to put it together for you," Sparks said. "It ain't going to do it on its own, doncha know."

"But…it's like two in the morning."

"What's the problem?" Father Bob asked. "We're at an airport. There's no one around to wake up."

"Well, you woke me up."

"Oh, yeah."

"Stop your moaning. Now, get in to hold the front end while we grab the tail," Sparks ordered.

We got the plane out slowly and into the brightly lit hangar. Then Sparks and I rolled his red Craftsman tool chest down the ramp and into our pit.

I shaded my eyes from the bright overhead hangar lamps. "Does it have to be so painfully bright in here?"

"Come on, move out of the way. I got work to do." Sparks yanked open one of the drawers on his tool chest.

I looked around and saw a couple of other crews quietly working on their planes. Scotty's red Cassutt was already assembled, parked down the line. I also saw Ax's yellow Shoestring with Peter and Manfred hunched over the engine. I was willing to bet Ft. Wayne wasn't going to be a repeat of his fiasco in Waco.

"It's way too early. I'm going back to bed," I said.

"Don't you move." Sparks pointed a wrench my way. "You need to help Bob hold the wings while I bolt them in place."

Sparks grumbled numerous expletives as Father Bob and I struggled to hold the wings level while he tried to lock them into place.

He growled, "Hold it still, damn it."

"Why don't you grab this thing and I'll turn the wrench?" I replied.

"Yeah…well, do you want this done right or what?"

"Or what."

"Funny man."

"Now, boys," Father Bob scolded us like a parish priest admonishing the altar boys "Let's play nice and get our work done correctly."

"There. Done." Sparks stood up and put his fists on his hips after we got the left wing in place.

"Good. Now, can I get some sleep?"

"Yes, yes. By all means," Father Bob said. "I'll get you up for your practice laps."

Sparks and I didn't say another word. We just gave each other the high noon stare.

Then I went back to bed.

~~~

I hosed the road dust off of me later that morning, then went in to check on *White Hawk Redux*. It looked like my airplane again—thank God.

Sparks and Father Bob had their heads stuck in the cowling. Down the line, I saw Scotty and Ed polishing up his red Cassutt.

I walked up to them. "Did you have any leftover parts when you put it back together?"

"Hey, you finally made it," Scotty said. "We were starting to wonder."

"Had a show with Allison up in Sacramento. Flew home, then drove straight through Tuesday night."

"That's a long haul." Scotty pointed at Ax, Peter, and Manfred down the way. "As you can see, our very special friend made it."

"You worried?" I asked.

"Nope."

"Yeah. Me, neither, too. Just keep him away from my plane."

"Lots of new faces around here." Scotty looked around at the other crews surrounding their planes.

"Different part of the world, I guess."

"So, think you can take me this time?" Scotty taunted me.

Racing the Dream

"We'll just have to see what Father Bob's come up with."

"Mmm. Well, it's good to see you."

"Yeah, you too." I turned back to my pit. "See you at the briefing."

All the pilots signed in for the briefing and got the usual time hack, weather, operations, crash-and-rescue info, along with Jack's air boss update, then we headed out to the planes on the east ramp.

I watched Ax strap into his canary-yellow plane. He fired up his engine.

I pulled my canopy down, went through my pre-start checklist, then signaled Sparks to pull the prop. Idled at a thousand and looked over to see Ax staring my way. He gave me a toothless grin, then taxied to the runway.

A couple of other planes headed out and I followed along in trail to Runway Three-Two. After my run-up, I was fourth off in a group of eight planes. I climbed to two hundred feet and rounded the first pylon, watching Ax in the three-plane pack ahead.

Father Bob redesigned the air intakes on the front end of my cowling. Sparks polished the cylinders and matched the airflow. I saw a definite improvement in speed over Antelope Acres before coming to Indiana.

I lowered down on the pylons at 3,000 RPM, finding my marks and feeling my way into a rhythm around the course to find my groove.

Scotty came up on me quickly from behind, over the top, and settled down in front of me. On the back straight he waggled his wings, then accelerated away.

I'd show him in the Saturday heat.

After our half hour of practice was done, I parked in the pits and told Father Bob and Sparks, "We're ready."

I qualified on Friday on the outside of the first row.

~~~

At ten o'clock Saturday morning, eight of us were idling on Runway Three-Two under the red flag waiting for the heat one race to begin.

A new guy, Steve Wittman, was on the pole. Scotty sat in the middle of row one and I was on the outside. Ax was in the second row on the outside behind me.

I closely watched the oil pressure come up, then closed my eyes and took a deep breath. I looked back. The red flag came down and the pit crews left. The green flag was raised. My right leg twitched holding the brakes on the rudder pedal.

I brought the throttle up slowly to three thousand. Then again to thirty-five hundred.

Just fly your race…fly your race…

I glanced quickly at Scotty to my left.

He acknowledged me with a quick nod, then we both stared at the flag man.

As the green began to drop, I was off the brakes. Somehow Wittman pulled ahead of us as Scotty and I paralleled down the right side of the runway. His tail came off the pavement and he climbed.

I lifted off and accelerated in ground effect, sliding to his four o'clock position.

Now it's every man for himself.

Racing the Dream

Wittman rounded pylon one in the lead. Scotty pushed me up and outside a bit as we banked into the course.

Steve's yellow *Bonzo* opened up a two-length lead on the backstretch. I settled in at a hundred feet behind Scotty, staying up in the clear out of his wake turbulence.

We arced around pylon six to the start/finish line in front of the stands on the north ramp, officially starting the timing of the race.

Working the stick and rudder to fly as smooth a line as possible, I was careful to keep the yarn on my nose pointing straight back at my face.

Didn't know what Scotty's tach said, but I was staying on his tail with some power to spare. I'd give him a run for his money—and maybe catch up with Wittman, but made sure I saved my engine for the finals on Sunday.

I was a plane length behind Scotty coming across the start/finish line for the fourth lap. On the backstretch, I noticed a shadow on the ground from behind but stayed in a high echelon on Scotty's red Cassutt.

Around pylons two and three, the shadow came way too close. I did a quick double take to the outside and saw Ax's Shoestring creeping in.

I turned in a bit early on pylon five—then a crunch on my right wing. A flash of canary yellow in my peripheral vision.

Full right aileron—the windscreen filled with corn stalks.

Right rudder—banking into the inside of the course.

"Mayday, one-four."

Easy on the controls. Maintain a hundred knots.

I brought the plane gently around for Runway Five.

Fly the airplane—fly the plane—one hundred knots—easy right pressure on the stick—level out over the runway…

I set down, rolling out on the centerline. I shut down the engine and coasted to a stop at taxiway Charlie Three, where the fire and rescue trucks surrounded me.

I gave them a thumbs-up and popped the canopy. "I'm good…I'm good."

One of the firemen leaned in over me and asked, "What happened?"

"I got hit."

Another walked around my right wing aiming a fire extinguisher at it. "Holy crap. Look at that."

I glanced over and saw the shredded wingtip. Pushing myself up out of the canopy, I took a couple of steps away from the plane, then just bent over, putting my hands on my knees, and closed my eyes.

"Jesus."

"Hawk—thank God," Father Bob said as he and Sparks climbed out of a pickup truck.

I stood up and looked at the planes overhead as the race continued.

Father Bob put his hand on my shoulder. "You're okay, right?"

"Yeah. I'm fine. But…" I pointed at the right wing.

Sparks peeled back the fabric and checked the struts. He looked over at me and asked softly, "How did you land this thing?"

All I could do was shrug my shoulders.

Sparks and Father Bob lifted the empennage onto the tailgate of the pickup truck. I climbed up and collapsed on my back in the bed beside them. The planes raced by up above as we towed my plane to the hangar.

Back in the pits, I slouched down in a director's chair with my eyes shut, while Sparks and Father Bob started taking the prop off of *White Hawk Redux*.

I was done for the weekend.

When the race was over, crews brought their planes into the hangar and I saw Ax walk by staring straight ahead as Peter and Manfred pulled the tail of his Shoestring into his bay.

I got up to head that way, but suddenly Sparks was in my grill.

"Out of my way," I growled.

He put his hand on my chest. "Stand down. *Now.*"

"But—"

Father Bob grabbed my arm and pulled me back towards the main hangar door. "Come on."

"But—fangs, man. Fangs out."

"I know. I know." He dragged me across the tarmac to the FBO's office, then into the empty pilot's lounge, and closed the door. "It's not going to do any good at all. None. Got it?"

I paced around angrily.

"Sparks and I are going to pack up the plane and load it in the trailer, then we're heading home. Simple as that." He followed me back and forth with his eyes. "What were you going to do? Smack him?"

"Yeah…I don't know." I stopped in front of Father Bob. "Maybe."

He shook his head. "You need to call Allison and let her know you're okay. That's what you need to do."

There was a knock at the door.

We frowned at each other, then Father Bob went over and opened it.

Ax stood outside. "Yes. You are here, then."

Father Bob stepped aside.

"I am terribly sorry. It was my fault for hitting you with my propeller today," Ax said mechanically, staring my way. "But that was not my intention to do so. I ask that you please accept my apology."

Boy, I really wanted to wring his neck. I stared him down. "It's a goddamn plastic trophy, man."

Father Bob looked back at me.

"Yes…yes, I know," Ax mumbled.

Finally, I shrugged my shoulders. "Stuff happens."

Ax took a deep breath. "Yes. I have heard that before."

I didn't say anything else.

"Very well, then. I, ah…Thank you." Ax turned and walked away.

I stared at the empty doorway.

"You need to call Allison," Father Bob reminded me softly. He stepped out and closed the door.

I did. Then we headed back home to LA.

Mulholland Drive

Once Father Bob pulled into Stitch's mansion in Beverly Hills at two in the morning, I was practically out the door before the Dodge-Mahal stopped rolling.

Sparks came out, gave me a quick nod, then quietly left in his pickup truck.

Father Bob stepped down from the motorhome and asked, "You going to be okay?"

I just nodded.

He paused for a moment or two, then headed inside to Elaine.

I walked around the front of the motor home and just froze at the steps leading up to my casita, staring at the door.

After thirty hours in the Dodge-Mahal, I felt like an animal suddenly released from a cage.

The back door slammed shut on the mansion.

I couldn't go back inside again.

Not into the tiny, cramped living room with the dusty shutters…Not into the claustrophobic bedroom with the peeling paint…Not to stare at my brother's artwork…

I just can't go in…

I turned toward my Corvette. Jumping in, I hit the ignition key and put the top down. Maybe the engine should have warmed up some more, but I had to go. And go right then.

When I got to Cold Water Canyon Road, turning south to

Sunset would have taken me to Allison's apartment. Instead, I turned right on Mulholland Drive heading north and drove…and drove…and drove…

I didn't know where I was going, just that I was going. The wind in my hair felt good, like shaking the Indiana dust off of me.

There were no thoughts of my midair crash with Ax in Fort Wayne. I had worked through it over and over again on the trek back home. Somewhere in the cornfields of Nebraska, I gave up worrying over it, staring at the dashed white lines leading me on and on west on Interstate 80.

I stayed on Mulholland, south of the San Fernando Valley, through Topanga Canyon, south of Calabasas.

I didn't think about Allison, either. Maybe I didn't want to—not just then, anyway.

Just drive…just drive…on and on …

I wound through the darkness of the Santa Monica Mountains, shifting up and down, pushing my speed to the max around the tight corners of the highway, kicking up dust and gravel behind me.

Before I knew it, I ran out of road coming up to the Pacific Coast Highway at Carrillo Beach, south of Point Magu.

My watch said it was just after four in the morning.

I must have sat at that intersection for five minutes, then turned south, back towards LA, this time at a more leisurely pace.

Passing Zuma Beach, I cut across Point Dume. When I got to Malibu, I thought of Allison. Maybe she was heading up to catch some waves.

On a whim, I swung right down Malibu Road and cruised the oceanfront properties at twenty miles per hour. Seeing the road ahead merging back onto the Pacific Coast Highway, I took a right down a side street that dead-ended into Malibu Point.

Racing the Dream

I parked for—I don't know—fifteen minutes or so.

Kicking off my shoes and socks, I hiked out onto the empty beach through the dying waves. There were no surfers, yet. No sun for tanning. No swimmers. No seagulls flying. Nobody. Nothing.

I sat down at the water's edge, looking west over the Pacific Ocean. Moonlight made the crest of the waves glow. The low rumble of the surf seemed to cleanse my mind.

Laying back, closing my eyes, and listening, I must have quickly fallen asleep, until an hour or so later, the rising tide crawled over my feet and woke me up.

Morning light broke to the east.

I got up and walked the beach south, cut through on the path around the abandoned Adamson House, and worked my way down to the Malibu pier.

By the time I got there and turned back, the sun was up and a few surfers were paddling out to catch the first waves of the day.

Dawn Patrol.

I didn't see Allison or her Woodie.

Coming back around the path, I headed north again. When I got to my car, I took a last survey south of the beach and up the side road, then down Malibu Point again.

I didn't know how or why, but I made a decision, then headed to Van Nuys airport and found Al McGuire in his office.

"Really?" he asked.

I just nodded my head.

"I'll make it happen."

~~~

"There you are," Allison said walking up to the FBO office as I came out. "I saw your car in the lot and went by the hangars looking for you."

I went up and grabbed her in a bear hug.

"When did you get back?"

"Like, two this morning."

"You didn't sleep, did you."

"No. I did not." I kissed her, then we headed back towards the parking lot with my arm around her shoulders. "Let's get some flapjacks and I'll tell you all about the trip."

~~~

Mohave Airport

I was on fumes the rest of the day, until I finally did a *stall-spin-crash-burn-and-die* in my bed, auguring into a deep sleep at seven that night, while Allison paged through a biography of Abraham Lincoln.

And she was still up before me rattling around in the kitchen. After coffee, she drove off in her Woodie to the beach and I headed back to the airport.

Sparks and Father Bob already rolled the fuselage off the trailer in front of the hangar and were wrestling the right wing panel out.

I could only stare at the frayed wingtip.

"Need I say more?" Sparks asked as they set it down on a pair of sawhorses. Then under his breath, "Lucky son-of-a-bitch."

"It sounded like a car crash," Father Bob said. "I sure don't want to hear that again at an airport. Ever."

"So, now what?" I asked.

"We go to work. The Cleveland race is next, but we've got a couple of months to get ready," Father Bob said. "And, ah, I want to talk to Winston."

"Who?"

"You know, Allison's dad."

"Why?"

"He's a test pilot, right? And he had some ideas I want to hear more about."

I scratched my temple. "Yeah…okay. I'll ask."

~~~

One week later, I came by the hangar to gather up Father Bob.

"Come on. Let's go," I said.

"Huh? Go where?" he asked. "I'm in the middle of something."

"You wanted to meet Allison's dad, right? Well, we're going to get together with him for lunch at Mojave Airport."

"When?"

"Today. Now."

"For lunch?" He looked at his watch. "It's almost eleven. We'll never make it there on time—not even in your Corvette."

"Oh, we're not driving."

"Then, how…" He scowled back at me from his drafting board. "Oh, no. I don't think so."

"Come on. It will be fun."

"You know how I hate to fly."

"I'll take care of you. No problem."

"In the Stearman?"

I just nodded. "You wanted to meet Winston."

"Yeah, but—"

"Yeah, but nothin'. Come on." I went back and grabbed Father Bob off his stool and dragged him out towards my other hangar.

Sparks stood up and watched with an evil kind of sneer on his face.

I got Father Bob up on the wing, then strapped him into the front cockpit, ignoring his protests.

"But there's no top on this thing."

"Just put on your helmet and goggles," I said.

"But—"

I was already buckled in back, flipping the switches as quickly as possible to get started up before he could climb out.

Father Bob covered his eyes when the Continental radial fired up, covering us in white smoke.

"I told you to put your goggles on," I said through the intercom as he rubbed his eyes.

He coughed. "I don't like this at all."

All I could do was laugh. "Please place your seat backs and tray tables in their full upright and locked position."

We taxied out to One-Six Right. After a quick run-up, tower cleared us and we rolled south. I lifted off, banking gently—just twenty degrees or so—north along the highway, then on towards Magic Mountain.

"Come on, man. Open your eyes and take a look around," I said.

"I don't like this."

"Yeah, you do. Come on, admit it."

I climbed slowly to fifty-five hundred feet, keeping everything as smooth as possible.

Finally, Father Bob gazed around. "I guess it's not so terribly awful."

"What did I tell you?"

Forty-five minutes later, I crossed Runway Two-Six for a right-hand downwind, easing the Stearman around on base-to-final to a gentle three-point landing.

"There. Not so bad, huh?" I said after we parked and I helped Father Bob down off the wing.

"Ah, *terra firma.*"

"Don't embarrass me by kneeling down and kissing the ground."

We headed to the restaurant. Winston was not there, so we got a table by the window and sat across from each other. Just as the waitress brought us our coffee, the windows rattled with the scream of a jet engine overhead. A few minutes later, an F-104 Starfighter taxied up next to the Stearman with the canopy raised and parked.

We watched the pilot take off his helmet and saw Winston climb down and head inside. He seemed a lot more impressive marching our way in his green flight suit than dressed in khakis and a blue blazer the first time I met him at Van Nuys airport.

"Gentlemen. Glad you could make it." He sat down and the waitress set down a glass of Pepsi in front of him. Without asking. "Thank you, darling."

"I like your ride," I said, pointing at the stubby-winged F-104.

"And it pays, too." Winston took off his aviator sunglasses. "Father Bob. It is quite good to see you. How are you today?"

"I am very well, thank you. And thank you for meeting with us."

"Not a problem. But time is short and I have to get the bird back to the barn soon."

The waitress asked Winston, "The usual?"

"Chili dog with onions and cheese."

She pointed at me. "I'll have the same."

Father Bob looked at Winston, then at me, and back to Winston, like we were crazy or something. "You guys are crazy. I'll just have some dry wheat toast with my coffee, thanks."

I looked at Winston and shrugged my shoulders. "Whatever—but could you bring me a chocolate shake, too?"

"So, how can I help you?" Winston asked.

"When you were down at Van Nuys, you mentioned something about, I think you called them tip sails, on airplane wings."

"That I did."

"And you said they would increase efficiency by cutting induced drag."

"They can, indeed. But there are some limitations. While the tip sails can dial it down, increasing range and maybe payload, they also add parasitic drag—and you want to go fast, right?"

"Yes, that is the whole point. So, I'm thinking of remodeling the wing on the plane," said Father Bob.

"Well, first of all, you don't see them on any fighter planes, now do you?" Winston pointed outside at his F-104 Starfighter.

"He's got a point," I said.

"And they are meant to go fast. Very fast."

"Yeah, but—"

"While induced drag decreases with airspeed, parasitic drag increases. Thank you, ma'am," Winston said as the waitress served our lunches. "You have to manage the trade-offs."

"So, it's really not going to be of much help," Father Bob said.

"Now, I did not say that." Winston took a bite of his chili dog. He chewed a bit and swallowed. "You just need to get creative about redesigning your wing."

I took a huge slurp of milkshake through the straw and eyed Father Bob.

"But how?" he asked, waving his pathetic triangular-cut hunk of dry wheat toast around like a crippled sparrow.

Winston grinned as he swept his plate my way. He flipped his paper placemat over and pulled a number two pencil out of his flight suit. "Have you ever heard of Hoerner wingtips?"

"No."

Winston took another bite of chili dog and with the precision of a draftsman, drew out the squared-off end of a wingtip—like on Scotty's Cassutt—then turned it around to show Father Bob. "Your wing probably looks a bit like this, right?"

"Well, okay, it does."

"The low pressure off the top of the wing curls off in vortices—and that's your induced drag, right?" Winston mimicked the motion with his pencil over the drawing. He then drew a second upside-down wingtip with the top end arcing down to a shorter span on the bottom. "Now this is a Hoerner wingtip. It helps accomplish the same thing without curving the end of your wingtip up and increasing the front profile of your plane. It pushes the flow out a bit from the high pressure under the wing, cutting down the intensity of the induced drag."

It made sense to me. I finished off my dog and made that gurgling sound when my straw found the bottom of the chocolate shake.

Winston and Father Bob gave me the look of embarrassed parents.

"Sorry," I said. "You were saying."

Winston shook his head and chuckled. "What is it that she sees in you, son?"

"Well, I make her laugh."

"Yes, I can imagine that you do, indeed." Winston gave me a toothy smile.

"This Hoerner thing looks interesting," Father Bob said.

"Wing rakes might help. So could some wing sweep on the front end. Lengthening the wing span might be an option, too. You have to get creative." Winston finished off his chili dog. "I assume you've figured out the C-L and C-D of your wing."

"Lift and Drag? Of course."

Winston nodded. "Have you figured out the Oswald Coefficient?"

"No, I haven't," Father Bob admitted.

Winston started scrawling out math equations and at this point, it was time for me to check out of their conversation. I rested my chin on my hand and looked out on the flight line.

Winston's F-104 parked right next to our biplane was a crazy arc of aviation history in a single scene. The Starfighter can do Mach 2. You have to give the guy credit—I never got to fly jets. But he is.

Good for him, I thought, as a Piper Aztec rolled down the runway and rose into the desert air. A Cessna 150, obviously with a new student on board, did crash-and-dashes around the pattern.

"Now, it seems, I had best get myself and my steed back to Edwards," Winston finally said. He shuffled through three different placemats scribbled up with the drawings, formulas, and notes he had made. He rolled them up and handed them to Father Bob. "Good luck."

"Thank you so much," Father Bob said.

Winston pointed at me. "Your treat this time, right?"

"You got it," I said. "Thanks for catching up with us."

"And take care of that little girl of mine, you hear me, son?"

"Always."

"Or else…"

We all shook hands and Winston left, heading out to his plane.

"Get what you needed?" I asked Father Bob as we headed up to the cash register.

"I did indeed." He grinned broadly.

As I paid the bill, the General Electric J79 turbojet fired up. We turned and watched Winston release the brakes and taxi away. By the time we got out on the tarmac, he was rolling down Runway Two-Six. He leveled off in ground effect and accelerated, then pulled the nose straight up, kicked in his afterburners, and climbed skyward.

~~~

Muscle Beach

What was that knocking on my front door? I hoped—no, prayed it was just a dream. It had to be three in the morning. Maybe pulling the blanket over my head and ignoring it, the rapping noise would stop and whoever was there would go away already. It was probably just Father Bob, anyway.

Forget him.

The knocking stopped and I could feel my eyelids uncrinkle. My muscles relaxed.

Thank God.

I was just dozing off again when a rapid tapping on my bedroom window yanked open my eyes.

"Hawk! Come on. You promised me," Allison said through the window. "Let me in."

I sat up and rubbed the sleep from my eyes. I looked at her through the glass. "What?"

"You promised me."

I slid my feet off the bed, slowly stood up, and shuffled towards the front door, scratching myself then stretching my arms and twisting at the waist to loosen up my back.

"What?" I grumbled as I opened the door.

"You promised me."

"When? Last night? Maybe I was drunk."

"Maybe—but it doesn't matter. You promised."

Allison was dressed in a tank top, shorts, sweat socks, and tennis shoes. Her hair was pulled back in a ponytail.

Maybe this is a dream—maybe a very good dream.

"You look nice." I reached out for her.

"No, you don't." She came in, pushing by me. "Now, let's get dressed."

"Dressed for what?"

"You were the one who suggested it—*Fatso.*" She grinned and poked me in my waist with her index finger.

"Hey! I am not fat." I pushed away her hand.

"You swore you would come with me."

"Oh, yeah…PT…" I reached out again to hug her. "I thought maybe we could, you know, ease into it some."

"Nope. Not a chance this time." Allison spun out of my arms. "Maybe later…*maybe.*"

"Promises, promises."

"Yeah, promises, remember? Like to me?"

"Can I at least get some coffee first?"

"Get dressed and you can drink it on the way." She headed into the kitchen.

I washed up and got dressed in gym shorts, a T-shirt, and running shoes, then slurped down the coffee as she drove us out to Venice Beach.

"You know, I used to be a lot better at doing this—back in Africa. Of course, I didn't have any other distractions at the time." I winked at her. "Not so much in Alaska. Way too cold up there. And dark."

"You'll thank me later."

"Yeah, sure."

"Doug used to work out with me when he didn't have any

early morning lessons. It kept him in peak shape, too."

"What a prince."

Allison parked and I finished off the last of my joe.

"Come on. Don't you want to be a lean, mean, flying machine?"

"You are hilarious."

"I guess I am."

We headed to the Strand. There were way too many people out on the beach exercising this early in the morning.

Allison spread her feet and bent over touching her left toes with her right hand, stood up, and touched her right toes with her left hand. "Aren't you going to stretch out?"

Standing behind her, I silently mimicked her, mouthing 'Aren't you going to stretch out.'

"What?"

"Oh, nothing." I knelt down pretending to tighten my shoelaces.

"It's your funeral." She suddenly started running south on the footpath.

"Hey, wait for me."

She was faster than I thought and it took me a quarter mile to catch up with her.

"Are you stalking me?" she asked when I matched up with her pace.

"And how far do you run?"

"Five miles. Think you can make it?"

"No sweat."

Allison looked at me and gave me a wicked grin. "We'll see, won't we."

Okay, I was a little out of shape, maybe panting some as we jogged toward Marina del Ray. "Are we there yet?"

"Almost."

"You're right, though. I do feel better."

"You say that now," she said.

We ran for another mile, then Allison pivoted west out onto the beach. "Now back up in the sand."

"What? Are you kidding me?"

She turned back north at the water's edge. "Come on…*Fatso*."

"What happened to the beautiful young girl who once brought me donuts—in bed?"

She laughed, maintaining the same pace as on the walkway.

I lumbered on behind her, my feet churning through the sand as she headed north. I called out, "I think this is where we parked."

She turned around, jogging backward and grinning. "We're not even halfway back."

"I hate you."

Allison turned around and picked up her pace, leaving me behind.

I slowed down to walk the last half mile, as I didn't want her to see me huffing and puffing when I got back to Muscle Beach.

She was doing pull-ups.

"Are you kidding me?" I flopped down on a bench nearby, still breathing heavily.

She dropped to the sand and came over. "You know, you really need this. It will help your racing, too."

"Yeah, yeah, you're probably right." I stared out at the waves.

"And it'd be nice to have you hanging around—for a little while longer, anyway."

"You do this every day?"

"Three times a week. And the other days, I'm out on my board. And that's a workout, too. But, you know, I gotta do it."

"I had no idea," I said, massaging the tops of my thighs as my muscles started tightening up.

"That's going to smart a bit. The sand is tough. So you just relax, while I finish my routine."

I watched her do push-ups, sit-ups, and pump some iron—it was all too exhausting to watch, so I lay down on the bench and eventually nodded off.

"Hey, Hawk," she said standing over me, nudging my arm and glistening with sweat. "Thanks for coming out."

I squinted up at her. "Well, I promised."

"Do it again Friday?"

"Yeah…I suppose."

Allison reached out.

I took her hand and she helped me up to shuffle on my aching legs back to the Woodie.

"Can we stop and get some donuts?" I asked.

"Sure."

~~~

Head, Hands & Feet

Oh, I ached all the next morning, but kept my word with Allison and worked out with her every other day. When I was finally ambulatory enough to show up again at the airport, I stopped by Al McGuire's office.

"Holy mackerel! It's like seven-thirty in the morning," he said when I rapped on his doorway. "Who are you anymore?"

"Very funny." I sat down across from him at his desk. "You should be a comedian."

"Somes got it. And somes don't. How's the rebuild on your plane coming?"

"Father Bob redesigned the wings. Stretching and angling them out. I think he's molding new fiberglass wingtips. And, of course, Sparks has the engine torn all apart—yet again. He said he's porting it."

Al McGuire nodded. "You know the engine's just a huge air pump. That should pull you through the sky a little faster. What's next?"

"Cleveland. Over Labor Day weekend."

"You'll be ready?"

"Father Bob promised me we will."

"Then Reno—that's just a couple of weeks later."

"Allison got with the promoter in Ohio and Bill Stead to get our wing walking act booked for both shows."

"You'll be a busy boy in September."

"About that other thing…"

"Still working it. Getting a little closer."

"Just checking. I hope you can make it happen." I stood up. "Thanks."

"No worries." He rubbed his chin. "You know, you look good. Have you been working out?"

"I gotta go."

"No, seriously."

I waved him off and made my way over to my hangar.

Sparks was polishing down the cylinder bores and Father Bob was hunched over his drawing board with someone looking over his shoulder.

"Hey, Bob…"

They turned around. Winston stood beside him.

"What are you doing here?" I asked.

"Been talking off-and-on with Father Bob, here, and I thought I'd come down and take a look-see for myself."

"Actually, you should shake hands with the newest member of the team," Father Bob said.

"Team?"

"Now, hold on there just a moment or two, Bobbie." Winston held up his hands. "This here is Hawk's airplane, so that means it truly is Hawk's team. He certainly should have the final say in all such matters."

"You want to help us out?"

"I do, indeed. I like what Father Bob is doing here. And I believe it could be helpful to offer up my assistance and, frankly, it will be fun for me." Winston cocked his head as he looked at me. "But, well, honestly, maybe you just don't want Allison's old man hanging around and getting in your way around here. If so, I understand. Just say so."

"Winston knows a lot and has had some great ideas," Father Bob said.

"But you fly jets…at Mach two, and this is kind of, well, Mickey Mouse stuff compared to that—no offense, Bob."

"I must disagree with you there, Hawk. It is fellows like you, and Father Bob, here, and Sparks over there," Winston pointed each of us out as he spoke, "sweating out the details in hangars, figuring out how to go just a little bit faster than the next guy. Sure, I'm a jet jockey, but I just go up and do what I'm told. You are old school. Like two guys in a bicycle shop in Dayton or a crazy motorcycle racer in upstate New York. Traditional…if you catch my drift."

"You know, he came down and got me into the wind tunnel over at Lockheed to run models of my wing designs through it," Father Bob said.

"Of course, it was in the middle of the night." Winston winked at me. "But I do know a few people over that way,"

I nodded at Father Bob, then looked at Sparks. "What do you think?"

"The Colonel's got an idea or two about baffling the engine that will probably gain you a knot or two or three."

"Well, I don't have a problem with it," I said. "But you are probably going to get your hands dirty around here."

"Not an issue. Who do you think put Allison's Woodie back together?" Winston asked. 'That's why they make Lava soap."

"And what about *her*?"

"Well, now, I'll leave that up to you, Bossman."

"Then, welcome aboard," I said, reaching out to shake

Winston's hand.

"Excellent——*excellent.*" Father Bob turned back to the drawing board. "Let me show you what we've got here."

I looked down on a new top-view drawing of *White Hawk Redux.* Then I looked over at the fuselage, stripped of its wings. "That's going to work?"

"This fellow, here, is pretty ingenious." Winston patted Father Bob on his shoulders. "His wing is a little bit of jet with the sweep there and a little bit of glider, being longer and thinner with just a little hint of the wingtips there at the ends. But very low profile—low drag."

"The extensions on the ends are fiberglass, so it's light," said Father Bob.

"Well, it looks fast on paper," I said.

Father Bob nodded. "Of course, your stall speed will go up a bit."

"We figured somewhere around five to eight knots," Winston said. "We'll work that out for sure in the fly-off, once the wings are bolted back on."

"Pop? What are you doing here?" Allison's voice from behind startled us.

"Allison?" Winston asked.

The three of us slowly turned around, no doubt our mugs looking like kids caught with our hands in the cookie jar.

I noticed Sparks slide quietly out the left side of the hangar door.

"I believe we discussed this situation and it is your conversation to have," Winston whispered quietly in my ear, "*Mr. Bossman.*"

"Are you here to spy on me?" Allison asked.

Racing the Dream

"No. He's here to help us out," I said. "I told you, Father Bob and I flew up to Mojave and met with him about redesigning the wing. They've talked a few times and snuck into the wind tunnel at Lockheed, and—"

"Is this all true?" She pointed at her father.

"Guilty as charged." Winston shrugged. "And, you know, I don't have a project to keep my hands occupied anymore—and you can't grow grass in the desert."

"He's right about that," said Father Bob.

Allison squinted his way.

"Come on now, honey," Winston half-pleaded. "You know, me and Hawk are just a couple of old single-seat knuckle-draggers—"

"*I am not old.*"

For some reason that made Allison, Winston, and Father Bob laugh out loud.

"You hungry?" Winston asked Allison.

"I am."

"Great. Let's go grab some grub at Norms." Winston walked over, put his arm around Allison, and turned her towards the parking lot, but she squinted back at me over her shoulder. "Come on, Bobbie. Let's go."

"But what about Sparks?" Father Bob asked me.

"He got away clean. He's on his own."

~ ~ ~

It took a little while for Allison to warm up to having her father on the quote-unquote 'team,' but he steered clear of sticking his nose in where it didn't belong.

Winston flew his personal Beech Baron down from Mojave about every other day to help us out with finishing the wing panels. I offered to help paint them, but Allison said, "Oh no, I don't think so. I've seen you eat with a fork."

And Father Bob agreed, "She's right, you know."

So I sat outside in the sunshine drinking beer while they spray-painted inside the hangar.

Winston also worked with Sparks to shape and position the aluminum panels in the engine compartment, channeling the intake air close around the cylinders, then out through the bottom of the cowling, making the cooling much more efficient."

He sat me down in the cockpit and made me talk him through a race to understand what is going through my mind around the pylons.

"You ever race go-carts? Me and Stitch grew up chasing each other around the neighborhood in Chicago, aggravating the neighbors. It's kind of like that."

Winston nodded. "But what is going through your mind? What are you thinking about?"

"You know, this sounds a lot like Allison forcing me to go through our wing walking routine in my head over and over and over again."

"She did that?" Winston asked.

"Yeah. It drove me damn near crazy. Why?"

He chuckled. "Well, I taught her and Doug that technique. A little habit I picked up during the year I ran the Thunderbirds. See, sometimes you don't know what actually stays with your kids."

"Yeah, I guess."

"Well, you can't just be a stick-and-throttle actuator in the middle of a race. You've got to have situational awareness, too.

Otherwise, you'll end up dead. And Winston's number one rule of aviation is…"

"Don't get dead."

"Head, hands, and feet, my boy…head, hands, and, feet."

Winston's ideas and wrench-turning definitely moved our redesign and reassembly along a lot faster.

Being summertime, Allison and I had weekend show dates up and down the west coast—and I did keep my promise to work out with her at Muscle Beach during the week.

On a Tuesday, the third week of July, she went surfing up in Malibu and I headed to the airport. As I wandered over to my hangar, I saw Scotty following Father Bob as they walked around my finally finished airplane parked out front.

"Hey, don't drool all over my new paint job," I called out.

"Wow," Scotty said. "But…*wow.*"

Father Bob beamed like a new dad in a hospital nursery.

"Are you giving away all of our secrets?" I asked Father Bob.

"It looks fast just sitting here in front of your hangar," Scotty said. "Have you had it up yet?"

I looked at Father Bob.

He said, "Today's the day."

"We fly?" I asked. "Seriously?"

"As soon as Winston gets here. Should be any minute now."

As soon as he said it, we heard his Baron overhead entering downwind. We looked up and watched him turn base, then final.

"Are you ready?" Winston asked coming up to us by the hangar.

"We are," said Father Bob. "Thanks for coming down."

"Wouldn't miss it for the world."

"What about you?" Winston asked Sparks, who rocked back and forth on his wheeled stool.

"I ran all my engine and prop tests. It's full of gas and full of oil. Not much more I can do right at the moment."

"Let's do it," I said.

Winston, Father Bob, and I did an extra careful walk-around, especially checking the attachment nuts and bolts on the flight controls.

"Okay, we've been through the first flight a hundred times." Winston knelt down beside me as I strapped into the cockpit. "First do the high-speed taxi tests, then if you are good to go, radio me and I'll be your chase pilot in the Baron. Got it?"

"Got it."

"Here, take this bag with you."

"What's that?" I asked.

"It's our car keys." Winston winked at me. "An old Lockheed tradition."

"So, if I don't make it back, you all walk home?"

Winston grinned. "Something like that."

"You know, I'm not really on board with this crazy idea," Sparks said, getting up and walking over to the prop.

I pulled the canopy shut and locked it. then I went through the start-up checklist.

Master on. Mags on. Mixture Rich. Primed the engine three times. Throttle open a quarter.

I pointed at Sparks and he pulled the prop through once…twice…and the engine came to life on the third one and the cockpit filled with a snarling Continental C-85. Sparks stepped off to the side.

I saluted the boys and pushed the throttle in to test the brakes, then taxied away towards One-Six Left, the short runway.

Ground Control cleared me for a series of high-speed taxi

tests, accelerating down the runway five miles per hour faster each time, up to eighty percent of stall speed, which we figured would be around ninety miles per hour. Then a few more times at that speed to get the feel for when the tail comes off the ground and noting the rudder requirements for P-factor. Finally ready to go, I taxied back to the approach end and called Winston on one-two-three point four. He fired up the Baron and came out to join me heading out to Antelope Acres.

"One-Four-Echo, cleared for take-off, One-Six Left. Left turn after departure. Good day—and good luck."

"One-Four-Echo, cleared for take-off. Thanks."

Full power…seventy miles per hour…tail up…a hundred miles per hour…

The plane leapt off the runway and climbed beautifully.

I was grinning hugely as I banked towards Magic Mountain. I didn't hear Winston's departure clearance behind me but his Baron quickly appeared on my right wing. He gave me a thumbs-up. I nodded and returned the sign. As we cleared the Airport Traffic Area he radioed to go to Company frequency on the way out to the desert.

Winston and I had gone through the first flight over and over again, so the maneuvers were definitely branded into my gray matter. So we went to work.

Maintaining one hundred sixty miles per hour, I checked all the flight controls.

Rudder five degrees right, then left.

Elevator three degrees up, then down.

Stabilized level and banked the ailerons left five degrees, then right.

Engine instruments all green.

Three hundred sixty degree turns at ten, then fifteen then twenty degrees in increments, left and right.

Slow flight at one hundred ten—climbing, descending, and turning. Then a series of power-off approach to stalls.

The wings buffeted at ninety-five, just as expected.

Winston finally called out an hour in the air, so we headed back to Van Nuys and landed.

Popping the canopy at my hangar, I told Father Bob and Sparks, "It flew great. Awesome job, guys. Awesome."

We debriefed the flight and watched Sparks check the engine and open the inspection panels. He gave me a thumbs-up. I topped off the tanks and went out in the afternoon, flying the exact same flight maneuvers as the first morning flight with Winston shadowing me.

When I got back to the hangar after another hour of flight, Allison was standing with the boys.

"Why didn't you tell me?" she asked when I popped the canopy.

"I didn't know until I got here this morning. Father Bob had it pulled out, gassed up, and ready to go."

"Yeah, well, he knew." She pointed at her father. "Didn't you?"

Winston just shrugged and smiled. "You didn't want to stand around here on the ground worrying, did you?"

I stepped out of the plane and gave the car keys back to Father Bob, Sparks, and Winston. "Well done. Well done."

~~~

Most days, I flew the racer twice a day, expanding the flight envelope in measured steps worked out with Winston. In between times, I practiced with Allison over Antelope Acres, and every other weekend we flew air shows.

Racing the Dream

We verified the stability, stall speeds, Vy and Vx, climb speeds, and, of course, the engine performance. Then we flew test squares, equal legs north-east-south-west to measure our airspeeds at different RPMs. Definite improvements over the previous design.

We were ready to race.

At the end of August, it was time to pull the wing off and trailer up the plane to head to Cleveland.

~~~

Cross Country

We were up early on the Tuesday before Labor Day weekend, in the PT-17, warming up the engine on One-Six Right to barnstorm our way to Cleveland. In the baggage compartment, we loaded a tent, sleeping bags, and a small overnight duffle bag. The rest of our stuff was on the road with Father Bob and Sparks in the Dodge-Mahal.

It was two long days of flying—eight hours plus a day—so we split the legs up trading off around an hour and a half each on the stick. Of course, we climbed to eleven thousand five hundred feet VFR to take advantage of the westerly winds aloft with fuel stops the first day at Grand Canyon Airport and Four Corners Airport in Farmington. We headed east through New Mexico over the Red River Pass in the Sangre De Christo Mountains, then northeast over the high plains, and finally—*finally*—across the Arkansas River to runway One-Four at Dodge City. Coming down from eleven-five the late summer heat became suffocating on downwind.

"Man, I am beat," I said after we parked on the north ramp and climbed down off the wing.

Allison stretched her back and leg muscles. "Come on, say it: aren't you glad you work out with me?"

"And I'm starving, too. I think I need a steak."

A line-boy meandered over from the FBO office. "Hey, guys.

You parking overnight?"

"Definitely," I said. "We'll need her topped off and a couple quarts of Aeroshell, too."

"We can do." He removed his baseball cap and scratched his head. "Nice looking bird."

"Thanks," said Allison.

"Where you headed?"

"Cleveland. For the air show," I said.

"Really?"

Allison shook her head at me to cut me off. "I'm hungry, too. Don't suppose there's a restaurant nearby."

"Sure. Delmonico's is just down the road."

"For serious? You mean, like on *Gunsmoke*?" Allison asked raising her eyebrows. "Matt Dillon and Miss Kitty?"

"Well, not the same one, of course, but they've still got good food. Just grab the courtesy car. The keys are inside. The joint is right down Wyatt Earp Road out front. A few miles west."

We tied down the Stearman, grabbed the fifty-nine Chevy Impala with cool rear wings, and headed into town. We pounded down a pair of huge ribeye steaks—Allison's hunk of meat was every bit as big as mine and I grinned when she pushed away her empty plate—then settled up and headed back to the airport as the sun was going down.

Grabbing our sleeping bags and the tent from the baggage compartment, we wandered a quarter mile north off the tarmac to set up camp on top of a low hill in the fading twilight. Far to the north, thunderstorms silently rumbled over the prairie glowing with cloud-to-cloud lightning like lanterns. The heat was still too stifling to climb inside the tent, so we laid our sleeping bags out in the grass and gazed up into the galaxy.

"I'm glad you're along this trip," I said. "It just didn't feel right last time, going by myself to Ft. Wayne."

Allison looked over at me. "But you had Father Bob and Sparks."

"Yeah, well…"

She laughed and put her hands behind her head. "You know, you never see this in LA. Ever."

"What?"

"There. The Milky Way. Amazing."

"Oh…yeah." The hazy band of our galaxy cut clear across the horizon. I hadn't thought about star gazing for a long, long time. Not since Congo. "They call it The Backbone of the Night in Africa."

"I like that."

I don't know how long after—a minute or five or ten—Allison quietly said, "And listen."

"What?"

"Shhh…"

After a few moments, I whispered, "I don't hear anything."

"Exactly."

We stared straight up, my eyes wandered from star to star, from constellation to constellation.

"This is good," I said. "Real good. Don't you think so?"

"Uh-oh."

"What?"

Allison rolled over to face me leaning her head in her hand. "This isn't going to turn into one of *those* talks, is it?"

"Those talks?"

"Yeah, about the future and you and me and…you know, stuff."

"Hmmm…stuff?"

"You're not worried about any of that, are you? It's just a dash."

"What do you mean, a dash?"

"This. Now. What we have here." She smiled at me. "On our gravestones, there's the year we're born and the year we die. In between is just a dash. *Life*."

"Never thought of it that way."

"It's all we've got." She reached out and stroked my cheek. "You're happy, right?"

"Well, yes, of course."

"Yeah, me too." Allison slid my way and laid her head on my chest. "What more do we need?"

I shrugged.

"Exactly."

I put my arm around her shoulder and nodded slowly. I don't remember the sky fading away, but we eventually fell asleep beneath the stars.

Up with sunrise, we got out of Dodge and with fuel stops in Topeka and Lafayette, made our way to Cleveland.

~~~

Burke Lakefront Airport

We landed at sunset on Runway Six alongside the downtown skyscrapers in Cleveland at Burke Lakefront Airport. There was no sign of Father Bob's Dodge-Mahal, so we tied the Stearman down on the ramp, covered the cockpit, then dragged ourselves over to Captain Frank's Seafood House on the East 9th Street Pier overlooking Lake Erie. Allison ate scampi in garlic butter and I had the waiter yank out the biggest lobster they could find in the tank. Afterward, we caught a cab up to the Sheraton-Cleveland Hotel on Public Square.

No star gazing that night. I zoned out on the bed even before Allison finished her shower—with a belly full of lobster, ignoring the silent screams of crustaceans echoing in my ears from being boiled alive. Just a long night's sleep in a very dark, very quiet hotel room.

At ten the next morning, we walked down Euclid Avenue to East 9th Street, then over North Marginal Road to the long, low hangar on the east side of the airport where the Dodge-Mahal was parked. Inside, Sparks lay on a roller underneath the fuselage, tightening the bolts on the wing panels.

"Up by the crack of noon," Father Bob said with a snicker. "Back to your old ways, I see."

"Oh, great," mumbled Sparks, "just when all our work here is about done."

"Ah, Hawk…" Father Bob cleared his throat loudly when I ignored him. "I said, we're glad you finally decided to join us."

I was distracted, though. A dozen teams were already spread out in the hangar assembling their planes or wrenching on engines, but I focused on Manfred and Peter bent over the cowling of Ax's yellow Shoestring.

"He made it, too, huh?" I felt my molars grinding.

Father Bob and Allison looked over towards Ax's pit.

Sparks rolled out from under the plane. He got up and stood up right in front of me, blocking my view.

"What?" I growled up at him.

"People say kill 'em with kindness." He looked over his shoulder at Ax's plane, then back down into my eyes and grinned. "But I'd rather use a two-by-four."

"I'll get him on the course."

"You betcha."

"Hey, guys!" Jack waved at us from across the hangar and came over our way. "Really glad to see you again."

"Wouldn't miss it for the world." Father Bob shook his hand.

Sparks punched me a little bit too hard in the shoulder and slid quietly away.

"The first Cleveland air show since Forty-nine. And, of course, the first races in fifteen years." I'm sure Jack noticed me staring across the pits and ignored it. He turned to Allison. "And I am glad to see you here, too. You'll be doing your wing walking act, right?"

"Yup. That's our Stearman over there." She pointed outside at One-Delta-Mike. "We're on the show schedule at one-thirty."

"Excellent. Excellent. Should be severe clear all weekend," Jack said. "And it looks to me like you've made some *special* modifications to your plane, Hawk."

"Wait 'til you see her run," Father Bob said. "She's going to be hard to beat. That's for sure."

"Great. Our crew is setting up the pylons today. First practice is tomorrow morning." He put his hand on my shoulder. "I'm glad you're back, Hawk. I'll see you at the briefing tomorrow. Okay?"

"I'll be there, Jack."

He shook my hand, gave me a smile, then headed over to talk to another crew.

"So, where's Scotty?" I asked.

"Don't know. We pulled out of Van Nuys at the same time," Father Bob said. "He should certainly be here by now—since his pickup truck moves along quite a bit faster than we do in the mobile home."

"Huh…That's not like him."

"Where did Sparks go?" Father Bob scanned the pits. "Anyway, practice early tomorrow. Qualification Saturday, then two days of racing."

"We'll get him this time." I looked over at Ax's plane again. "For sure."

"I'm not scared," Allison said, pulling my arm toward the hangar door. "Come on, we don't want to miss our practice slot."

Allison and I got twenty minutes to run through our wing walking routine. Afterward, we climbed to the top of the grandstands to watch the rest of the air show planes arrive and get marshaled to parking. The Blue Angels practiced their show in their F11-F1 Tigers. The six-plane Delta Maneuver was amazing.

We had dinner with Father Bob and Sparks at the Brown Derby in the terminal, then walked back to the hotel.

~ ~ ~

The next morning, I saw Scotty's red Cassutt parked in the pits. He slept on the floor beneath the wing with his head on a duffle bag. Ed's face was stuck inside the cowling.

"Got her ready?" I asked.

"Almost there," Ed said. "Almost."

"Where the heck have you guys been?"

"Transmission problems with the truck in Omaha." Ed stood up. "Got in at one-thirty this morning."

"I'll bet Scotty wasn't too happy."

"To put it mildly. It was a long ride in. Never heard so many swear words in my life."

"He knows them all." I kicked Scotty's leg. "Come on. Get up. Briefing is in an hour."

"Oh, yeah. Yeah. I'm on it, okay?" Scotty sat up and rubbed his eyes. "But, man, it seems early."

"It is. Like four in the morning California time. How much sleep did you get?"

"A few hours. I'll tell you, I am in serious need for some caffeine."

"Jack's got coffee and donuts over in the corner. Remember, the briefing is at eight. Don't miss it."

"I got it. No problem."

I went over to my pits and met up with Father Bob. "Where's Sparks?"

"Don't know. He was up and over here early. Looks like he got things all set up. You're ready to go."

I looked around the pits, which were bustling with activity. Mechanics were making final adjustments and buttoning up the cowlings. Others were polishing off the wing surfaces yet again. "Let's do this thing."

Racing the Dream

Father Bob and I headed over to the North American Air Racing Association briefing and signed in. Scotty straggled in right at eight o'clock, sucking down more black coffee. I studiously ignored Ax sitting up front in the second row.

Jack reviewed the course layout, especially the pylons mounted on boats floating in Lake Erie. Unlimited ceilings and visibilities. We would be using Runway Six for take-offs with a direct entry on the course this morning.

Sparks stood in our pit when we got back after the briefing.

"Where've you been?" Father Bob asked.

"Around. Just around." He looked over at Ax's Shoestring. "Never you mind, anyway. Let's get moving."

"Okay. Help me out here with the plane," I said.

We lifted the tail, rolled it forward, then backed it out onto the tarmac.

Scotty was already in his Cassutt, strapping in.

I walked over and shook his hand. "Good luck."

"Yeah…won't need it." He grinned his cheesy Eddie Haskell smile. "Eat my dust, pal."

Sparks and I did our usual walk-around, then I climbed in *White Hawk Redux*, pulled my belts tight, and ran through my pre-starting checklist. I pulled the canopy down and locked it, then signaled Sparks to pull the prop through.

Scotty was already idling when my engine fired up. I motioned for him to lead the way to the runway.

At the west end of the airport, I ran the throttle up to seventeen hundred and checked the left mag. Then back on both. Checked the right mag. Barely a drop of seventy-five between the two.

Tower cleared Scotty onto the runway and instructed me to hold short.

"Six-Six-Sierra, cleared for take-off Runway Six. Closed course."

"Cleared for take-off, Six-Six-Sierra," Scotty responded.

"One-Four-Echo, position and hold behind the departing red Cassutt."

"One-Four-Echo, position and hold."

Sitting on the runway numbers, I checked the engine instruments. All green. All good.

Looking to the east, I saw Scotty lift off and climb.

"One-Four-Echo, cleared for take-off."

I slowly pushed the throttle all the way forward and held it in. "One-Four-Echo is rolling."

The airspeed came alive. Moments later, the tail wheel lifted off the ground. A touch of back pressure on the stick to lift off into ground effect. I accelerated one wingtip above the concrete, tracking the centerline.

I looked up, ready to follow Scotty around the first pylon, but he was already well east of it over the water, climbing up through the hard top of two-hundred fifty feet.

"What the hell..."

In the blink of an eye, a piece of airplane separated from the tail of his plane and spun around crazily in the prop wash, then fell away.

The nose of Scotty's red Cassutt arced up. He rolled left.

"Six-Six-Sierra, Tower."

Gaining on him quickly, I swear I could see the airplane shudder as it began to stall.

"Scotty—"

The plane keeled over, spun a half-turn, and slammed into the water.

"Oh, God...Oh, God..."

Racing the Dream

By the time I got overhead, plywood hunks of the wing panels floated on the surface of the lake and the fuselage was sinking underwater.

I circled overhead. Rescue trucks raced to the departure end of Runway Six and parked, the firemen helpless as he went in a half-mile offshore.

"One-Four-Echo, Tower."

I strained to see any signs of movement in the bubbles below.

"One-Four-Echo."

"Nothing," I radioed. "Nothing at all."

Waves began rolling over the impact point.

An orange-ringed Coast Guard Response Boat sped east behind the break wall.

I circled fifty feet over the crash site.

Burke Tower quickly began landing racers off the course.

The northeast pylon boat upped anchor and headed my way.

"One-Four-Echo, we've got a helicopter coming on-scene. Give them some space. Report a left downwind for Runway Six."

"Roger," was all I could say. I climbed to five hundred feet on a left crosswind.

As I turned downwind, an orange helicopter hovered ten feet over the crash site. A diver jumped into the water.

I turned base and looked east. The Coast Guard boat came on scene.

"One-Four-Echo cleared to land Runway Six. Wind zero-four-zero at six."

I closed my eyes for just a moment, then banked onto final.

"One-Four-Echo for Six."

I landed and taxied as fast as I could to the east side of the tarmac. Killing the engine, I popped the canopy and climbed out of the cockpit in a flash, running as fast as I could down to the edge of the shore.

Standing on the rocks piled up at the end of the landfill, I watched helplessly as divers dropped off the side of the Coast Guard boat.

A tug slowly pushed a recovery barge over the crash site and dropped the cables of a giant crane into the water.

The divers resurfaced, gave a thumbs-up, and with a horrible diesel grind, the fuselage of Scotty's Cassutt broke out of the lake, spewing water out from inside. Four or five guys guided it down on the barge. They unhooked the plane and quickly covered it with a tarp.

Eventually, after collecting as much debris as they could, the barge and the Coast Guard boat sailed away.

Allison finally found me out there with my head in my hands. We sat for a while, then walked back to the Dodge-Mahal with my arm around her shoulders.

"What do we do now?" Allison asked.

I shrugged my shoulders. "We fly."

~~~

Afterward, everything got a little foggy.

I talked to Jack and his technical guys and told them what I saw. I guess an FAA guy was there, though I'd probably have to talk to the NTSB, too. I sat in the back of Jack's impromptu briefing with just us racing pilots where, of course, everyone decided to continue with the races. I don't even know if I voted or not.

Allison and I eventually headed back to the hotel. We ordered room service, but I just laid on the bed with my head on her lap, staring a long, long time at the ceiling. She didn't speak and just rubbed her hand through my hair. There wasn't anything to say. I did not feel my eyes close or fall asleep or even dream.

Rolling down the runway…lifting off…Scotty's nose rose up and up…then arced over—

I startled myself awake before he hit the water.

Just a dash…

"Relax," Allison whispered. "Just relax,"

"Yeah…" I closed my eyes and took a deep breath. "What time is it?"

"Never mind. Just sleep."

~~~

The next morning, I met Father Bob and Sparks at the pits. I qualified seventh, in the middle of the third row. I just never found my groove on the course. When I got done, nobody said anything—not even Father Bob.

Allison met me at the pits and we lost ourselves in the air show spectators, walking among the static aircraft displays on the tarmac. In the grandstands, we watched Bob Hoover do aerobatics in his *Yellowbird* P-51 Mustang. Then the Air Force did ten minutes of flybys in one of its F-4 Phantoms. Once Stan Segalla started his Flying Farmer routine, pretending to "steal" a Piper Cub to perform a heart-pounding low-level show that seemed to defy the laws of physics, we headed to the Stearman. At ten after one, We strapped in and taxied to Runway Two-Four to wait. Then the air boss called and it was our turn.

Rolling down the runway, it all went away from me—Scotty's

crash…qualifying so poorly…racing Ax the next day—I turned it all off and flew, steadily clocking off all the mechanics of the aerobatics in the show—and then, finally, Sitting On Top of the World and we were done.

Allison smiled at me as she stepped back into the front cockpit from the wing.

All I could do was nod. We landed. I put the tail wheel down and she climbed quickly up on top of the wing to wave to the crowd.

After we parked, she gave me a big hug and we were done for the day.

~~~

Sunday morning after the briefing, I rode on the tailgate of the pickup truck as it pulled my plane out to the runway for the first heat race. Father Bob sat beside me. Sparks walked along following us but stared up ahead. I looked and he was eyeballing Ax's yellow Shoestring.

I closed my eyes and lay down in the bed of the pickup.

"Nice day," Father Bob said.

I looked up into the deep blue sky. "Looks like you could see a hundred miles or so."

"No wind, either. That's good."

"Smooth rides—except I'm way back in the pack."

"You'll be fine."

I just nodded.

We dropped my plane in the middle of the back row.

Ax's plane was up ahead in the middle of the first row.

I hung back and listened to Jack's final briefing with the eight of us before we headed out to the planes.

"Look, let's just have a clean race. Okay?" Jack looked at Ax, then at me. "Put on a good show. Fly fast and turn left."

Nobody said anything to me. A couple of guys patted my shoulder as we headed out to strap ourselves in the cockpits.

Honestly, Ax didn't even register with me as I pulled the five-point harness down over my shoulders. Pushing my earplugs in and putting on my headset, I pulled the canopy shut and locked it, thankfully quiet for the moment, anyway.

The red flag went up. I stepped on the brakes and signaled Sparks to pull the prop through. The engine fired right away as he stepped back.

Idle to a thousand RPM. Oil pressure coming up.

I bore a hole staring at the oil temperature gauge as it slowly wound up.

There was a sharp rap on the top of my canopy.

Outside, Sparks held his baseball cap down on his head in the prop wash. He pointed at me and gave me the Churchill V for victory sign. Old school stuff. Just like back in England during the war. He knew. Pilots come and go and sometimes die. The next day you go up again.

I mirrored his victory sign back.

The red flag came down. Sparks and Father Bob walked off the runway.

Engine to seventeen hundred. Left mag. Good. Back to both. Right mag. Good. Oil pressure—green. Oil temp—green. Controls free and clear.

The green flag went up.

Throttle full forward. Roll back the mixture just a bit.

I took a couple of deep breaths, staring at the flag man.

As the green flag started coming down, I was off the brakes

and got a jump on the two planes beside me.

Eyes left and right and left and right as we rolled down the runway. I closed the gap halfway with the second row of planes, ending up fifth into the first pylon, falling just a bit behind as they arced out over the lake. But I expected that with the change Father Bob made in the prop. Once we passed back around the start-finish line to start the timing on the race, I started closing the gap with the leaders.

On the back stretch of the second lap, I climbed out of the turbulence of number four. I rode his right wing around pylons four, five, and six, then traded the altitude for speed to pass him on the front straightaway.

Up ahead, I saw Ax starting to make his move on the race leader to take first place, but I was closing the gap with him as well. In another lap and a half, I caught them and passed a white Cosmic Wind into second behind Ax.

I slowly reeled him. I climbed on the straightaways, then worked up on his wing around the first turn, staring down at his yellow plane, carefully holding my distance off his wing,

I came around pylon six, crept ahead of his wingtip, and looked over at him. He glanced at me. No expression on his face. Then I couldn't see him anymore, but I could feel him at my eight o'clock around pylons two and three.

Fly my race…Fly my race…As tight on the pylons as I can.

Just one more lap.

On the front straight, Ax slid out and climbed up on my right. An echelon together around the first turn. Rolling level heading west on the backside, he suddenly found a burst of speed and quickly passed me.

He grinned my way and closed in around the final pylons,

then crossed the finish line two plane lengths ahead of me to take the checkered flag.

Dammit.

I slowly raised the nose to climb up to three thousand feet behind Ax, holding off on my turn to downwind, shaking my head and wondering how I suddenly lost a race I clearly won.

I turned base-to-final behind Ax on the hot side of Runway Six. He landed, slowed, and taxied over to the right.

I set down behind him and followed him over to the cold side. Turning on Taxiway Charlie, I noticed Sparks standing on the tarmac with Jack and several other race officials. A marshal signaled Ax over to the group of officials on the tarmac.

I taxied back to the pit area, where Father Bob met me.

"So, what's going on with Ax?" I asked.

"Oh, I think they're going to find out exactly how he found the extra speed to beat you. Come on."

I climbed out and we hiked back to Ax's plane with the other pilots and crew members from the race. We made our way over to Sparks.

Ax had shut down the engine and sat inside the closed cockpit.

"Sparks, what's going on?" I asked.

He grinned. "A tech inspection pop quiz."

Jack walked over to the canopy and motioned Ax to open. "We need to take a look at your plane."

"Ah…right now at this very moment?" Ax looked at the small crowd that had gathered around him on the tarmac. "Out here. Not back at the hangar?"

Two technical inspectors walked up behind Jack.

"Yes. As a matter of fact, we do. Right here. Right now. Could you please step out of your plane?"

Ax unbuckled himself, awkwardly pushing himself up to step out of the cockpit. He limped kind of stiff-legged back to the tail followed by one of the technical directors.

"Watch this." Sparks chuckled coldly.

Jack stood back and watched the other technical director lean into the cockpit. A minute or two later, the inspector called out, "Found it."

Jack looked at Sparks, and we all pressed in around the plane. He leaned into the cockpit, looking at the rubber tubing hanging down behind the instrument panel. The inspector pulled a screwdriver out, opened the cowling, and traced it to the carburetor.

"Peter and Manfred always seem to be the last ones out of the hangar at the end of the day." Sparks grinned. "Except last night."

"You found it?" Father Bob asked.

"They had to know where to look and maybe—just maybe— I helped them out with that just a little bit."

Jack walked over to Ax. "Come on. Where's the bottle?"

Ax scowled at me and Sparks and Father Bob.

"They could never find the nitrous," Sparks said. "Because he hid it inside his flight suit then pulled it out and connected it during the red flag when no one could see it, except his guys by the plane. When the race is over he yanks the hose off the engine and pockets it while he taxis back for inspections. Nobody ever thought to check him for the bottle of nitrous."

"Don't make us search you." Jack waved back towards the grandstands. "Out here in front of the crowd."

Ax unzipped his flight suit, reached inside, and handed the other inspector standing beside him a small, slender high-pressure tank.

Racing the Dream

"Nitrous oxide?" Jack asked.

Ax stared at Jack, then at me and Sparks.

Sparks gave him a wave.

Jack scowled at Ax, then turned and walked away.

"You may be sly…" Sparks muttered. "But so am I, you weasel."

~~~

Without Ax and Scotty in Monday's final race, there was no competition and I handily won the race from the pole position, but it was an empty feeling standing up top on the podium with my trophy.

Mid-morning, a cold front out west lowered the ceilings with alto-cumulus clouds over the airport.

"I don't know, do you think we should do the show?" Allison asked, looking around at the line of clouds pushing in overhead.

"We'll be alright," I said.

"I'm not so sure."

"I talked to the Blue Angels flight leader and their weather guy. He said the front won't come through until after six tonight. By four, the weather will probably be ten thousand overcast, so the Angels will do what they call a low show. And, you know, we can still see the Five-Mile Crib out in the lake, so visibilities are okay. I think we should be good, especially since we don't really go above pattern altitude."

"Well, okay. Then I guess I'll go get dressed."

"I'll preflight the Stearman."

Forty-five minutes later, we were at the approach end of Runway Two-Four, staring at mammatus clouds out to the west, but still not over the airport.

"We'll be good," I said over the intercom. "Just twenty minutes."

"Let's do this thing," Allison replied.

The Air Boss cleared us for take off, so I released the brakes to roll down the centerline.

Allison waved her hands over her head as we flew by the half-filled grandstands still in ground effect. The threatening weather had somewhat dampened the crowd turnout on Labor Day.

Holding fifty feet, the air seemed smooth. Over the departure end of the runway, I climbed in a turn back over the lake, then Allison unbuckled. She turned towards me and gave me a huge smile and a thumbs-up, then stood up, planted her foot in my windshield, and climbed up on the top wing, maneuvering into the struts and strapping herself in.

There were a few bumps, but nothing really out of the ordinary. I slowly banked right and descended to fifty feet passing back in front of the crowd.

Allison waved, then we started our routine as I pulled up into a loop. The Stearman struggled a bit climbing through a downdraft to the top of the loop. Coming back down we caught a couple of pockets of light turbulence. The air got a bit rougher as we finished the rolls and hammerheads.

Allison climbed down from the top wing and slowly crawled out to the end of the left wing. I held the plane as steady as I could fighting the air pockets. Turning out over the lake, I noticed a waterspout to the north.

"Uh-oh," was all I could say when the bottom seemed to fall out from beneath the airplane.

The left wing fell.

Racing the Dream

Stick right. Power in. Easing back.

In my peripheral vision, I saw Allison slip.

"NO!"

I quickly shot my eyes her way. She wrapped her arms around the flying wires, then reached out for the wooden strut. Bringing the wings level again, her head banged hard against the horizontal javelin strut, but she held on.

I powered back, slowly raising the nose.

"Allison!" I yelled pointlessly behind the roar of the radial engine.

She didn't look at me. Allison's arms were wrapped around the strut with her legs pushed back and flapping in the wind.

"Come on!"

I leveled off heading east along the shoreline and slowed down to minimum controllable airspeed to take as much air pressure off her as I could.

Allison pressed her forehead against the wing fabric, then looked my way. The fear in her eyes chilled me.

All I could do was smile, reaching out with my left hand to wave her to me.

She nodded, then pressed her forehead against the fabric again.

I radioed the air boss, "One-Delta-Mike breaking off. We've got a problem."

"Say your intentions."

"Wing walker is down—maybe hurt. Need some time, but I have to land, ASAP. Maybe Lost Nation."

"Or Cuyahoga County. Five miles southeast."

I looked over and saw the runway. "We'll take it."

"One-eighteen, five. I'll call the tower and advise."

I held the plane as steady as I could. A shallow bank to the southeast.

"Come on—come on—come on—" I muttered to myself as I watched Allison wrap her right arm around the first flying wire to her right, crooking it in her elbow and pulling herself inches closer to me.

"County Tower One-Delta-Mike inbound."

"Are you declaring an emergency?"

"Affirmative."

"How many souls on board?"

I closed my eyes for just a moment. "Two."

"Cleared to land Two-Four. Wind two-seven zero at twelve. Gusts eighteen."

Allison slowly crawled towards the cockpit using her arms and legs to hold on and pull herself from wire to wire.

She reached out and I grabbed her, clenching her forearm as hard as I could and pulling her towards me.

She kneeled and locked her left arm over the front cockpit.

I couldn't let her go, but I had to so she could get inside.

I pulled her arm into my side of the plane, released her, then quickly grabbed the back fabric of her flight suit.

Allison pulled herself up and dove head-first into the cockpit.

I pulled the power and we sank like a refrigerator.

"One-Delta-Mike right base-to-final."

"Cleared to land."

I really don't remember landing or taxiing off the runway. I stopped on the tarmac. Fire trucks and an ambulance pulled in behind me.

I cut the engine and when the prop shuddered to a stop, the rescue squad guys jumped up on the wing.

Pointing to the front cockpit, I watched them pull Allison out and down off the wing.

Racing the Dream

Her eyes were closed and her head flopped about.

Before I knew it, she was on the gurney, loaded into the ambulance, and driving away with the red lights flashing.

I finally unstrapped. I wanted to get out, but I couldn't—I didn't have the strength in my knees to push myself up off the seat. I closed my eyes and leaned my head into my hands and finally—finally exhaled.

I opened my eyes and saw Doug's placard on the bottom of the instrument panel, "Don't do nothin' dumb."

~~~

Maggie

"Who is Father Bob?" the skinny fireplug of a woman demanded at the door of the Cleveland Clinic waiting room at six-thirty the next morning. Her nearly baritone voice sucked every bit of quiet right out of the room.

"Huh? What? Ah, I am." He sat up slowly.

We had been stretched out on the couches trying to sleep, waiting to hear more from Allison's doctors after morning rounds.

"And who the hell is this Hawk character?"

I looked over and slowly raised my hand. "That would be me?"

"You don't look like a nurse," Father Bob said.

"I ain't no damned Candy Striper." She marched over to me, put on a set of horn-rimmed glasses hanging from a chain around her neck, and stared down at me. "I'm Maggie. Allison's mother."

"Uh-oh," I moaned and closed my eyes. "Mama Bear."

"You're damned right, partner."

"I had to call Winston and let him know," Father Bob said.

"And Douglas got me on a United red-eye last night. Now what in God's green earth is going on here?

"Well, we—" I started to say.

"Not you, Birdman." She pointed at Father Bob but glared down at me. "You. Father. Give me the scoop. And don't take all the damned day about it."

I think she even growled at me, as Father Bob quickly told

her what happened yesterday afternoon.

Maggie pulled her glasses off and looked around the deserted waiting room. She pointed at me, then out the door. "You. This way."

I got up and she led me out into the hallway, then backed me against the wall, standing uncomfortably close, looking up at me.

"You…" She poked her finger into my chest. "…are relieved."

"Excuse me?"

"Winston claims you have a race coming up—in Reno, I guess. Well, I suggest you get to it."

"But Allison—"

"I am her mother. And I am here for her now. So, head on down the road."

"Yes, ma'am, but I don't think so."

"I raised them kids on my own while her father was out saving the world during the war. Don't need you. Don't want you. Move along."

I leaned out from the wall pushing into her index finger. "Tough. I'm here and—"

"Hawk," Father Bob called out from the waiting room door. "The doc's here."

Maggie and I stared one another down, then went back into the waiting room.

"I am Allison's mother. Now, you tell me, what is her condition?"

"She's still unconscious, but stable. No doubt she suffered a pretty severe concussion when you said she hit her head against the wing strut." The doctor pointed at me.

Maggie growled my way.

"Anyway…" The doctor reflexively stepped back. "No fractured skull. Her breathing is normal—which is good, so no brain stem issues. Right now, we are going to let her rest and recover. If she remains stable, we'll look at moving her out of the ICU this evening or tomorrow into a regular room, then you can visit with her. Any questions?"

"You a neurologist?" Maggie asked. "Not some medical student or intern or anything. A real doctor."

"Yes, I am."

"Okay, then. Thank you." Maggie walked over to the chairs, sat down, put on her glasses, and pulled a *New York Times* crossword puzzle book out of her purse.

"She'll be okay, right?" Father Bob asked.

"There may be some confusion or amnesia, blurred vision, and headaches. We'll have to wait until she's conscious to learn more."

"Thanks, doc," I said. "Appreciate it."

"It may take a while, but she should be fine." The doctor looked at Maggie working her crossword. "We'll talk again later today. Okay?"

We nodded and he left.

I pulled Father Bob out of the waiting room. "You and Sparks need to get back to California to get ready for the Reno race."

"What about you?"

"I'm staying."

"Okay, but…" Father Bob looked at Maggie in the waiting room.

"Like I said, I'm staying."

Father Bob shook his head. "We'll see you in Reno, then."

"One more thing. Make sure Ax gets in the race."

"But Jack said they're going to suspend him from the Association for cheating."

"I don't care. Talk to Al McGuire. Talk to Bill Stead. Just make sure he's on the starting grid."

"Why?"

"It's not done until I beat him across the line."

"Okay. I'll make it happen. And, ah…" Father Bob flashed his pearly whites at me. "…good luck in there." He pointed at Allison's mom, chuckled to himself, then left.

I took a deep breath, then went back into the waiting room. I sat on the other side of the room from Maggie, who studiously ignored me, so I picked up the first of several LIFE magazines to pass the time.

Reading every single story, studying every photograph, and pondering the sales pitch of each and every advertisement took a long time—and thankfully kept my mind from churning over and over what happened the day before.

I really didn't know how much time had passed or not, until Maggie cleared her throat. I glanced at my watch: seventeen-twenty, Greenwich Mean Time. Doing the math, it was twenty after one, local.

"Seven-letter word for little wing."

I lowered my third LIFE magazine below my eyes and saw her pondering her puzzle.

Seriously? You are married to an Air Force Colonel who is now an Edwards test pilot—and you are asking me that?

"Aileron."

"Yeah. That works." She wrote it down with a pen.

"In ink?"

"I don't often make mistakes." Maggie looked up at me. "I'm hungry."

"Me, too—but it's hospital food."

"Well, it's either that or I gnaw my own arm off."

I stood up.

"A corned beef sandwich will do just fine."

"You may be asking for a lot."

"No egg salad. No tuna salad. Real food. And *no jello*."

"Got it."

I found my way to the cafeteria and returned with a couple of roast beef sandwiches, chips, Cole slaw, and coffee.

"I took a wild guess that you drink yours black," I said, handing over her lunch.

"Well…sort of." Maggie took a flask out of her purse and poured a shot of bourbon into her coffee. She held the flask up for me.

I shook my head.

"Well, damn it all anyway, sit down already. Nothing worse than breaking bread alone."

I stared at the chair next to her.

"I ain't gonna bite—well, not you anyway."

I think I got a sliver of a smile out of her, so I sat down and we ate.

Eventually, Maggie said, "Allison told me about you and I didn't like it. Not one bit."

"Why? Because I'm…older?"

"Damn it, no. Because you bought Douglas's plane just when he was out getting a real good job for himself and let her continue on with this cockamamie wing walking nonsense. And look where it's gotten her. I never approved of it. Ever."

"This wasn't part of the plan."

"No plan survives contact." She looked over at me. "Winston always used to say that."

"Smart guy."

"You bet your ass he is." Maggie took a deep breath and exhaled. "And for some reason, he seems to like you. Go figure."

A nurse stepped into the room. "Are you two here for Allison?"

"Yes, indeed. I am her mama."

"She woke up a little bit ago and we're moving her down from ICU. You'll be able to see her in a half an hour or so. I'll come back when she's in her room."

"Great," I said. "Thank you."

After the nurse left, Maggie said, "I gave you an out. And you didn't snag it."

"Of course not."

"Like I said, I don't often make mistakes."

"Forget about it."

"Anyways, I'm here for her now and Winston is right. You have a job to do in Reno, so after we visit tonight, you head back west to take care of business."

"Is this another test?"

"Damn it, don't you make me mad at you again."

~~~

National Championship Air Races

Reno.

I lowered myself into the cockpit, rolled the earplugs into my ears, then put on my headset. I went through the checklist, then pulled down the canopy and locked it. I double-checked it was secure.

Master on. Mixture rich. Prime the engine. Throttle open a quarter inch. Ignition on.

I signaled Sparks. He pulled the prop through once. Then stepped back up and yanked it down again. The engine roared to life, filling the canopy with that low-throated idling sound. It made me smile—each and every single time.

Oil pressure green.

Father Bob gave me a thumbs up. I saluted, tested the brakes, then taxied to the runway behind an orange Cassutt and a white Whirlwind.

I rolled onto the short dirt strip behind the Whirlwind and was cleared for departure while he lifted off in a cloud of dust from the sandy runway. I eased up to a hundred and fifty feet and followed him around the first set of pylons to the backstretch, staying twenty-five feet above him in the clean air, but gaining on him easily.

Up on his wing in turns three and four, I easily passed him on the front straight, accelerating as I dove down to seventy-five feet and into the first turn.

The half-hour of practice went by fast. I pulled up to three thousand feet to cool the engine, eyes definitely outside the cockpit, because returning to the airport is always the most dangerous part of these flights. On the course, everybody is flying predictably, between fifty and two hundred fifty feet, always turning left. Afterward, though, each pilot seems to have their own ideas about getting back down on the ground. Some go long. Some turn a short final. It's way too easy to lose situational awareness and get tangled up with someone if you aren't paying close attention.

I rolled in behind Steve Wittman's *Bonzo*, giving him a little extra space on final as he set down on the hot side of the runway, then slowed and cleared to the right side to taxi in. I followed a half mile behind him over the runway numbers and headed back to the pits.

As I taxied up to the hangar on the west side of the airport, I noticed Manfred and Peter rolling Ax's plane into his pit area. Then I noticed Jack standing next to Bill Stead, pointing at the yellow Shoestring. That made me smile. No funny business this time.

I came to a halt in front of Father Bob, Sparks, and Winston, standing on the brakes and pulling the mixture all the way out to kill the engine. I popped the canopy and pulled off my headset.

"You done good. You done real good. Runs like a champ." I pointed at Winston. "What are you doing here?"

"Part of the team, right? Just here to do my tiny bit for aviation history."

I climbed out of the cockpit and said to Sparks, "We could do it."

"Yeah, and what's that?"

"Two hundred. I can feel it. It's there."

Racing the Dream

Spark just grinned.

"Would you look at that. Why, it's…" Winston pointed over at Al McGuire and the red-headed beauty on his arm, walking up to Bill Stead and Jack. "…*Jill St. John.*"

"The actress?" Father Bob asked.

"McGuire's a hound dog." I shook my head. "Evidently, she is the official Queen of air races, and this here Nevada Centennial Celebration."

"She'd make a bulldog bite his chain," Sparks muttered.

"That she would…that she would," Winston said, as we all wagged our tongues on the ground. "Anyway, you'll be happy to know that Allison is heading back home. The docs finally released her from the hospital and Douglas got them on a plane heading back to California."

All I could do was smile.

"And I heard you held your own with Mama Bear."

"Oh, I got myself a couple of nasty claw marks, but we made out just fine in the end."

~~~

The next morning I sat on the runway waiting for my turn to qualify. Sky was deep blue. Wind calm. A perfect morning for time trials.

During my run-up, I played a bit more with the mixture setting. Seeing as how we were at forty-five hundred feet field elevation, we ran leaner than normal and I worked to get the engine set for maximum power.

A blue and white Cassutt zoomed overhead, then climbed. With the course cleared, the flag man signaled me to take off.

Full power. Off the brakes. On the roll.

It took a bit longer to get up to speed due to the field elevation, but I lifted off and leveled at fifty feet, banking left down the back straightaway. Around pylons three and four, I roared down to the start-finish line.

I angled in slowly for the first pylon—just like Winston briefed me to minimize aileron drag—and fell right into my groove, looking down quickly on the pylon, keeping on the outside, then angling for number two and easing my wings level down the back straightaway. Stick slightly back to keep level, banking hard around pylons three, then four.

Coming up to the home pylon, I radioed, "Race One-Four, on the clock."

Across the start-finish, the timing started.

I didn't think at all. I just reacted. Anticipating my turns. Full power. Locked in my groove. Stick-and-rudder flying, keeping the yarn on my cowling pointing straight back at my nose.

Forty seconds or so later, I crossed the start-finish line and climbed up to three thousand feet.

I rolled right to circle over Sky Ranch airport, pulling the power back off of maximum to allow the engine to cool, paralleling the runway, descending slowly down to pattern altitude. Looking down, the ramp was filled with airplanes, pilots, and crew members crawling all over them like foraging ants.

I banked around on a right upwind, then crosswind to downwind. I did a long curving base leg to final, then set down and taxied back to the pits and shut down.

Father Bob was there when I popped the canopy. "Two hundred three."

"Seriously? I did it?"

Racing the Dream

Sparks came up behind him, grinning. "Two-oh-three, point seven, to be exact."

"Excellent. Think it will hold up?"

"Well, right now, you are definitely on the pole."

And Friday morning I was still on the pole for the first heat race, as Ax came in second at one-ninety-six with Wittman third at one-eighty-eight.

I went out of my way to ignore Ax during the pilot briefings and in the pits, but there on the starting grid, it was a little impossible with his Shoestring parked right next to me.

I stood alone by my plane, soaking in the blue skies and breathing the clear, clean desert air that morning.

"Congratulations on your qualification time," Ax said as he came over beside me. "Two hundred miles per hour is very, very good."

"Two-oh-three…point seven." I smiled.

"Yes. Yes, of course. Very good for you."

"And, well, you are right here beside me in the front row."

"And, so, we will race here today, again."

"No funny business?"

Ax looked down at his feet. "No. No funny business. We will race you clean."

I squinted my eyes at him from the sun.

He looked up at me. "Honest."

"Okay. That's all I want."

"Yes, then. Okay." He started to turn back towards his plane.

"Good luck." I extended my arm.

Ax looked down at my hand, then finally shook it. "But, of course, I will work hard to be the first, you know."

"Of course." I grinned. "I came here to race…and to win."

"I understand. It is every man for himself." Ax gave me a nod, let go of my hand, and walked back over to his plane.

"Still don't trust him," Sparks said from behind me.

"Yeah, neither do I. But there he is." I stepped into the cockpit, slid down, and strapped in.

"Remember," Father Bob said. "It's a ten-lap race. Not eight like before."

"Got it." I winked at Father Bob. "Make sure I don't accidentally land early."

He shook his head. "Just watch for the checkered flag. Do I have to explain everything?"

"Oh, yeah." I chuckled as I closed the canopy and went through the checklist.

The red flag went up and I signaled Sparks to pull the prop, then jammed on the brakes while the engine temperature came up to green.

I looked over and watched Manfred pull the prop on the yellow Shoestring to my right several times before his engine caught. Ax looked over at me. I gave him a salute, then did my run-up.

The red flag waiting is usually the hardest part. Anticipation builds because you're ready to go race, but holding back, knees shaking some as you cram down on the brakes against the thrust of the engine—but not this time. Crazy. I sat there smiling, humming a tune over and over and over in my head.

Da do ron-ron-ron, da do ron-ron...

The red flag came down. The green flag came up. Full forward on the throttle.

Da do ron-ron-ron, da do ron-ron...

Green flag down and I was off, first into pylon one and

immediately in my groove, not once ever worrying about who might be on my six, until, ten laps later, I took the checkered flag, singing to myself.

"Da do ron-ron-ron, da do ron-ron…"

~~~

After the race beside my plane, shaking hands with Father Bob and Sparks, Winston pulled me aside. "Come on."

"How about that? Number one."

"Yeah, yeah, great. Now, let's talk?"

"About what?"

"About what was going on behind you that you couldn't see." Winston dragged me over to a picnic table outside the pit hangar and sat me down. "Remember, you've got two more races tomorrow before this thing is over."

"Yeah. Got it."

"Your main competition is Wittman, Ax, and Porter."

"I figured that."

"You clocked out at one-ninety-three. Wittman was second at one ninety. Ax's *Miss Munich* was third at one-eighty-nine—"

"*Miss Munich*? That's his plane's name?" I asked.

"You never noticed before?"

I shrugged. "News to me. Never paid attention before."

"Bob Porter in *Little Gem* was in the mix, too. Of course, you didn't see any of it 'cause you got off to a great start and never had to look back, but it was a catfight back there."

"Hopefully, I'll stay out of it if I can."

"But if you can't, you need to know what's going on. Wittman is smooth. He finds his groove. It's a little on the high side, but he sticks to it and nails it every time. And he's clean on the passes. Porter tends to stay low and he's pretty aggressive on the corners. He's very tight on them. I thought he cut pylon number three, but the officials didn't call it. It was close."

"That's a twenty-second penalty, right?"

"It definitely hurts you. Knocks you out of the race, so be careful."

"What about *Miss Munich*?" I sneered.

"He's very precise in his runs—almost too much though. Mechanical. Robotic. Though when someone gets on him to pass, he gets sneaky. He'll loft a bit and try to push you outside on a longer track, so you have to stay up on his wing to get by."

"Good to know."

"It looked pretty rough back there. A lot of jumping around. Lots of turbulence."

"I'll stay out of it if I can."

"But if you can't…"

"Yeah. Thanks."

"Now, hey, I gotta get going."

"Where?"

"Got an errand to run. I'll be back later."

"What for?"

"Never you mind. I'll see you tomorrow."

~~~

Formula One had two races scheduled for Saturday, the last heat race and the final Championship.

I was on the pole again for Heat Race 1B with Wittman beside me and Ax on the outside of the front row. Porter's *Little Gem* was behind me in the second row. I looked around for Winston, but it was just Sparks and Father Bob there with me on the starting grid.

"Where's Winston?" I asked, pulling the five-point harness tight around my body.

"Probably in the grandstands to watch the race," Father Bob said. "Like yesterday."

"Yeah. I guess." But I wondered what errand he had to run.

The red flag went up and we started the engines. Got the V-victory sign from Sparks as the engine warmed up. Into the green, I ran the tach up to seventeen hundred and messed with the mixture settings over and over again trying to set best power. There was a bit more RPM drop in the left magneto. I brought it back to both mags, then played with the mixture again. The left was down almost one hundred. I played again with the mixture.

I looked at Sparks. He scowled and looked at the engine like he heard something in the pistons firing. He twisted his hand, but The red flag came down and he had to leave with the rest of the pit crews.

The green flag came out.

I brought the power up, still tweaking the mixture—a half turn in—a quarter turn out—when the green flag came down.

Full power.

The engine surged, then slowed. I pushed in the mixture and the power returned, but I was slow off the start. Ax and Wittman beat me to the first pylons.

As we came around three and four, Porter made a move up on my wing and came around on the front straightaway.

Now fourth.

Detonation in the engine. Oil temperature running high.

Up ahead, Wittman led Ax with a two-plane lead.

I messed with the mixture a bit more to find more power, gaining a bit on *Little Gem*, but I was still off my usual pace, late into turns, sliding back with the distraction of the engine. I never found my groove.

I tried passing Porter a couple of times, but he held me off and I ended up in fourth across the finish line.

I wasn't singing this time.

Parked on the tarmac with the engine shut down, I closed my eyes and popped open the canopy, waiting for the grief I knew would come my way from Sparks.

Finally, a familiar female voice came from behind, "Boy, you really blew chunks in that race."

"Elaine?" I turned around to look back.

Standing next to her was Allison, shaking her head, but smiling at me. "Yeah, you know, that kind of sucked."

"What are you doing—"

Allison came over and planted a big wet kiss on my face. "Good to see you again. Now get out of there."

I unstrapped and stepped out of the plane. She grabbed me in a huge bear hug.

"I told you, I had to run some errands," Winston said. "They wanted to see you race, so I ran down to LA in the Baron to get the girls."

"Ah, where's Mama Bear?" I asked.

"Back home on the ranch, shooting coyotes, no doubt." Winston put his hands on his hips. He said sarcastically, "Nice job, by the way."

"Yeah, what the hell happened?" Sparks demanded.

"Operator error. I screwed up big time with the mixture

settings and ended up with some detonation issues."

"Damn it all, anyway." Sparks popped open an inspection panel on the cowling and reached inside. "Man, those mags are hot. Come on, Bob. Help me get this into the pits."

Father Bob simply shook his head and helped Sparks pull the plane into the hangar.

"Man, it is great to see you, Allison."

She gave me another quick kiss.

"The Championship race is this afternoon."

"Go on. We'll be in the stands with Dad. Just, ah…"

"What?"

"Don't do…" she winked at me "…nothin' dumb."

Arm-in-arm with Elaine, she headed back towards the grandstands.

~~~

For the Championship Race, I was on the inside of the second row, getting ready to eat the dust of Wittman, Ax, and Porter. Sparks stood out front. Father Bob and Winston were next to me as I got ready to get in for the red flag.

"You know, Stead's got this set up like boat racing and I've gone through the whole points thing he's got going on here," Father Bob said. "And, I think, even if you come in right behind Ax—second or even third—you'll have enough total points to be the winner."

"You know, that's not how this works." I climbed into the cockpit and strapped myself down. "I won't race to be second."

"I'm just saying…"

"Hey." Winston knelt down beside me and leaned in.

"Remember the debrief. You won't have a problem with Wittman and Porter. Ax will run you out if he can."

I nodded. "Got it."

"Go get 'em, Hawk."

"Thanks for getting Allison."

"Yeah, right, like try to stop her once her mind is made up." He stood up.

"Yeah. I know." I grinned and closed the canopy.

I took a deep breath, then ran through the engine start-up checklist. The red flag went up and Sparks pulled the prop through three times before the engine fired up.

I ran the engine for five minutes, then did my run-up taking extra care adjusting the mixture. When the red flag came down and the green went up, my knees were knocking on the rudder pedals. I was back in the pack now, so getting to the front would be no cakewalk.

The grounds crew had watered and rolled the runway before the race, but it was still a dust bowl when the green flag dropped, so I plowed straight ahead—eyes ahead—eyes right—eyes ahead, checking the directional gyro to keep on the centerline. Tail off—almost blind like taking off in the English fog. Finally, up and around the scatter pylon, I was fourth, but out of the dust storm.

I jockeyed my altitude on the back straightaway, trying to find some smooth air, watching Ax crawl up on Wittman coming around three and four on the pace lap, then across the start-finish line to start the race.

Three lengths behind Porter, I concentrated on slowly reeling him in, climbing bit by bit on his tail around the pylons. I rode his right wing up around pylons one and two, then dove past him down the back straightaway.

Around three and four, I saw Ax up ahead crawling all over Wittman's six for the lead.

At sixty feet, I settled in, anticipating my turns early, watching for my shadow on the ground and steadily closing the gap with the two leaders.

Ax held his high line into the lead, with a plane length and a half over Wittman. In the clean air, I clawed my way up on second place. On lap four I passed Bonzo, now less than half a lap behind Ax. Back down to fifty feet, clipping along in the smooth air behind him. I had the extra power I needed.

Holding the throttle all the way in. Oil temperature—Green. Early roll into the turn—minimum stick to the left, yaw dead center, bank set, looking directly down on pylons three and four…Closing the gap.

It was down to Ax and me. He held his usual higher line up at eighty or ninety feet, so I slowly climbed five to ten feet per lap in the turns, keeping in the clear air above his vortices to position myself in an echelon on his right wing. Two lengths behind, I pointed my nose inside his yellow Shoestring, cutting a shorter line on his track. I had the airspeed on him and knew that this time he didn't have any nitrous to dump into his engine.

Two laps to go.

Into the first pylon and just like Winston told me, Ax began to loft into my wing and push me outside as I closed on his wing, trying to stay up and outside to pass.

Uncooperative formation flying…Ax's fangs coming out.

But I wasn't going to let him flip me inverted like out over Antelope Acres. Not this time.

Left wing dipping—rudder to correct…

I climbed with him, my eyes on his right wing, holding the echelon.

Neck-and-neck down the back straightaway, inching ahead. Around pylons five and six, Ax tried again to push me out over the cut line, but I had him then. I looked at his cockpit and grinned as I closed the door.

I could see it in his face: the recognition of defeat as I moved by him.

I crossed the start-finish line ahead and took the first turn. It was just stick-and-rudder flying now.

Tight around three and four, then down to fifty feet, first across the finish line.

I climbed, rolling the plane twice, and keyed my mike.

"Da do ron-ron-ron, da do ron-ron…"

~~~

I got mobbed after I landed and parked the plane—pilots, crews, and fans, shaking hands, patting me on the back, taking photos, and getting a huge hug from Father Bob.

"You did it," Father Bob said in my ear. "You did it."

"No—we all did it." I squeezed him back hard, but, honestly, I was really interested in just one thing: finding Allison.

From the top of the podium, I finally saw her with Winston and Elaine, walking over from the grandstands. Elaine waved. Allison hugged her dad while photographers got their endless shots.

The glory didn't really last long. There were other air show acts and Unlimited heat races, so Allison and I slipped away hand-in-hand, wandering down the flight line.

"So, how does it feel," she asked. "Mister National Championship winner?"

"Great, but…"

"But?"

"You know, Scotty and all. He should have been here, too."

We walked past a few parked planes.

"So, what happened?" Allison asked.

"Jack said he talked to the NTSB guys and it looks like a loose bolt on the elevators came off, causing a flutter and then the separation. After that, there was nothing Scotty could do."

"But how could that happen?" Allison asked.

"Ed must have missed it in the rush to get the plane ready to race, 'cause they were so late getting in."

"God, he must feel awful."

"Yeah, Father Bob's reached out to him." I shook my head. "Boy, I don't know how I'd feel about that."

Up above, Bob Hoover's *Yellowbird* led a line of P-51s and Bearcats down the front straightaway for an air start of the Unlimited heat around the grandstands.

"Gentlemen, you have a race," Bob Hoover's voice was broadcast over the show's loudspeakers.

We watched the planes dive onto the course and start their heat.

"Maybe you should get a ride in one of those for next year," Allison said. "That might be fun."

"Yeah, maybe, but I think I'm good for now." I watched them chase around the course. We walked down the show line and I led her around to where I had parked our Stearman. "You know, I'm sorry you missed getting your wing walking act on *The Wide World of Sports.*"

"The thrill of victory…" Allison rubbed her temple. "The agony of defeat. I definitely get it."

"I'm sorry about Cleveland. I—"

"Not your fault. But my dad said that's what you get for listening to Naval aviators." Allison grabbed my arm as we looked at the plane "I'm good with it. I'm just glad to be here with you again."

"Me, too."

We didn't say anything as the Unlimiteds finished their heat and climbed skyward.

I asked, "Do you want to hang around for the last two days of the show?"

"Nah, let's make this pop stand a memory." She gave me a kiss. "Fly me home, okay?"

And I did.

~~~

Malibu Colony Road

I sat beside Allison in her Woodie as she navigated north on the Pacific Coast Highway toward Malibu. She was finally ready to get back up on her boards.

As we passed the beach parking, I said, "Let's go up ahead a bit."

"But there's a spot right there, real close. I won't have to carry my board so far."

"Trust me. I know what I'm doing."

I told Allison to drive another mile down the road, then turn west onto Malibu Colony Road.

"Head on out to the end, there."

"But we can't park down this way. People live here."

"Yeah, I know. Pull in behind that Cadillac there." When she parked. I opened the door. "Come on."

"About time you got here." Al McGuire leaned against the rear quarter panel of his black El Dorado, looking out on Santa Monica Bay through his mirrored aviator sunglasses. "Well, it's a done deal."

"Deal? What deal?" Allison asked as we walked up to the Cadillac's rear bumper.

"You didn't tell her?" Al McGuire pulled down his sunglasses and gave me a friendly scowl over the top. "You dog, you."

"Tell me what?"

"How would you like to live on the beach," I said.

"Where?"

"Here. I'm tired of being out back in the casitas behind Elaine, so I bought the last lot right here and I'm going to build a new place for us."

"Us? Live together? You and me?"

"Yeah. Exactly."

"I don't know what to say."

"It's just a dash. What more do we need?" I smiled at her. "Just say yes."

Allison gave me a huge hug. "Yes."

"Great. Now grab your board and go surf."

~~~

Thank you for reading my story.

Special Thanks

I appreciate all the help I got in writing this story, especially from Jack Dianiska, Juan Browne, and Scott Holmes for their insights into Air Racing.

The National Championship Air Races for sixty years of racing and permission to use the cover artwork from the original 1964 inaugural race poster, the photos of Bill Stead, and the 1964 Formula 1 Results page.

Bob Holmes and the International Formula 1 Air Racing Association for their support.

Mike Henniger of www.AerialVisuals.ca for the images of *Fraed Naught* and *Limitless* at Reno/Stead Airport (KRTS)

Jack Dianiska for the photos of *Miss Cleveland* at Elyria Airport (1G1) and her builders.

Juan Browne for his photo.

Air Race 1 for the photo of Scott Holmes.

Lora Mosier for the photo of N914E at Thacker Field (11LL).

Dariusz Jezewski for the photo of N521DM at Oshkosh AirVenture (KOSH).

Lori Patzke for the photos of Uncle Wallace and Uncle Don in their cars.

Mark and Dawn Patzke for the photo of Arthur Patzke.

Our Racing Days
by
Arthur Patzke

**Uncle Don #3 & Uncle Wallace #39
Racing at Angell Park Speedway
Sun Prairie, Wisconsin**

I have given this a lot of thought, having had so many great experiences and met so many people from an environment that few attain, I want to tell about them ere they are lost forever. I have read and re-read what has already been written and in order to create some sort of continuity have decided to ignore all previous accounts and from scratch tell it like it was. There will no doubt be much repeated, but I hope to make it interesting enough to make you want to read on.

Now it all began when my father gave me a car chassis that he had replaced. I build a race car body on it and soon had visions of competing with Frankie Lockhardt, Ralph DePalma, and Barney Oldfield on the sands of Daytona Beach. Many years later, I did ride the sands at Daytona but somehow they were not in evidence. My equipment was such that it soon found its way to Gordon's Junkyard. Other activities put this endeavor on the back burner. A family was started and when a son became old enough, a car (pedal) was given him, hopes were revived, and something more potent in the days to come.

Another interruption to my dreams, the raising of a family, and a devastating economical depression again put them on hold, our financial position became such that hopes were all but abandoned. We were ever grateful when some relative would invite us for a Sunday drive and one Sunday our brother and sister-in-law asked us to join them for a ride. We wound up at State Fair Park in West Allis. It so happened there were auto races that Sunday, so we parked on the backstretch allowing the kids freedom to enjoy the outdoors, while enjoying the events on the track. Of course, this again sparked a dormant desire, and soon made every effort to attend races held there. It became evident that a car was a must for work and family pleasure, so a 1925 Dodge became our pride and joy. With this transportation, we were always on the backstretch during races there. The car had a soft top and we would perch on the top of the car, allowing the kids to wander atop between events. A few holes were made in the top but this was no problem in dry weather but rain seeped in. I carried a few bricks to place over the damaged spots. On one occasion while at work a storm came upon us, so I hurried out and placed the bricks on the car top. A man hurrying by saw what I was doing and asked if I was afraid the car would blow away.

As Milwaukee was a dirt track used mostly for horse races at Fair time, it was pretty dusty when the cars held events there. I don't know who were the pioneers in racing there but Carl and Judy Marchese, Geoge Young, and Frank Briscoe were prominent participants. On one occasion, the first two cars made the first (south) turn but created such a cloud of dust the rest of the field, unable to see, went through the fence, ending in the now-empty horse barn. I don't know how organized it was at that time, but I think Tom Marchese took the initiative and became a promoter for Milwaukee. Under his leadership, many of the country's leading cars and drivers were running there under the AAA section. Such drivers as Billie Winn, Joe Russo, Muari Rose, Chet Gardner, Doc McKenzie, Wilber Shaw, and many more, I just can't recall them all who appeared there.

On occasion the I.M.C.A would appear at the West Allis track. This was a rival group whose star drivers were Gus Shrader and Emory Collins. As uncommitted or free-lance drivers were welcome to participate such boys as Cowboy Hardy, Byron Salspaugh and a host of hopefuls from the Chicago area were there. I must add my personal opinion to this, I feel that Gus Shrader was one of the greatest dirt track drivers I have ever seen. It could be that his competition was so inferior or he was that good. He could go top speed into a turn, never backing off during the turn and out onto the backstretch. Just Great!

The time came when our transportation had to be updated and this enabled us to venture to other tracks. A 5/8 mile track was constructed at Carrolville. This attracted free-lance drivers from Chicago and northern Indiana, as well as local drivers. The only local I can recall was George Young. Even then the metric system didn't fare too well and soon the 5/8 mile oval was abandoned. One Sunday our travels took us to the Cook County Fairgrounds, Mannhein and Wolf Roads. With the wind in the right direction, we soon were caked with dust. State Fair Park offering top-notch drivers became the stalwart in the area. Tom

Marchese corraled the top finishers at Indy, for a still date the first Sunday after Indy, with an agreement for State Fair Week. With Illinois State Fair ending, with a racing program on Saturday, the participants moved to the Milwaukee track. Races were held on Sunday, Thursday, and Sunday with the Minnesota Fair next this brought the best drives from far and near. From far came Chet Grdner, Doc McKenzie, from near Johnny Sawyer, Jack Matts, and many more. The Marchese boys acquired a Miller straight-eight race car, that was entered and finished fourth at Indy with Carl at the wheel. This car toured the circuits with Johnny Sawyer doing the driving. With new techniques invading the race car designs, soon the Miller straight-eight had become obsolete and shunted from corner to corner in Marchese's garage, too good to throw away but what to do with it? Eventually, it was heard from again.

A new form of racing was soon to appear. Racing had gained the public's craving for excitement and to satisfy this small track activity was the answer. The Milwaukee area had several abandoned dog tracks and some knowledgeable boys created mini cars to use these facilities. The midget race cars were born and at least in the Milwaukee area and the parents of this offspring were to my knowledge, can only mention a few: Louis Frank, A.J. Breecher, Johnny Martin, Erdman and Hil Ermer. On Sunday with a place selected, they would gather and run their efforts of the past week, compare notes, and improve. Soon competition set in, an association was formed, schedules prepared, members were solicited, and though it remained a helpful group the atmosphere changed.

I would like to leave Badger Midget Racing Association for a moment and return to our part of all this. When Chevy announced the Soap Box Derby we proceeded to enter. As we had to register under a Milwaukee address, Racine did not participate, we made two events in Milwaukee and one locally sponsored event in Racine. The result of our efforts was not too flattering. In due time two cars were built with wash machine motors that we could run on dead-end streets in the immediate neighborhood without any danger to anyone. This was exciting as it taught both Wallace and Don the basics of driving.

Midget racing had taken a firm hold on the public and with weekly shows became a must for us at Horlick Field in Racine on Thursdays and Milwaukee on Friday evenings. A new crop of drivers emerged, such boys as Tony Wilman, Ted Duncan, Frank Burany, Tony Bettenhausen, Myron Fohr, Wallie Zale, and an endless list whose names became household names. With the country emerging from a devastating depression the world seemed rosy, but alas in 1939 war clouds erupted in Europe and soon the U.S. became involved, calling many young men into service. One such was Joe Chek who had a race car ready to run but wasn't sure if he would return, he advertised it for sale for $100.00 including the trailer. We bought it and now were on the brink of the other side of racing, performing instead of just watching. Thus our racing days began and an exciting period of our life was only beginning.

After becoming acquainted with our newly acquired equipment, though very inexperienced Wallace and Don took the car to Chicago Amphitheater on Sunday for races there they found a driver, and cannot say just how much was gained, a foot in the door was. The boys were contacted by Badger Midget Racing Association relative to becoming affiliated with them. Our next event was at Singer Speedway a family-operated track at

Joliet, Illinois. With various members of the Singer family with seven cars in the field, I soon found out an outsider didn't have a chance. Quickly we were crowded into the fence and out of the running. Taking it into the Amp it was bent back into shape, and though not really deserving, by fate were awarded first place in a shortened semi.

As both Wallace and Don indicated they would join Badger, our next appearance was at Sun Prairie a half-mile flat track hemmed in by cornfields. As we had no one to drive we got a fellow from Madison by the name of Friday to do the driving. The next Sunday having acquired a helmet Wallace took his first ride in competition. When the races were over he was offered Hil Ermers Copper Kettle to drive so his performance couldn't have been so bad.

We made many Sunday afternoon races at Sun Prairie though our financial return was quite meager, we were enriched with know-how and rapport. Too we took part in races in Racine and ventured to State Fair Park in Milwaukee. Here everyone who didn't make the feature was eligible for the semi-(main) commonly called the Cast Iron Derby. In these events here's how you paid your dues to prepare for the big time. One Thursday the family took the car to H.A.F and I got there later. When I reached the track during warm-up I soon found Wallace, but no car. Soon it came by in a cloud of dust. Who is driving, I asked? Don was the reply. I knew immediately a driver was in the making. A few words of fantasy could be injected here, somehow, somewhere we obtained another car #16 and entered it at H.A.F. No driver so borrowing a helmet from Steve Russo I proceeded to be both an owner and a driver. Took the green flag and immediately ended on the infield hay bale. I was aware I needed more experience but the opportunity didn't come for a long time. When it did come I made the most of it, but that will come later.

With the war in Europe gaining momentum all racing was stopped for the duration. There was no activity trackside, enthusiasm remained high, meetings were held, equipment was improved, and plans were made for when the ban was lifted. Many firms formerly involved, but for the duration doing war work, were not napping and firms such as Edelbrock Curtis, Wico, and Offenhauser, were ready with special components when again the green flag indicated "go." As this specialized field developed the Marchese taking the never-discarded Miller engine, made two four-cylinder engines, mounted them in midget chassis, and with such pilots as Shorty Sorensen, Myron Fohr, Chuck Stevensen, Harry McQuinn gave Zale Bettenhausen, Burnay plenty of competition. Weekly races were held in Racine on Thursdays, Milwaukee on Fridays, and Farmer City on Saturdays or Riverview Park in Chicago or St. Louis on Sundays. Yes, this type of racing had become of age.

As the competition centered around the metropolitan areas, leaving the areas away from the big cities hungry for the sport. With this demand Badger, by now quite well organized, moved into this area. Races were booked at various fairs as well as still dates. Such places as Darlington, Verogua Antigo, Luxemburg, Manitowoc, Rico Lake, and Philips all were in Badger's list. Two names were intentionally omitted as a comment should be made. On our appearance at Marshfield, Wallace had the date at Seymour, Wisconsin was in itself unique, the track carved out on an Indian reservation. As this was government property, gambling slot machines were prevalent. The highlight of the occasion was the races and as the race track was anything but acceptable it was decided to barnstorm the show with competitive positions paid according to the finish of the feature. As a storm was brewing my car headed for home leaving Don to collect our share of the purse. Near Clintonville, the storm really hit, so I wisely pulled off to wait it out. With visibility at less than zero, a car parked aside us, and when the storm cleared, who was aside us but Don. Seymour was unique in more ways but it was an interesting day. With a weekly program scheduled at Sun Prairie on Sunday nights and De Pere on Saturday nights our concentration was to make as many of their schedule as possible.

Must deviate a bit to mention our equipment. We started with a Stude engine which was strictly stock. If any special equipment was available I didn't know, but soon it became evident that the Ford V8 60 was the way to go. Despite this decision with a tour over a July Fourth weekend, we planned our week well. With races at De Pere, a half-mile flat track on Friday, Saturday at Rice Lake, Sunday at Sun Prairie a good tour was expected. We had the misfortune of an end-over-end flip that put our driver in the hospital and ended our tour. After gathering our possessions together, Gene and I make a stop at St. Vincents Hospital in Green Bay, headed for home with a pretty bent-up car in tow. Trying to reach our home was somewhat difficult, so every city we went through on 57 we attempted to call. Eventually, we did reach home by phone and said we would be home sometime during the night. Yes, Saturday was a very troublesome day with no word from St. Vincents. At about 3:00 pm our phone rang, it was Don. I have been released, come and get me. By 3:15 we were on our way and though the ride was tortuous as Don was bent up some and quite bruised, but I'm sure he was as well as we were happy to have him home. After a week or so for recovery, he was soon on the prowl for another car to drive. He found and soon was driving for Sam and Fino Sacuula. The car was quite rapid, but it seemed to be plagued with all sorts of problems. He had a pleasant relationship driving the car.

In due time, my car was repaired and Wallace finished the season as my driver. As our success was continually in the lower bracket, it became evident to improve or get out. The latter was not to be, so improvement was the way to go. The Stude was replaced with a V8-60 engine. With this new power plant and somewhat unfamiliar with it we were strictly stock and while others were measuring with micrometers we were using a yardstick. We ran this equipment for several seasons, but just could not crash that charmed circle of the twelve fastest to make us eligible for the feature race. About this time the schedule was Sun Prairie on Sunday nights, a new improved semi-banked, lighted track. Slinger on Wednesday nights, Milwaukee on Friday nights, and De Pere, a new quarter-mile flat dirt track on Saturday nights, a rather full schedule. Fair dates as well as still dates that were scheduled were in addition. We made most races.

There was a motor block being worked on in the basement most all the time. One Wednesday night at Slinger we blew an engine so Thursday we started to install a new one. While busy with this we got an invitation to run a new track at Farley, Iowa about twenty-five miles west of Dubuque. We worked till midnight on Saturday, loaded the race car not knowing if it would even start. About 2:00 AM Don came home from De Pere and had the Piermans and their car. He had driven it that night as his car failed to show up. They experienced gearbox problems to set about to correct them. How long they worked I don't know but at 7:00 AM on Sunday, we left for Iowa, with two cars for an afternoon race at Farley and an evening race at Sun Prairie. We were guaranteed appearance money plus all we could make in the events and with a small field of cars we were in most races, our take was considerable. Don had the misfortune to flip his car, and not too badly damaged, Gene and I proceeded to get it back in competition while the Pierman brothers just wrung their hands, exclaiming, "It was such a pretty car." They just could not conceive that it would ever run again. The program over, we got out fast, headed for Sun Prairie, and though arriving late, qualified between heats and placed fourth in the semi. Not too bad for a weekend.

We appeared again the next Sunday at Farley but found this schedule too strenuous so gave that up. We did appear at Davenport, Iowa but had the misfortune of breaking the drive shaft so this ended as a dry run. We continued to make most Badger meets and though not getting rich were aware we could do better with an improvement to our equipment. Little by little we gathered parts to better our performance both on the track and at the pay-off window. From Bill Fitch, I got a chrome crank and a pair of Offenhauser high-compression heads. Through Don's influence, Martin Jacks loaned me a magneto. I don't know where the Edelbrock Dual carburetor valley cover came from. A lot of help came from Mick Nagy and Gus Weasel. We converted from Gasoline to alcohol to keep the engine cooler. We put these components together, proceeded to Sun Prairie, and I'm sure at the time trials a few eyebrows were raised. For the first time, Wallace had a car that run with the best. From that time on he always put it in the feature race.

We were permitted 2-3 pit passes plus 2-3 grandstand passes and as Gene and I were absorbed this left one vacancy. A friend was eventually to be our third member, Joe Porcaro. This was an environment he was surprised to find himself in and he just loved it. Yes, he proved his worth by being an aid at loading and unloading, pushing into our starting spot, and just having around, such as company on the 100-mile drive home. At Sun Prairie I could always count on a being with Don while Joe would treat the rest of the party to hamburgers, malts, ice cream, or whatever. On weekly races, if he could get away, his greatest thrill was to treat our party to chocolate malts on the way home. Yes, Joe filled that third spot in our crew quite well.

When Wallace indicated he would like to end his driving days, Eugene said he would like to try. As he was underage, I got the clearances required by Badger. As he took his first green flag, on the first turn he spied a competitor upside down on the outer rail. He did not finish the lap, but wisely pulled into the pits and declared that was not for him. Wallace took over and with now better equipment had a most successful season. With Eugene away at school it was time to bring up Dave into the pits. Soon he too wanted to drive, but by this time the competition had become so cutthroat only the experienced could hope to survive. He did get the opportunity but, his desire soon turned to zero. Again, Wallace came to the rescue and filled the vacant seat in the #3. Don too shared in this and when Don won the Kenosha Fair trophy we were contacted if we would sell the car. A buyer with a driver was interested, a deal was made to be completed at Muaston, Wisconsin. When the buyer took over there, Wallace Jr. cried when someone else was taking his Daddy's car away and I must say it was a rather somber trip home. Though this ended our participation with the #3, it did not mean we were retiring from racing. We shall eventually see how this continued.

Back to memory lane, while we were having fair success,

Don too was doing well. His association and friendship have endured to this day with Sam Succula. When he relocated to California a new car was sought. An opportunity arose, and Don met Gus Wessel who had access to an Offy owned by Martin Jacks. With Gus as mechanics and Don as driver, the car was taken to the 1/8 mile indoor track at the Chicago Amphitheater. A field of 50-60 cars, out of which Don time trialed among the 24 fastest. As his heat got underway Paul Russo starting directly in back of Don put the nose to tail and pushed him through the turn, no doubt an intimidation tactic. Now Don had met the best and survived.

A friendship developed between Gus and Don. The #10 was retained, the Offy engine was replaced with a V8-60, and they ran the Badger circuit. At season's end, I don't know what happened, but with Gus employed by Bob Wilke who was sponsoring an Indy car, the opportunity to be part of the big time, may have been the reason the car was returned to Jacks. Don having kept a good relationship with Martin Jacks, the #10 was loaned to Don. He bought an engine from Mick Nagy which was installed in the car. He ran the Badger circuits and had fair success. At this time we too were active and gave whatever help we could. In a 100-lap race on a 1/2 mile track at Peoria, Illinois, despite gearbox problems, he finished fourth a satisfying finish for that kind of race. Don and Betty returning to home territory to run Oshkosh on Sunday afternoon and Sun Prairie on Sunday night. Mother and I headed for Athens, Ohio to attend the graduation exercises of Gene at the University of Ohio. With the season completed the engine was removed, and the chassis returned to Jacks. The engine having many features for better performance, these were incorporated in our equipment.

Racing the Dream

With a new season, Don decided to drive for others and found owners that could and did use his ability. Among those that entrusted their equipment to him were Billy Johnson, Elmer Zeloff, and Bob Steinman, no little accomplishment in a field where a wrong split-second decision could mean disaster for equipment as well as participant. To select any one performance would be unfair, but one race deserves mention. Driving Zeloff's #39 he time trialed either 5th or 6th fastest putting him in the Handicap (6 fastest). At the drop of the green flag, the front four, as near as I can recall, Carl Hunter, Gordy Frey, Don, a the fourth I can't recall, took off and a bed sheet could have covered the four for the entire 15 laps, stealing the thunder from the first and second qualifiers who were left far behind. An outstanding job by four determined drivers.

A mutual friend had a car that was not too potent, so having the dollars as the technical equipment and knowledge decided to go for the best. He acquired a Kurtis Craft chassis and spared no expense to the engine and gear train. After several attempts it became evident his driver could not handle this equipment so Bob Steinman tried other recognized drivers, eventually settling on Chet Morris. A previous roll at Slinger weakened Chet and was ordered not to drive for X number of weeks. With the #31 without a driver, Chet talked Bob Steinman into letting him drive it. During the feature race, Chet completely demolished the car and himself. The car was rebuilt and with Don looking for a hot car to pilot and Bob looking for a qualified driver they soon got together and soon Don was driving the #31. Steinman was very selective and would only appear when the purse warranted. Bob became involved in late model stocks which occasionally took him away from Badger meets, but with an efficient pit crew, he would send the car with his wife (Lorraine) with instructions to Don as to his performances and following then aim his wife toward Oconomowoc.

As Milwaukee was one of the tracks we raced at and the #31 was no exception on Friday nights, the #31 was primed to crash the 100 lapper scheduled for Friday. This was no easy task as all the local and traveling names and cars were in attendance. When the fumes cleared and times were announced the #31 was among the 24 to start the main (100 lapper). An attempt to eliminate this upstart was made, Don was crowded and upset on the inner rail by Bettenhausen, if this was intentional or something that developed in the heat of competition I don't know. So once again he met one of the best and survived. The car was righted, damage assessed, and with no obvious damage was readied for the feature. The #31 held its own during the race and when the checkered flag fell was in 6th place. There may have been others but Frank Burany was the only one who expressed his displeasure of Ford outrunning the Offy. This had to be one of Don's greatest efforts.

With a new season, Wallace and Don shared driving the #3 but somehow the desire was not there anymore, and when Don won the Kenosha County Fair trophy at Wilmot an opportunity to sell appeared and was completed the following Saturday night at Mauston, Wisconsin. So our active racing days came to an end.

This period of our lives has gone full circle. We started on the backstretch of a race track and evidently getting homesick for this area found ourselves on the back stretch at Indy. We progressed to the stands to get sprayed with dust and dirt and now a visit to Hels Corners Speedway can get us the same treatment. Time spent in the pits in competition just can not be evaluated. It was exciting, pleasant, prayed, nursed, and applauded our efforts. Without them, there would be no racing days. Finding ourselves back where we started can now sit back, reminisce and take part live or on TV.

There is no doubt many have crossed our paths. A few that we admired from afar are Rose, Gardner, Winn, Shrader, Collins, Horn, Mays, Chitwood, Nalon, Roberts, Hanks, McKenzie, an endless list. With Midget racing catching the fancy of the public, a whole new crop of drivers became household names. Zale, McQuinn, Wilman, Burany, Mills, Chandler, Nelson, Russo, Sorensen, Stephenson, Tomske, Marcheses, Richards, Fohr, Duncan, Easton, Bettenhausen, Carter, this could go on and on.

With our entering the competitive field we soon met and continued to meet a group of people that were helpful to us in our endeavor. Breecher, Erdman, Ermer, Asten, Sneeberg, Frank, Goetzke, Martin. These were the roots that Badger grew from. As Badger grew so did the memberships and I would like to mention a few that we rubbed elbows with—Scot, Frey, Woods, Hunter, Ladd, Balastriri, Fisher, Richie, Stahl, Alberts, Conners, Redman, Babicke, Lange, Dietz, Hamberger, Fredenburg, Peters, Johnson, Melius, Adams, Burany, Welsh Ellis, Morris, again an endless list. Of many a story could be told, but for now, I hope I haven't offended anyone by omitting them.

It was a pleasure to relive these days again, and though they say nothing is forever, these memories will to Art (Pop to many) Patzke.

~~~

**Art "Pop" Patzke
with my Grandmother**

Uncle Wallace

Uncle Don

Jack Dianiska

Jack Dianiska (Right)
With George Larsen (Left) and Nick Stanich (Middle)

Jack Dianiska is a seven-year U.S. Army veteran and helicopter pilot, from 1956 to 1963. After his discharge, he became interested in getting into air racing and building Formula 1 planes with the help of his associates. They competed in national and international events with their home-built Formula 1 racers. Eventually, Jack became the president of the newly formed U.S. Air Racing Association [USARA] dedicated to promoting and preserving the sport of closed-course air racing. He has also been involved in organizing and sponsoring air racing events all over the eastern United States and as far west as Waco, Texas. Dianiska is passionate about sharing his knowledge and experience with other pilots and enthusiasts, and he has also been a mentor and a leader in the air racing community for decades. He is also a supporter of STEM education and aviation history and has participated in many air shows and exhibitions.

~~~

Jack's Cassutt — Miss Cleveland
First Flight at Elyria Airport (1G1)

Juan Browne

Juan Browne, also known as Blancolirio, is an Airline Transportation Pilot and a YouTube creator from Nevada County, California. He makes videos about aviation, outdoor adventures, community events, and other topics that interest him. He has gained popularity for his coverage of the Oroville Dam Spillway incident and repairs, as well as other aviation accidents and incidents. He raced biplanes at the Reno Air Races and currently flies a Husky A-1 and a Boeing 777 for his work and recreation.

https://www.youtube.com/user/blancolirio

Scott Holmes

Scott Holmes is a Formula 1 air racer from Edmonton, Canada. He started flying when he was a child and got his pilot's licence at age 17. He joined the Formula 1 Air Racing tour in 2016 and has competed in several international events, such as the Air Race 1 World Cup in Thailand and the National Championship Air Races in Reno, Nevada. He is currently building a new plane that he hopes will break speed and altitude records.

https://www.youtube.com/@Holmes540

Aircraft Credits

N914E — Vans RV-7A
Pilot/Owner/Builder: Bernie Ockuly

N521DM — Cessna 172L Skyhawk
Pilot/Owner: Jim Allison

Bill Stead
and
The National Championship Air Races

Bill Stead and Little Miss Reno

Bill Stead was a rancher, pilot and hydroplane racer who had a passion for aviation. In 1964, he organized the first Reno National Championship Air Races, a five-day event that featured various classes of aircraft and attracted thousands of spectators. The races were held at a former military base near Reno, Nevada, and became an annual tradition that ran for sixty years, until 2023. Stead also competed in the 1965 race himself, flying a modified Cosmic Wind called *Little Miss Reno* in the Formula 1 Class. He died in a plane crash in 1965, but his legacy lived on in the Reno Air Races.

https://airrace.org/

**Bill Stead in Little Miss Reno on the Starting Line
1965 National Championship Air Races**

1964 National Championship Air Races
Formula 1 Results

QUALIFYING TIME TRIALS - SEPT. 15, 16 - 1 LAP OF THE 2-3/8 MI. COURSE

PL.	RACE NO.	PILOT	AIRCRAFT	TIME	SPEED
1	#14	Bob Porter	Miller "Little Gem"	42.6	200.70
2	# 1	Steve Wittman	Wittman "Bonzo"	45.4	188.08
3	# 6	Bob Downey	"Miss Cosmic Wind"	46.4	184.27
4	#31	Art Scholl	"Miss San Bernardino"	48.6	175.93 (a
5	#94	Mike Dewey	"Little Mike"	49.6	172.38
6	#19	Jerry Quarton	"Quarton Lil' Rascal"	54.7	156.31

(a) This aircraft previously raced as Kistler "Skeeter".

HEAT 1A - SEPT. 17 - 10 LAPS OF THE 2-3/8 MI. COURSE

PL.	RACE NO.	PILOT	AIRCRAFT	TIME	SPEED
1	# 6	Bob Downey	"Miss Cosmic Wind"	8:08.9	174.88
2	#31	Art Scholl	"Miss San Bernardino"	8:10.2	174.42
3	#19	Jerry Quarton	"Lil' Rascal"	8:21.5	170.49
4	#94	Mike Dewey	"Little Mike"	DNF	(a

(a) Dropped out during the race with engine trouble.

HEAT 1B - SEPT. 18 - 10 LAPS OF THE 2-3/8 MI. COURSE

PL.	RACE NO.	PILOT	AIRCRAFT	TIME	SPEED
1	#14	Bob Porter	"Little Gem"	7:20.9	193.92
2	# 1	Steve Wittman	"Bonzo"	7:29.0	190.87
3	# 6	Bob Downey	"Miss Cosmic Wind"	8:11.4	173.99
4	#31	Art Scholl	"Miss San Bernardino"	8:33.6	166.47
5	#19	Jerry Quarton	"Lil' Rascal"	8:48.2	161.87

CHAMPIONSHIP RACE - SEPT. 18 - 10 LAPS OF THE 2-3/8 MI. COURSE

PL.	RACE NO.	PILOT	AIRCRAFT	TIME	SPEED
1	#14	Bob Porter	"Little Gem"	7:22.0	193.44
2	# 1	Steve Wittman	"Bonzo"	7:36.2	187.42
3	#31	Art Scholl	"Miss San Bernardino"	8:17.8	171.76
4	# 6	Bob Downey	"Miss Cosmic Wind"	8:33.3	166.57
5	#19	Jerry Quarton	"Lil' Rascal"	8:45.0	162.86

https://reports.airrace.org/1964-1984/1964-1975.Formula.Report.pdf

International Formula 1 Air Racing

Imagine flying over 200 mph only 50 feet above the ground in a steep turn while battling 7 other top-level pilots for first position. Our Formula 1 pilots and their aircraft will do just that while powered by the same engine used in a simple Cessna 150 training airplane. These pilots and their crew chiefs build and maintain their airplanes, modifying what can be changed by reducing drag and increasing power all while staying within strict racing association rules.

https://www.if1airracing.com/

About M.T. Bass

M.T. Bass lives, writes, flies, and plays music in Mudcat Falls, USA.

www.mtbass.net

White Hawk Aviation Adventure Stories #1
Available in Paperback & eBook

Hollywood, 1950 — Former P-51 fighter pilot A. Gavin Byrd is on location for a movie shoot, when he gets a call from the police that his older brother, a prominent Beverly Hills plastic surgeon, has been found dead on his boat. The Lieutenant in charge of the investigation is ready to close the case as a suicide from the start, but "Hawk" doesn't buy it and decides to find out what really happened for himself.

With help from a former starlet ex-girlfriend, a friendly police sergeant whose life was saved in the war by his brother and a nosy Los Angeles Times reporter, Hawk's search for the truth takes him through cross-fire, dog fights and mine fields in Hollywood, Beverly Hills, Burbank and Las Vegas, and leads him into some of the darker corners of his brother's patient files and private life that he never knew existed.

www.mtbass.net

White Hawk Aviation Adventure Stories #2
Available in Paperback & eBook

"There are only two types of aircraft: fighters and targets."
~Doyle 'Wahoo' Nicholson, USMC

Sweating it out in the former Belgian Congo as a civil war mercenary, with Sparks turning wrenches on his T-6 Texan, Hawk splits his time flying combat missions and, back on the ground, sparring with Ella, an attractive young missionary doctor, in the sequel to My Brother's Keeper.

www.mtbass.net

Available in Paperback, eBook & Audiobook

She was one in a million…and the day I met her I should have bought a lottery ticket instead.

Griffith Crowe, the "fixer" for a Chicago law firm, falls for his current assignment, Helena Nicholson, the beautiful heir of a Tech Sector venture capitalist who perished in a helicopter crash leaving her half a billion dollars, a Learjet 31, and unsavory suspicions about her father's death. As he investigates, the ex-Navy SEAL crosses swords with Helena's step-brother, the Pentagon's Highlands Forum, and an All-Star bad guy somebody has hired to stop him. When Griff finds himself on the wrong side of an arrest warrant he wonders: Is he a player or being played?

Lawyers and Lovers and Guns…*Oh, my!*

www.mtbass.net

Available in Paperback & eBook

People ask me where I get the ideas for my books. In this case, I recall reading about Alaska bush pilots for fun. I must have watched *Animal House* and *Treasure of the Sierra Madre* around that time and…a few months later—Eureka! The words for the prologue and first chapter just started spilling out of my head. ("Clean up on aisle five.")

Seriously, what could go wrong?

Love & Betrayal…Murder & Mayhem…Friendship & Double-Crossing Partners in Pursuit of Buried Treasure…

www.mtbass.net

Available in Paperback & eBook

Kansas City, 1965 — Y.T. Erp, Jr. can't wait to leave for college at the University of California, Berkeley to escape not only the work, but especially all the phlegm-brained idiots at his father's aerospace company. Leaving behind a pregnant auburn-haired cheerleader, a sensuous red-headed siren plotting to usurp his familial ties, and his two best friends—one who ends up in Vietnam and the other in the Weather Underground—his "trip" on the wild side of the Generation Gap takes him from the psychedelic scene of Haight-Ashbury to the F.B.I.'s Ten Most Wanted list. Meanwhile, his father is consumed by the task of managing his unmanageable corporate team in the quest to help fulfill a President's challenge to "land a man on the moon."

www.mtbass.net

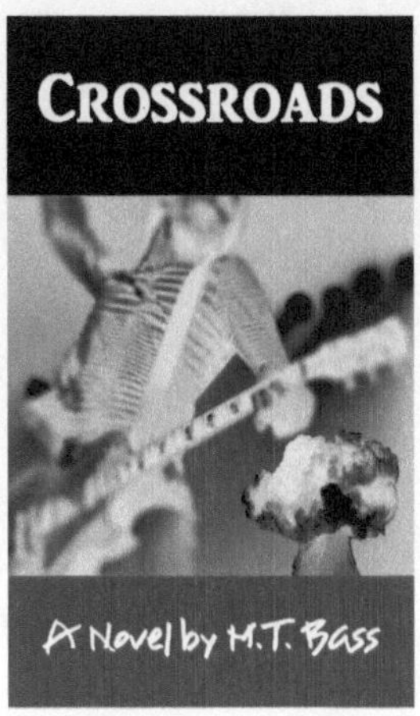

Available in eBook

Cleveland, 1977 — Grappling with a foreign policy crisis, the U.S. Government targets a hapless rock-'n'-roller as a Russian spy in a classic case of mistaken identity for an innocent, 'Wrong Man' hero…or *is he?*

Think of an unholy fictional union between the Rolling Stones and Alfred Hitchcock's *North by Northwest*.

Unlike any novel you have ever read, this one has a soundtrack. After all, a story whose characters are musicians should have…well…*music*. Right?

www.mtbass.net

Murder by Munchausen Sci-Fi Thriller Book #1
Available in Paperback, eBook & Audiobook

50

When androids are reprogrammed into hit men, detectives of the Artificial Crimes Unit repo the AnSub and track down the hackers. Partners Jake and EC's case of an "extra-judicial" divorce settlement takes a nasty turn with DNA from a hundred-year-old murder in Boston and a signature that harkens back to the very first serial killer ever in London.

Artificial Intelligence? *Fuhgeddaboudit!*

Artificial Evil has a name…*Munchausen.*

www.mtbass.net

Murder by Munchausen Sci-Fi Thriller Book #2
Available in Paperback, eBook & Audiobook

It was the case of a lifetime…but then it went sideways on her. The serial killer Maddie put behind bars might have been crazy but it turns out he was innocent, and now she finds herself hunting robot killers in the Artificial Crimes Unit. Worse yet, she's partnered up with Jake, her former lover.

When androids are hacked and reprogrammed into hit men, Maddie and Jake investigate and track down the hackers. But now, an evil genius is using droids to recreate the infamous Jack the Ripper murders.

www.mtbass.net

Murder by Munchausen Sci-Fi Thriller Book #3
Available in Paperback, eBook & Audiobook

Now unleashed, the "Baron" is resurrecting history's notorious serial killers, giving them a second life in the bodies of hacked and reprogrammed Personal Assistant Androids, then turning them loose to terrorize the city. While detectives Jake and Maddie of the police department's Artificial Crimes Unit scramble to stop the carnage with the Baron's arrest, the cyberpunk head of the Counter IT Section, Q, struggles to de-encrypt his mad scheme to infect world data centers with a virus that represents a collective cyber unconsciousness of evil.

www.mtbass.net

Murder by Munchausen Sci-Fi Thriller Book #4
Available in Paperback, eBook & Audiobook

Just when you thought you could trust the robots again…

A senator's son is strangled by a synthoid in AsiaTown and, just like two other victims, tattooed with an indecipherable barcode.

Jake and Kim, his new partner, battle political corruption, the Chinese Triad, and Internal Affairs, discovering a disturbing Fourth Law of Robotics as they decode the tattoos to stop the deviant series of murders.

www.mtbass.net

Available in eBook

*Lodging — bending of the stalk of a plant (stalk lodging)
or the entire plant (root lodging)*

While World War II engulfs every nation on the globe, Rebecca and her high school friend Sarah can only dream of escaping a dreary, wind-blown existence in western Kansas, until their boring, stodgy old hometown fills with handsome young men learning to fly Army Air Corps bombers known as Liberators, and their lives are suddenly filled with temptation and, perhaps, true love.

www.mtbass.net

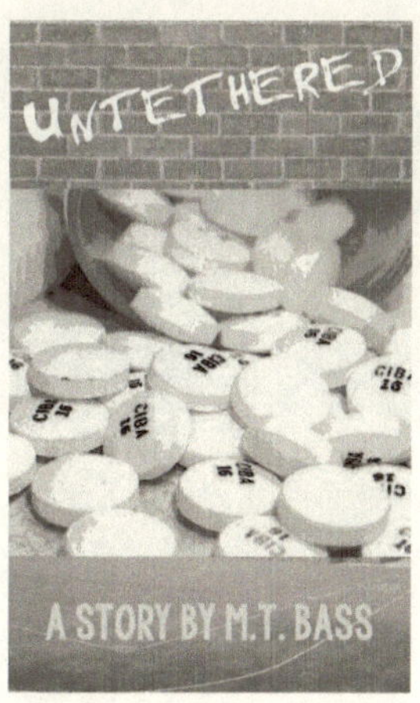

Available in eBook

At District High School #6241, Connor wants only to get close to Liz, the cheerleader whose locker is just across the hall, and forget the suicide of his father in jail, but his family's dark past and a rebellious nature force him to the fringes of student social circles and into an unlikely alliance to fight back against a tyranny of conformity.

www.mtbass.net

Available in eBook

The collected songs and verse of M.T. Bass

www.mtbass.net